SILVER LADY

TRAVELS ALONG THE RIVER ROAD

SUSAN E. SAGE

Black Rose Writing | Texas

This is a work of fiction. Names, characters, businesses, places, events, and incidents are either the products of the author's imagination or used in a fictitious manner. Any resemblance to actual persons, living or dead, or actual events is purely coincidental.

ISBN: 978-1-68513-523-2
PUBLISHED BY BLACK ROSE WRITING
www.blackrosewriting.com

Printed in the United States of America
Suggested Retail Price (SRP) $20.95

Silver Lady is printed in Garamond Premier Pro

*As a planet-friendly publisher, Black Rose Writing does its best to eliminate unnecessary waste to reduce paper usage and energy costs, while never compromising the reading experience. As a result, the final word count vs. page count may not meet common expectations.

PRAISE FOR
SILVER LADY

"Sage has crafted a unique near-future, post-pandemic world where Art is vanishing and the world is chaotic. The *Silver Lady* drifts downriver in a dreamlike state, slipping through time and reality, past and present, in a world with ever-changing rules, making you question what is real..."
–Lena Gibson, author of *The Edge of Life: Love and Survival During the Apocalypse*

"This delightfully enchanting river tale, full of woe and wonder, will keep you guessing what lies around the next bend. I often caught my breath at Susan Sage's bright, lyrical writing."
–Milana Marsenich, author of *Shed Girl*

"You can always count on Susan Sage to create characters with a few fascinating flaws, interacting in a setting both realistic and mysterious, to keep you reading late into the night."
–Sandra Sperling, author of *The Stash*

"An amazing woman's struggle to make sense of a world gone horribly wrong and a dose of magical realism combine to make a river voyage on the *Silver Lady* a trip worth taking."
–Gail Ward Olmsted, author of the *Miranda Quinn Legal Twist* series

"Close the door, turn off the TV, and send the kids to grandmas. Once you board the *Silver Lady,* you will find yourself on a surreal journey into a possible and not too distant future. Capt. Cassie Navrone skillfully steers us through a world damaged by our recent past in such way as to give insight and hope. As she navigates the watery River Road, Cassie takes us on a deceptively slow ride on a river full of reflection, mystery, and mystique."
–Gin Coleman, author of *Desert Brave*

ACKNOWLEDGMENTS

After writing *Dancing in the Ring,* I decided to switch gears and write in a genre that I've always enjoyed reading: Magic Realism. It could also be considered 'upbeat Dystopian,' or more aptly described as Protopian.

First, a HUGE thanks to my editor, Gia Scribes! This isn't the first manuscript of mine Gia has fine-tuned. Her comments and suggested changes continue to be incredibly helpful and wise.

A big thanks to my beta readers! Much gratitude to author and friend, Milana Marsenich, for reading the MS, at least twice, and inspiring me with more than a few imaginative possibilities that I took her up on (in particular, making Silver Lady, sentient). A big thanks to my dear friend and reader extraordinaire, Jane Cameron, for her careful reading and enthusiastic response. Also, many thanks to three other early readers: Sandra Sperling, Patty Duffy, and Faye Turner-Johnson. Both Patty and Faye are friends and fellow writers, as well as members of my writing group, *Instructors as Writers.*

And once again, my heartfelt gratitude to Reagan, David and the entire Black Rose Writing team!!

Last, but not least, thanks to my husband, Tom, for 'rooting me on,' and reading another one of my books, even though it isn't his usual fare.

"All that we see or seem is but a dream within a dream."
~Edgar Allen Poe

SILVER LADY

DAY 19

From the Captain's Log

Although the engine quit working, the water damage isn't as bad as it was after our first storm. This time, mainly small objects got scattered around and a little soggy: table lamps, flashlights, hoodies, and flip-flops. The storm hit while the *Silver Lady* was docked, but within minutes the moorings detached, and the wild river took us on a thrill ride downstream. One which none of us would dare repeat. After being tossed about for hours, the boat ran aground.

And now we gaze at each other, tired, dazed, and waterlogged on a beach. We have no idea where we are. The opposing riverbank seems farther away than usual. Festivities of the river gods must have gotten out of hand, as they've spewed their guts on the vessel.

It appears we're all okay, but then I notice one of my five passengers is missing. Panic sets in despite our weariness.

A FEW YEARS INTO THE FUTURE: THE GREAT COLLAPSE AND THE VANISHING

Heading down the mighty river on a sunny spring morning is a luxury houseboat, the *Silver Lady*. Cassie Navrone is at the wheel, although she isn't the boat's owner. It's the first day of a long journey. One moment, she's wide-eyed in anticipation, and the next, wistful.

At first glance, her two long, mostly silver braids appear attached to her captain's hat. There are a few black strands mixed with silver, but not many. The hat's a little mismatched with her purple caftan. Following her cat, Jezebel's, recent demise, she applied for a temporary job as a houseboat captain. The day before, she completed a brief instructional lesson at the marina where the seventy-foot vessel has been docked. It's now her responsibility to drive the boat to its owner—almost two-thousand miles away.

Cassie is a retired teacher and doula. She's also a widow with a grown daughter, Melanie. Like many, Melanie only leaves home when necessary. Until now, Cassie had little going on, except for creating Qigong videos and having coffee once in a while with two friends. Truth be told, she didn't leave home much either. Now feels like the right time for her to do something new.

Many refer to what's been taking place as the Great Collapse or simply the Collapse.

Cities have been seeing a dramatic spike in violence—especially gun violence. Daily mass shootings occur, especially in cities across the nation. There is chatter about the states turning into separate countries and getting rid of the now completely feckless federal government. Travel between states is permitted but strongly discouraged. Little doubt the sky-high prices and less availability of goods and services led to the now daily rioting and looting, especially in what many are calling the 'DSA'—the soon-to-be, Disunited States of America.

The most recent pandemic, three years ago, was caused by a virus more deadly than any previous ones. Its most virulent phase lasted only a year, but in that time, almost a billion people died. Deaths occurred in cities on every continent, though few places were immune. The virus infiltrated even the best-made masks. It struck mainly at night and became known as the Strangler Virus, as its victims woke up struggling to breathe. Over half died within hours. The rest of the infected experienced such intense brain fog that they lost most of their long-term memories. While those infected could talk, walk, recall their names, and where they left their keys, few kept memories of their lives before the Strangler Virus came to town.

Humankind hid for the first year, and a great many remained isolated for the next two. Both climate change advocates and skeptics alike hoped climate change would magically go away during this time of resettling. Sadly, it was discovered that it was happening faster than anyone expected.

If that weren't enough to grapple with, there's also, the Vanishing. People have vanished, by the hundreds, if not thousands. Here one moment, but gone the next. No one knows how much artwork has disappeared. Paintings and books vanish or disintegrate right before the eyes of their creators. The exact number of missing artwork and people is unknown since the crisis continues. It is commonly believed that the pandemic is somehow connected to it, as it started happening after its much longed-for, but abrupt, departure. Anxiety levels have reached new and alarming heights, but anxiety meds are as rare as rhodium.

Hot spots are popping up at an alarming rate. It is in those places where the Vanishing occurs. Artists and poets—at least those in the know—continue to search for cold spots where creative works seem to last. Artworks aboard boats on freshwater lakes and rivers are safer, at least to some degree. The hope is that keeping works above water rather than on the ground level will help preserve them.

Four of the six travelers aboard *Silver Lady*—except for Zona and Cassie—are artists or poets.

YEAR 2033

DAY 1

From the Captain's Log

I've always longed to write 'From the Captain's Log.' Another cross-off from my bucket list, though I'm not a real captain. You don't need a special license to operate a houseboat, but since I organized this journey, I'm proudly claiming the rank as captain of the eighty-foot *Silver Lady*.

She isn't my craft. The owner, George Sherman, hired me to drive her home. My father always navigated the river in various kinds of boats. A few summers of my youth were spent assisting him. I adore rivers and river travel. Guess that was enough to convince George of my capability.

She is a sleek and elegant lady—charcoal gray fiberglass with dark windows. When I first saw her, her bow resembled a face. Two window-eyes separated by a pinch of fiberglass for a nose, and below was a porthole-mouth. Her name—*Silver Lady*—was painted in large black calligraphy on her stern. She has the demure look of a lady ageing well, sure of herself and where she's going.

There are three levels. The house part includes two sections, with outside decks near the bow and a larger one on top. Living room, kitchen, small reading room/office, and a bathroom are on the main deck. There's even a fireplace in the living room—a fake one, of course. All five sleeping cabins are on the second deck. They're all the same size: cozy. Additionally, a chair and nightstand are included in the ones with single beds. An upper deck on the third level is great for viewing the river and riverbanks. The hardtop canopy, no doubt, a helpful shield from strong sunlight. At the front of the main deck, you'll find the driver's cab near the bow. One other person can sit comfortably next to the driver.

While there are five small cabins, or sleeping quarters, the boat can sleep up to twelve, as a few cabins have double beds. If needed, you can use the beige sectional couch as two beds. I know technically, beds are berths on a large vessel, but it doesn't sound correct to refer to them as 'single berths' or 'double berths.' (While I'll try my best to use correct Captain Log terminology, I'm not going to sweat it.)

Everything from the fiberglass to the furnishings is modern and stylish. No obvious stains or rips; no visible damage at all. Nothing appears broken, which I indicated on my checklist. I had to inspect the entire boat before the passengers set foot on board since I will be held responsible if *Silver Lady* is the "worse for wear" when we arrive at her new home.

George reassured me he doesn't expect his boat to be spotless after the long journey, but maintained as well as possible. While I'm aware of how to drive the River Road, I can't believe I signed up for such a lengthy trip.

. . .

Once all were aboard, I gave the five passengers the grand tour. I'd expected them to ask more questions. Afterward, I tried to tantalize them with the upcoming travel experience by describing the peaceful beauty of the river scenery. Who was I fooling? They knew this was my debut as captain; I'd been honest when interviewing them. I guess I was playing tour guide because I didn't know what else to talk about. After having socialized so little these past few years, I'd lost my ability to converse—at least in a relaxed way. Also, too, my nerves were on edge because of the gloom-and-doom talk of the Collapse. It could be the others felt the same.

The passengers consist of two couples and a young woman. While they are passengers, they're also crewmates, as I may well need their youthful energy to help me swab the decks now and then. They've agreed to relieve me occasionally at the wheel. It was part of the deal, as I only charged them a nominal travel fee. For all that, I put them through a lengthy interview process. I initially planned to accept only women on board, but later changed my mind. I hope I don't regret my choices.

As I said, this is the largest group I've been around in a long time. I've avoided them ever since the last pandemic. Do the others feel anxious about socializing, too? If they've been getting together with family or friends, they're probably doing okay. I wouldn't be so off my game if I'd had more opportunities to socialize—not that I've been a total recluse. Maybe I'll ask them, but I don't want to pry. It often feels like I have marbles in my mouth. Self-consciousness is driving me nuts: *Am I too friendly? Do I sound stupid? Have I already said something to annoy them?* I'm worse than a teenager who has just smoked pot for the first time.

For two nights before we set sail, I didn't get any sleep. A zillion questions occurred to me. Of foremost concern: Will I feel like I'm living someone else's life?

I can't help but want to observe them and try to figure out who each of them is, as well as their habits. This takes time and patience. Daily meditation should help relax me. If I remember to do it, that is. So often in the past, I've tried to make it a habit, a way of life, but failed in my attempts.

· · ·

We've now docked for the night. For several hours, the scenery here along the upper part of the river was lovely, with many bluffs and tree-lined banks. We saw prehistoric-looking cranes and herons, plus a host of smaller birds. Trees closest to the water's edge seemed to watch and wave at us as we passed by. The area's serenity and simplicity reminded me of a classy woman at a party, not overly made up, and wearing a gown of simple design. If I was a poet, I'd write about the way the pink ribboned sky dipped into the river and floated down it like a wedding gown train. Maybe I'd rather paint sunsets. I'd sure love to capture this transient beauty.

But then we saw smoke above the tree-line and heard the familiar sirens. It must have been coming from a town a few miles away, but close enough to remind us how the world has changed. Violence lurks, even along the river.

I can't wait to be cradled by the water; for it to both sing me its watery lullaby and rock me asleep. We all need a little nurturing in this difficult world—especially since the latest pandemic. Besides the pandemic, the Vanishing and the Collapse, there's now talk of war breaking out. I hope being on the river will help me, at least temporarily, forget about the pointless destruction. If this is a con job, it's a necessary one.

How I wound up here:

The fear of the Strangler Virus caused many of us to only leave our homes when necessary. It subsided a little, only to be replaced with fear of a civil war. The absence of drinkable water is a significant factor. Bottled water is now a precious commodity, often available only to the wealthy. Violent social unrest erupted in the larger cities; nightly curfews were imposed in many. Gunshots and sirens can be heard day and night—despite the curfews. Some people dismissed what was going on, convinced it was fear-mongering. How could you dismiss what you were hearing and seeing? I sure couldn't. My nerves curtailed me from venturing out a few times. Still, I tried to keep up with routines: the daytime walks, making it to appointments, shopping for groceries—that is, when I didn't have them delivered. But I also lost a few pre-pandemic friendships.

After a couple of years of near seclusion, I decided that making Qigong videos, having occasional get-togethers with Janet and Sasha, and phone chats with Melanie, weren't enough. I was spending too much time watching the clock on my fake fireplace mantel. Changes needed to be made. Thus, I became a houseboat captain.

Aboard *Silver Lady*, I note time by the sun's rise and fall, only checking the hour and minutes when needed.

DAY 2

When the scenery grows tedious, I look for other boats. We passed several earlier in the day, though we've only seen one since mid-afternoon. I'm stunned and downright stupefied by the fact that the journey has finally begun, after several months of planning. Surprisingly, we've seen little evidence of the Collapse. Perhaps the news has been exaggerated, making things seem grim. At least I hope so.

The river's still high from earlier spring storms, though it crested weeks ago—overflowing its banks in several places. While it's lovely to gaze at, there's an occasional stench of rotten eggs, no doubt from all the organic matter being churned up. One moment the water's pitch-black, but then it's blue or green. It's so clear we can see the bottom, but then—for no apparent reason it turns murky. Maybe it's like a crystal ball and we'll be able to see events before they happen or as they're happening elsewhere. To read a river—what a gift that would be!

I wonder if we'll see much debris from shipwrecks. (I think it's called flotsam and jetsam, even if it's not from the ocean.) If we do, I'll note it in the log. How fun it would be to go aboard an old deserted boat washed up on a shore! One that we could wander around in and discover all kinds of treasure...

We'll be heading southeast aboard *Silver Lady*, traveling through several states, or is it more correct now to call them countries? Two curious places we should see along the way are the Land of Doze, as well as the Island of Lost Children. Both sound intriguing.

Thankfully, George Sherman doesn't expect us to arrive any sooner than two weeks, and not to worry if we take a little longer. He added he has no immediate plans to take *her* out, so if we needed more time, it should be fine, but to let him know. He said that he and his wife were vacationing in the North last summer when the Collapse began. Worried about encountering river pirates, they flew back south to their home. Should I be taking the pirate threat seriously? Certainly, there's more to fear in this new bizarro world. Based on this info, and the fancy *Silver Lady* herself, I'd wager that George must be pretty well off. Like me, I'm sure the others wouldn't be able to afford such a trip, as houseboat rental prices are beyond ridiculous these days.

• • •

I interviewed many people online to determine who would be the best fit to join me on *Silver Lady*. It amazed me that my Facebook ad only ran for less than a week. I didn't expect so many applicants, since I presumed a fear of the pandemic resurging was still out there. I stipulated how I was hoping for those who longed to travel but couldn't afford a 'big' vacation; creative folks who enjoyed the outdoors; and those in good physical shape. Hard to believe there were over one hundred inquiries.

The passengers: Margot Bryson, Vincent Kennings, Leon Stewart, Kali Turnell, Zona Workes, and me—Cassie Navrone. Almost everyone who applied has roots in the Midwest. No point for someone from either coast to travel here for a long boat ride, especially now. I'm from Minneapolis; Leon and Kali are Detroiters; Zona was born and raised in Wisconsin— she refused to specify which town or city; and Margot is from upstate New York. Vincent moved there from Toledo, Ohio, a few years ago. It's hard to process that soon we could well refer to the states not as states, but as separate countries.

I also chose ten alternates to be on my standby list in case any of these folks changed their minds—or I force one of the chosen to walk the gang-plank!

My somewhat popular YouTube videos of my Qigong practice helped give me a little name recognition. In fact, I'm looking forward to conducting occasional morning and evening workouts on the top deck or even on the occasional pristine riverbank. This is something I mentioned to prospective passengers.

I narrowed down my list of applicants by eliminating those who weren't creative, though I made one exception. I got rid of dozens this way. Then I conducted a second interview and came up with a list of five who met my qualifications. My choices were subjective. Someone else would have, no doubt, made different decisions. But trust me, I didn't choose the winners on a whim.

Zona is the only one who isn't all that creative, apart from me. Mind you, I've always appreciated all art forms, but not all forms of any particular one of them. Take music, for example. I dislike Italian operas and Blue Grass. We can't like everything, right?

"Think it's possible to become imaginative if you haven't always been?" I ask Leon and Kali. They've been discussing what inspired them to write. Three of us are sitting at a table, nearly large enough for six. For the first time since the trip began, I don't feel the need to keep tabs on where everyone is on the boat—that is when I'm not steering *Silver Lady*.

"I don't see why not," says Kali, putting her hand on my forearm. I feel myself stiffen. How strange it is to be touched.

It's daunting to be around so many imaginative people. I can't help but be envious. Being creative must make the human condition more tolerable.

"Think some of their magic might rub off on us, Zona?" I ask the girl who is walking by for a snack. Without answering, she gives Kali and me a hostile glance, though I swear she then bats her eyes at Leon. Earlier, she acted jumpy and unfriendly around Vincent and Margot. Maybe it was a mistake to have accepted her aboard. When interviewing her, I thought a river trip might benefit her, since it was her fist time on a boat and seeing a river. While she's only in her early twenties, this struck me as odd.

I've always had friends who were creative types. Creatives is the term I still apply to them. I realize now I've always divided adults into two groups: Creatives and Non-Creatives. Creatives, of course, aren't necessarily better people. Ego issues are especially higher among the Creatives. And yet they know how to use magical thinking to get by in this tough world. At least it's always seemed this way to me.

If I had enough friends, I wouldn't have had to choose strangers as passengers. I suppose it's telling that I don't. Even if I did, who knows if they'd be interested in this sort of journey—especially during these difficult times? I have two friends. Both had understandable reasons for not going: Janet couldn't leave her ninety-year-old mother, and Sasha hates water. Too bad they were forced to pass up, what I'm sure will be the trip of a lifetime.

. . .

I've now had several chats with my crew. Most were friendly enough, but short. Margot is the only one I haven't spoken with since the interview. The chats have been lively, but not very informative. I know it will take time getting to know each other, so maybe I should ask fewer questions. I don't want to appear over-eager, especially since they didn't seem curious about me.

Houseboat living should bring out the best in people and turn strangers into friends. At least I hope so. We've all been marveling at the strangeness of a river vacation—strangely wonderful—after years of near seclusion because of the plague and all the civil unrest. Will this remain a vacation, or will it become as difficult as life on parts of the mainland? It's anyone's guess, and I haven't expressed this fear to the others, but they must be wondering the same. I'm going to do my best to relax, and I hope the others will, too.

One thing always leads to another. Had Jezebel, my feline companion of twenty years, not died in my arms, I wouldn't have applied for this job. The pairing of the numbness from grief with the realization that I wasn't shackled to my pet caused me to take such a brash measure. I mean, I might as well have joined the circus! I'm almost always pragmatic, or at least someone who considers her options. She was a remarkable companion. Unlike most humans I've known, Jez was sensitive to my moods, and she enjoyed my singing voice (unlike my human companions). Even here on the water, I miss her.

. . .

Before boarding the boat, Zona had exclaimed, "This is a river, then? Sure hope the current is fast and it doesn't take forever to get where we're going."

Why hadn't I thought to ask my passengers whether they'd ever been on a river? Maybe allowing Zona aboard was a bad idea.

"This is *the* river! It's as changeable as a person and better than family," I'd responded. Had she not read *Wind in the Willows* as a girl? I guess she didn't catch my reference. She pursed her lips and rolled her eyes. The tattoos on one arm depicted dragons, spiders, and other unfriendly creatures I couldn't identify. Her other arm was decorated with butterflies and rainbows, as well as a few ladybugs.

"The river-branches are a little like your arms: though different from each other, they're both attached to the same body, right?"

Zona didn't respond.

. . .

Margot and Vincent are wild about each other. It's curious they aren't sharing a room. The cabins are small, so it's certainly understandable. Both are attractive in a hippie-ish sort of way. Tall and thin, with large soul-filled eyes, and long, tapered fingers. While I'm no judge of age, I'm guessing they're both around forty. (I didn't ask for ages on the applications.) They both strike me as being introverts, so living together with strangers might be even harder for them. Margot hasn't said a word so far. I hope she at least talks to him in private.

It's challenging to consider the world from others' perspectives, after years of living alone. Surely, I'm not the only one who's having a hard time walking in someone else's shoes. The main thing is that we try. I hope self-centeredness doesn't ruin the trip.

Leon and Kali are sharing a cabin. They're as attractive as the other couple, though in a different way. Leon must be near forty, too, though Kali's more likely in her early twenties.

Both couples admitted their relationships are new ones. Less than six months in both cases. Margot and Vincent strike me as being more romantically involved than Leon and Kali. The latter two were the last to board *Silver Lady*. Leon, who is Black, glanced around and said, "If I'd known there'd be so much whiteness, I'd have canceled my reservation!"

We laughed, but the friction in the air was thick as chowder.

"Just joking, y'all. Lighten up!" Leon said. This time the laughs got trapped in throats, and another one or two squeezed through taut lips.

Why did I choose not only to accept two couples, but two fairly young couples? Am I such a masochist that I wanted to experience jealousy? It's been forever since I was romantically involved. At least I'm not the only single person aboard. Zona and I will be able to commiserate when we feel bothered by all the romance surrounding us.

. . .

While I enjoy steering the impressive wooden wheel, the others have agreed to help, so I'm not stuck with the chore for any long stretches. The plan is to dock every evening by sunset, and set sail no later than 9:00 a.m. We'll spend part of the days in the more peaceful and attractive ports. If we want to stay a little longer in one port, occasionally, we can spend a night in a hotel, provided it's within walking distance of the docks. How risky these visits will be is anyone's guess. I heard about a few places to avoid— larger towns, which are more inland.

. . .

We often find ourselves sitting around the table when not on one of the outer decks. Earlier, I told everyone how meal planning will be as simple as possible: we'll make our own breakfasts and lunches from basic food in the galley.

"The owner told us to drink the rest of the bottled water on board," I announced. Their eyes grew large, like I was telling them he'd left us precious jewels. Finding good drinking water was an unexpected find.

Our larder includes cold cereal, oatmeal, and hard-boiled eggs, along with juice and coffee or tea for breakfasts—though we must limit hot beverages to one cup per day; and sandwiches and fruit for lunches. Eggs and fruit are expensive and not always available. For cost-saving measures, I've stocked up on cans of soup and tuna, as we're going to try to eat dinner together—a light supper in the evenings after we've docked for the night. Sometimes we'll eat our main meals in river towns. We've also brought several bottles of wine, though due to the limited space, we'll definitely have to stock up every few days.

Vincent then informed us that Margot and he are vegetarians, though they sometimes make exceptions. I already knew this from the interview.

"Not me! I'll eat about anything put in front of me," said Zona. I was surprised, only because Zona is pretty scrawny.

"How about fresh fish? That is when we can catch some." Leon's remark made some of our eyes light up. As it so happens, both Leon and Kali enjoy fishing. I'm looking forward to some fresh fish dinners, however infrequently. Still, there will be curries, pasta dishes, legumes, and vegetables (canned if fresh ones are unavailable), for everyone. Meal preparation will rotate, ensuring no one gets stuck in the galley for too long!

So far I haven't had much of an appetite. I don't think the others have had much of one either. At times, I've even been queasy. Once I'm used to the rocking motion of the boat, and I calm down a little, it should pass.

DAY 3

The others are still sleeping and I'm trying to be as quiet as possible. Being captain can be nerve-wracking, but I feel surprisingly at ease. My appetite's getting a little better and my stomach isn't rumbling so much. I'm writing this as I sip a steaming mug of coffee in the dining area inside the boat. The galley is separate and the living room/dining room is large and open. The yellow and blue furnishings are simple and ultra-modern in design.

While practicing Qigong and meditation helps, I've been on edge for the past several years, experiencing, like many, a general anxiety. Mine spikes and drops, only to rise again. I'm sure most others have experienced it, too, but the healthier folks have figured out ways to cope, and reduce, if not eliminate, fears spawned by both the plague and subsequent Collapse. Last night was a better one. I drifted off like a swaddled baby in a cradle. While I woke up a couple of times, unsure of my surroundings, the boat's gentle rocking allowed me easy re-entry to slumber-land.

A few of the others have expressed interest in joining me for Qigong. I'll hold off conducting my first session until the afternoon, since it's too chilly outside to sit out on the upper deck. While I'll wear my purple caftan at night, I'll don more practical clothing by day: black yoga pants, t-shirts, and a hoodie. Also, I will no longer sleep in my captain's hat.

· · ·

As the sun shimmies up the sky, the others, except for Zona, slowly begin to emerge from their cabins. We sit around the large table and on the two couches, sipping coffee from nautical-themed mugs. A few crewmates claim to have slept better than the first couple nights.

Excited for their company, I probably ask too many questions. Most of them are about how they'd slept. After discussing our previous night's slumber, the day's itinerary, and how far we might get down the river today, we discuss the Vanishing. I'm surprised not everyone has heard about hot and cold spots, and their effects on artwork. I truly thought this would've been the main reason artists would embark on a river adventure. Go figure why I didn't ask this on the application.

I tell them how the colder water in the north contains an unknown property that preserves paintings. Risking sounding like a know-it-all, I add, how as the water gets warmer, paintings and drawings have been vanishing at a much higher rate. Also, as bleak as it sounded, it's commonly believed there's something about being in a boat that causes artworks, of all kinds, to fare better.

"What about an anchored boat?" asks the lanky Vincent.

I admit to not knowing, but explain how the latest research hasn't been peer-reviewed.

Vincent slurps his coffee, sighs, and then says if some of his sketches vanish in the warmer waters, he won't be able to remain for the entire trip. Before I can respond, he thoughtfully adds, "Man, I hope it doesn't happen with the written word, too. Someday, it could all just evaporate as fast as writing in the sand. No permanence, but I guess nothing lasts, does it?"

He likely hasn't heard that the print in published books is disappearing, too. I decide against telling him. I'll bet Vincent's been wearing lumberjack shirts and torn-up jeans ever since he was a teenager. Bet he couldn't pull it off if he wasn't so handsome. Plus, he's artistic-looking like his girlfriend, though unlike him, she appears like she hadn't slept in what she's wearing. A more pulled-together look, if not exactly polished.

Next, Leon chimes in, "I've heard strictly digital work is disappearing as fast as the bees, but—at least so far—I don't know anyone having lost the hard copy of their writing."

Again, I am tempted to let them know what I've heard, but refrain. It isn't like I know for sure. He doesn't appear as concerned as Vincent. His tone is offhanded, unruffled. Strange, as Leon is a poet. He then says, in a somewhat muffled voice, how he hasn't yet published a book of his poetry. This explains his attitude.

"I do know a few writers who have lost their published works, though it seems to be affecting classical works more than contemporary. Sure, that could change in these crazy times. Bad enough our world's so battered and bruised, but now to lose our art? One of the few 'good' things about humanity...well, shit, just SHIT!" Leon says, flinging his glasses on the floor of the main floor outer deck. After retrieving them, he storms off. We can hear him cussing in his cabin. So much for what I wrote about Leon not being as concerned as Vincent!

Everyone is alarmed except for Zona, who only joined us after Leon's outburst. She has this little Mona Lisa grin on her face. After being pressed, she tells us how she hadn't slept well. She'd admitted to having severe sleep issues during her interview.

I absent-mindedly try to pour more coffee, but the pot is empty.

Will the men talk over the women on board? Had it been a mistake to allow them on board? They both seem caring and sensitive to others. Had I picked up a macho vibe during the interviews, I wouldn't have given them further consideration.

"We can at least memorize our poetry...plays...movie scripts. And poetry should always be memorized. Not all, of course. But the best and most important ones," Kali says, adding "Why can't copies of paintings or books be made and put in a vault or something?"

While I am relieved that Kali spoke up, am I dismissive of her thoughts because she twists a strand of her dark hair with her index finger? Maybe it is simply her youth. She could be onto something insofar as the memorizing, but I doubt there are enough vaults for all the artwork.

I can tell by the way Leon looks at her that he, too, finds her naïve. Maybe that's partly why he finds her attractive. She's pretty, with silky-smooth coffee-and-cream skin due to being both Asian and African American. I only know this because she told me at the interview. It wasn't something I would have asked on the application. I wonder if she was born with that dewy, wide-eyed expression or if it was acquired. She's like a young colt, unsure of itself and unable to physically contain the joy of being alive.

Then Kali adds how maybe no one should speak unless they have something profound to say.

I knock over my coffee mug. Good thing it is empty. My, but this girl sure is naïve.

"That will make it a pretty quiet boat trip, don't you think? Not that we're incapable of being profound, but even sages would have a tough time."

The others nod, but Kali appears simultaneously blank and defensive.

I change the subject, but soon afterward she takes me aside and whispers that she can tell I'm the motherly type and asks if it would be okay to use my shoulder to cry on, at least now and then.

"My shoulder's available, rent-free," I reply.

We both laugh, but knowing myself, I'm sure I'll take her words to heart and try my best at mothering. Still, her request almost took my breath away, as my own daughter has always refused to see my maternal side—though she knows full well, it's there. I guess we see what we want to see in others.

Neither Zona nor Margot give their opinions on the topic of the hot and cold spots. I can't help but notice how Zona avoids Vincent. Has he picked up on her iciness? Maybe he doesn't care.

Margot leaves the group, and heads for the upper deck.

While Zona keeps a diary, she has said nothing about expressing herself creatively. Something tells me she's at her most creative when using fancy expletives. While I swear a little, I lack her ability to string together juicy words and sling them at the world. Even Zona has a passion. At least we have something in common: neither of us has an artistic passion. She looks like she longs to spit at the world. That is, when she's not eyeing Leon. Has Kali noticed this?

My head is spinning as I try my best to keep up with all this social interaction. It could soon prove to be tiring.

What's happened to Margot's voice? The only time I've heard her speak was during the interview. Even then, she said very little. She plays haunting melodies on her flute. I think she composed them. Of the three women, I think Margot and I stand the best chance of becoming friends.

. . .

Maybe being a houseboat captain is my true calling. It's not too late at sixty-two, is it? I probably felt the same when I first became a teacher and, years later, a doula, but never was I *this* sure. Although I've always considered myself a natural teacher, I burned out after only a few years. I kept teaching long after I should have quit. While I enjoyed being a postpartum doula after retiring from teaching, I wound up feeling more used as a nanny by a few of the women whom I'd cared for. Because I'd suffered so with post-partum blues following Melanie's birth, my sole aim was to provide comfort for new mothers.

After a few days, I should ask the others to evaluate me. That way, I'll know for sure.

. . .

Once this river ride is over, maybe I'll conduct others, so long as civil war doesn't break out. I love being on the water, even more than when I was a child. Not to sound like I'm tooting my horn, but toot-toot! My personality is well-suited for the job of captain. Not only because of my leadership skills—I'm usually calm in a crisis—but because people seem to feel relaxed around me, and find me easy to confide in, as well. I've always wanted to take an extended boat trip, and I'm sure Melanie not seeing me because of her fears about the virus also has something to do with it.

I've only seen her a few times in the past several years, though we live in the same area. At first, we'd meet outside, in masks. Even then, we had to remain eight feet apart. How hard it's been not to hug my daughter! Little has been harder.

Except for Melanie, no one's waiting for me when I return. It feels like forever since I've been married. My late husband, Peter, died in the first Gulf War. I used to call him 'Peter the Great,' though he was neither cruel nor tyrannical.

· · ·

Again, we see smoke rising behind one of the bluffs. The sound of sirens greets us as we wind around a bend in the river. How close is the craziness? Is rioting going on in a nearby town? I don't bother asking the questions aloud, as we probably know the answer.

"I'm sure we're safer here on the river," I tell my crew.

Heads nod, but no one says anything. Did they hear the doubt in my voice? I've got to work on keeping any misgivings at bay.

Did I already mention that we plan on stopping for gas and provisions every few days? I've circled towns on the map that are close to the river, so that should be no problem—provided looting and general mayhem haven't spread. Fact is, due to the Great Collapse, there's little temptation to linger long on terra firma—as terra firma is none too firm. Supposedly, small towns aren't experiencing the violence found in urban areas. No one knows if it's true.

Some grocery stores are doing well, but many have only enough food on their shelves to keep people from going hungry. It's a relief, but not much of one, as it's believed the supply chain will one day go belly up. I'll have to resist the urge to purchase more than essentials, not only for cost issues, but also because the storage space on the boat is pretty limited.

If you're thinking back to my list and wondering about the wine, wonder no further: it's necessary—the essential ice-breaker in this sort of situation.

Despite the risks, a trip like this is the perfect solution for someone like me. In the past few years, I began to have a problem with hoarding. Books, old magazines, owl figurines, pillows, and pens—whether or not they worked. My place didn't appear all that cluttered, but my compulsion to squirrel away certain items is more than your garden variety packrat. I know I can't do this on the boat. This is part of my modus operandi: learning how to let go, and to go with the flow. Could there be a better place to learn it than living on a river?

. . .

We'll be traveling from the upper part of this great wide river, and according to the river chart, veer southeast, though our journey will end well before it meets the ocean. Not counting various tributaries and backwater areas, we will cover close to fifteen hundred miles. The river continues south for several hundred more.

The gorgeous region we've been passing through is known for steep, narrow valleys and tall bluffs. Just when we get used to one view of the river-road, it alters when turning down the next bend. There are supposedly many lagoon-type coves and backwater places off the main channel, some of which we hope to explore.

When I'm at the wheel, I want to be writing—but when I'm writing, I want to be at the wheel!

Melanie would love it here. When she was little, I took her on several camping trips. We had a pop-up camper she adored. If only she was here, seeing it with me.

My biggest fear is that we'll get stuck.

The chart plotter screen is broken and the aqua scope must be too, as it's showing only blurry images of the river bottom. Luckily, physical charts mark the larger underwater rock piles. There are way too many of them in this area. It's only when we're making our way from the shore to the channel that we need to worry about them. I hope that the spring rains will help prevent us from getting stuck, but it's important to be aware of the possibility.

• • •

I think I'm going to enjoy writing about the others here in my captain's log. I'll have to be discreet and not let them know, or fool them into thinking I'm jotting notes about the journey. Certainly, I'll also write about our daily adventures along with personal reflections. Best for everyone if I'm part of the group, and don't steal myself away when I'm not behind the wheel. The engine purrs. It's like we're floating downstream. While I need to keep a close eye on the water, I'm hoping there will be time for recording some observations.

(Early Afternoon)

I've already gotten a few hostile glances from some of my fellow travelers. I can't seem to help but call out "Ship, Ahoy!" whenever we pass another vessel. So far, we've only passed a few today. While I know this isn't the busiest part of the river, I thought we would've seen more boats by now. Sure, there are probably more thieves in this strange new world, but what's wrong with being friendly? I will not apologize for my extroverted tendencies, given the years of forced repression. Makes me realize how much I've missed seeing others, though I'd forgotten their inhibiting effect. No way will I allow myself to feel straight-jacketed because of my fear of being criticized. Still, I don't want to upset and annoy my passengers. As captain, I need to be sensitive, but realize it's within my rights to be friendly.

· · ·

"Make sure you stand with your feet hip distance apart, your back is straight, and your arms are hanging loosely at your side. Now, inhale and raise your arms above your head. Lower them as you slowly exhale. That's it. Good job!"

A short time ago, we docked for a brief break. While Margot napped and Zona read in the living room, the three others attended my Qigong session on the sunny top deck. Leon looked a good deal calmer than earlier. Our torsos were as stationary as tree trunks, but our graceful and fluid arm-branches danced in a stiff breeze. I felt self-conscious, as I didn't have either this crepey skin under my upper arms or breasts-past-full-bloom in my earlier videos. Maybe my imperfections aren't so apparent in soft lighting. If my current age makes this workout routine less attractive to them, that's their problem.

No one on board's discussed it yet, but I'm sure they, too, feel a sense of relief being out here on the water, despite varying degrees of social anxiety. While the Collapse hasn't affected everyone, it has spread to urban areas, leading some to argue that civil war is almost certain. "Sooner rather than later," is heard with growing frequency. I'd wager that most here have been affected, though so far, we've shied away from talking about it. We all want this trip to be fun, if not carefree. I wonder when the last time any of them enjoyed an outing or trip somewhere other than a grocery store or a doctor's office. Something tells me, it's been a while. I find this oddly reassuring. And I'll bet my new friends are worried, too, that we'll either witness violence or get swept up in a mob scene. Maybe we should come up with a plan about what to do, especially in the latter situation.

Outside of Melanie's fears about me contracting the plague, the main reason she objected to my river adventure was the Collapse. I tried my best to reassure her that the looting and rioting hadn't yet reached small riverside towns. We haven't heard gunshots or screaming. No doubt there's some piracy along the river, but I'm hoping it's something we won't need to worry overmuch. To my knowledge, the only weapons aboard are a couple of sharp kitchen knives, as well as a few boat repair tools that could do a little damage, if necessary.

Many of us came out of hiding only recently—intending to live out our lives to the fullest, before whatever happens next.

I tried my best to entice Melanie to join me, but I should have known better and realized by doing so, she would become even more resolute hiding out in her apartment. She's undoubtedly smarter than her mother.

She's been angry with me ever since I first told her about the river trip. Every time we spoke by phone, right up to the day of the trip, she'd implored me to cancel my crazy plan. I tried my best to listen to her, to not argue. She wondered if I had dementia from the plague. I might have been stricken once—a slight case from one of the early variants. It wasn't diagnosed.

I tried to reassure her that, indeed I did not, but it fell on deaf ears. These last few days, she's been texting me to turn around—to come home...My ears are plugged, so I can't hear you, Mel. La, la, la! Can you see me dancing? And she would say, "And who's the child, Mother? Really?"

It's my life and I don't give a flying fishcake!

(*Later Afternoon*)

Silver Lady is resting near a river town.

The entire group is chatting outside on the upper deck over coffee. The sun plays peekaboo from the clouds. I'm chilly one minute, but warm the next.

"Can't we stop in towns like once a day?" asks Zona.

Before the trip, I'd specified that we'd only be docking in towns every few days, because of the general unrest. Strangers eye each other a lot more warily these days, so why be uncomfortable?

"I agree with Zona. We wouldn't have to stay in any one place for long," says Kali.

"Why would this be necessary?" I ask, playing dumb, and knowing full well that a good part of the reason is their need to be connected to the internet. I sure don't miss the time-suck of social media. Why can't they see how stupid it is? Maybe it's because they're in their early twenties—both twenty-two, I only just discovered.

Despite the Collapse and the world's general craziness, the internet has still been going strong, so I'm sure we'll be able to get a good connection, at least in the bigger towns.

I reassure them we'll be stopping at marinas or riverbanks at least once a day—if not for gas, for a Qigong or yoga session.

Kali claims it's not only because she wants to get online, she simply must get out for walks and prefers towns to the boring countryside. Zona interrupts Kali, saying she just needs some space since the boat's a little cramped.

Thankfully, the other passengers refrain from discussing the matter.

Zona then again complains about not having slept well. She repeats what she'd told me in the interview about her sleep issues, adding that part of the reason she signed on was because her insomnia is so bad that she sometimes falls asleep in the middle of the day. Right in the middle of something.

"Could it be narcolepsy?" I ask.

"A less intense form of it," she says, "but close enough."

Poor girl! I would feel like a dormouse at a tea party. It makes me almost grateful for my garden-variety insomnia.

"Sounds like you're better off around others, then. Being on foot in a strange town might be—" I say, but am interrupted by Zona.

"Look lady, I'm just letting you know my preference."

"I was just going to add that going into a strange town could be dangerous. By the way, my name's Cassie."

"Whatever. It's not like we signed a contract before boarding your boat."

"No, you didn't, though you did sign an application form. While this isn't my boat, I am the captain and the one responsible for getting the houseboat to its owner. Let me think about how often we'll make stops. Is that okay with both of you?"

The two nod. Zona a little more reluctantly. She smacks her gum and has a problem meeting my eyes.

"Any of you others have an opinion on the matter?" I ask, not liking my role as issuer of edicts.

At first, no one speaks, but then Leon's deep voice slices the silence.

"How about getting info on which towns to avoid ahead of time? Maybe ask around and only stop when necessary. If we find ourselves getting restless to stretch our legs on terra firma, then we will."

Leon looks pleased to be the peacemaker. Vincent adds his opinion, which is pretty much the same, though worded a little differently. "Sounds logical. I know you younger folks have more of a need to be online than the rest of us. I get that. What do you think, Margot? Think we should stop more often or only when necessary?"

Margot answers by shrugging her shoulders. She's a pretty woman with eggshell skin, a long black braid, and large blue eyes. Something tells me bohemian skirts and off-the-shoulder blouses, like she's wearing today, comprise most of her wardrobe. Except for her braid, had Margot dressed in all black, she would resemble a friendlier Morticia Adams. She looks like a kind and empathetic soul, but it's hard to tell since she hasn't spoken. It's not the first I've noted her enormous eyes well up with tears. She wouldn't be here if it wasn't for Vincent; that much is obvious. But her silence is most curious.

The others glance at her. Waiting, but less expectantly.

"I don't bite. I promise," I tell her in as gentle a voice as I can muster. Do I have an intimidating effect? If so, it can't just be only my social skills that have fallen a few notches since the pandemic. Maybe she's shy because of the isolation. I get that, though it seems to be having the reverse effect on me now. Maybe Vincent and Margot had a falling out over the trip. While she'd spoken during the interview, her answers were brief. Vincent did most of the talking. I'd interviewed them right before questioning Leon and Kali.

"I'm sure Margot will find her voice one day soon. For now, maybe don't ask her much. She's had a pretty tough go of it lately," Vincent says on her behalf. At last he meets my gaze. While it was nice he defended her, he didn't have to snap. There's something about him I don't trust, despite his gallant behavior, especially regarding Margot. Maybe I'm just jealous as it's been a long time since I've been in a romantic relationship. But no, there's something more—he's always looking over his shoulder.

After assuring them both that I would respect her silence, I add that I've always been inquisitive. I tell the story about when I was only a few months old, how I'd point at everything with a questioning expression. My mother loved to repeat the story about how once I was told the object's name, I'd appear satisfied but become bored, and point at the next unknown. She was relieved when I didn't do the same when introduced to people.

Margot and Vincent silently chuckle over my memory, but then I notice the others observing a young boy wandering by himself on the river bank. He looks lost. Just as I'm about to run over to him, an older boy screams for him to join him. The smaller boy complies. A car horn blasts in the marina lot. Behind the wheel of a beat-up truck sits an angry woman, probably their mother.

Vincent finger-combs his blondish red hair back from his long forehead. With his deep-set blue eyes and shaggy beard, he could be a not-too-distant relative of Van Gogh's.

We return to our earlier conversation about how often to make stops. I let them know that we'll have to see how our journey goes. While we don't have the foresight to know what we'll find downstream, it would help if area locals could forewarn us of any possible impediments.

DAY 4

We are in our first actual town along the river. Hard to believe it's been four days since last on terra firma.

After speaking to a few friendly boaters at the marina, we decide it is safe enough to walk around shabby and tired-looking Byron. It looks so straight from the 1950s that I half expect it to be in black and white. At one time, the town square might have been pleasant enough, but not today. Not a single drop of water drizzles from the spout of the pond fountain. While some water remains in the pond, it is murky and covered with scum and litter. Over on Main Street, there are several empty window fronts. The thriving part of the business district includes a couple of bars, two small restaurants, a hardware store, and the Rialto, a theater. At least there is no evidence of recent looting.

It feels good to explore the mainland. After stretching our legs on the marina pier, we decide to split up before moseying our way through town. And after being told that Mama's on Main serves fresh homemade bread and soup, Margot and Vincent opt to go there for lunch, while Leon and Kali instead choose a small neighborhood bar. Our appetites seem to have returned.

Both couples invited me to join them, but I declined as I could tell they needed some time alone together. Also, I knew I wouldn't feel comfortable around Vincent and Margot, since Vincent does all the talking for Margot. Does she at least talk to him when they're alone together?

I doubt neither pair asked Zona to join them. I try to befriend her by suggesting we stop for a bite somewhere, but she turns me down.

"Uh...no thanks. See you later, ma'am—I mean, Cassie."

"See you back on the boat no later than 5:00, okay?"

Zona nods, but still no eye contact. Is she smacking the same piece of gum from earlier?

Is there something she's afraid I, or the others, will find out about her? It's like she's trying to hide something, though it could be she's shy and defensive. Maybe introversion just seems like this to those who, like myself, are friendly with everyone.

I saunter as slowly as possible up one side of Main Street and down the other. The loneliness pangs from the plague era still gripping me like a Braxton Hicks contraction.

I thought there'd be more hustle and bustle, but it's a sleepy town and only a few people are out and about. An older guy with a silvery goatee is playing a saxophone on a street corner. He gazes at me, stops playing, and smiles seductively before sounding some deep notes on his instrument. For a few minutes, I fall under his musical spell. I tell myself to snap out of it a couple of times, before moving on.

At least the weather is cooperating. It must be close to 80 degrees. Pretty warm for so early in the spring, but then true springtime has become a once-upon-a-time-ago place—a season that thrives only in another world. Winter, almost everywhere, now turns directly into summer.

After scarfing down a grilled cheese sandwich at Debbie's Diner, I buy some bananas, tomatoes, and Brussels sprouts at a market, then make my way back to the boat. Despite the high cost of most items, the fresh food makes me see in Technicolor again. I am hoping I'll see my passengers out and about, but our paths don't cross.

I am eager to be back on the water and hope the others are, as well. The locals are civil, but look at me with suspicion. It makes sense during these disturbing times.

Will the group dynamics change on the trip downriver? Will any of us become true friends? Will the two couples get a little tired of relating mainly to each other? Vincent and Leon appear to have bonded, though I wonder if Leon will exude anger like water from a leaky boat. Will those two get competitive with each other and do that chest-thumping all men do to assert dominance? While Leon has a short fuse, he also seems to quickly move past the ire-provoking issue. And Vincent acts a little too charming—too gallant. I've always been suspicious of men like that. Do the others, except for Margot, think so, too? Of course, I can't ask the always-smiling Kali. Zona appears to avoid any sort of interaction with Vincent, though I can tell she's attracted to Leon, since she's often staring at him. Does this bother Kali? I'll have to ask her when we get a moment alone.

Margot never remains in a room or on a deck if Vincent isn't by her side. No surprise there.

Kali seems to enjoy hanging around me more than the others. Maybe it will keep me from missing Melanie so much. Since Zona and she are so much younger than me, I'll have to take care not to treat them like children. Kali gave me this backward glance when she and Leon went into the bar in town. Could she have been sad I hadn't agreed to join them? Probably not, but I hoped so.

Suddenly, I'm tired out from having to contend with so many people. Maybe it's due to all the previous isolation. How long did I only have my cat, Jezebel, as company? Still, this new, but temporary life on the river is intriguing, especially watching the male/female flirtation dance.

• • •

My thoughts drift like an unmoored boat. No one's ever stayed in my life for long. I was an only child. My parents, two musicians, often left me in the care of someone who viewed me as a job. First, they left me with my paternal grandmother, but she died when I was in kindergarten. I loved nothing better than sitting on her lap telling knock-knock jokes and making her laugh. And then I was pawned off on various relatives. I was good at following their rules, which mostly involved keeping out of their way. I couldn't make them laugh like I could my grandmother; none had her warm lap.

My parents told me they loved me whenever I saw them—which wasn't all that much. But at least I have a few memories of boat rides with my father. My mother didn't like the water, so it gave me a good chance to get to know him better. It softened some resentment over feeling they could buy my love with souvenirs from their road trips. By age ten, I had more stuffed animals and postcards than my friends did. I was forever jealous of their close family ties. Feels like I've always been on the outside looking in at laughter and sheltering embraces.

I couldn't wait to have my own family. And for a minute, I did. The three years Peter and I were married and began raising Melanie are among my happiest. He was a wonderful father. We didn't have much, but we did have love. Melanie has several memories of him, though I don't know how many are actual or which are the ones I repeatedly told her about after he was gone.

She is tall and lanky like her father. Like him, she has enormous eyes that take too much of the world in at a single glance, forcing them to blink and look away. Their rosy unblemished skin always made my pallor paler, if that makes sense.

I like to remind myself that Melanie wasn't always self-sufficient. That once she needed me. Even as a baby, she loved nothing better than the solitude of her crib—she'd babble away for the longest time. Then as she grew, she loved her room and would spend the day building towers from blocks, and drawing sketches of houses, then later towns and cities. She always knew she was going to become an architect. We both did.

. . .

Hard to believe my last romance was with Giles, a whopping ten years ago. It lasted until a couple of years ago, but during that time I kept having dreams about my late husband, Peter. Giles was a good guy, a preacher. A passionate man. He was stocky, about a foot shorter than me, with wild brows and soul-piercing cornflower-blue eyes. We tried our best to keep in touch and remain friends, but it was impossible to sustain. Dreams about Giles began to replace the ones about Peter. There's been no one since, but one can always hope, right? In truth, it's nice to no longer need a man, though sometimes I miss being swept up in a romance. That rush from my own lust.

. . .

I'm writing this on the upper deck, open to the sky. The others are all chatting with each other. Besides me, Margot's the only one observing the passing scenery. I think she's secretly fascinated by life on the river. Green bluffs are on one riverside, and white pelicans dot both landscapes. The Balsam Poplars exude an intoxicating honey scent. How could anyone have problems with the sky so blue? Truly, the pristine serenity is enough to take your breath away. Something tells me the changeable river isn't going to always appear like a wholesome country girl, especially the further south we travel. We've been warned how the waterway can get pretty congested with other boats, be they for pleasure or business.

• • •

The last couple of nights, I slept well, though I woke up a lot in the wee hours. Gratefully, only long enough to peer into my dreams, before slumber once again took me away. And for the first time, none of my dreams have been about Peter or Giles. It's like they don't know I'm here on the boat and can't locate me. This thought, or realization, is liberating. Even after Peter's death and Giles had married another woman, I felt like I had to be accountable to them. If not, it was like I'd betrayed them. I used to dream about one or the other almost nightly; that is, on the nights when I slept long enough to dream. The idiocy of my guilt makes me feel giddy and free.

• • •

Silver Lady's hull has been stuck on trees and tree roots for almost an hour. It feels a lot longer. It feels like she is being stubborn and refusing to journey on. I gun the engine a little too long, and according to Leon, I've flooded it by giving it a little too much gas.

Vincent tells us we should all get out of the boat and push. Come on, Vincent, it's not like the entire vessel is stuck...You guys got this, right? Groans from the others are as noisy as a flock of angry birds.

It is Leon who comes up with a solution: the women can stay on board, and the two men will do the job. They try this first, but it doesn't do the trick.

"You got any other bright ideas, Leon?" Vincent asks.

"Nope, I don't. Okay, ladies, back to Vincent's plan. Time to all pitch in!"

So we do. Thankfully, the water isn't too cold or deep, although the problem in the first place was because of the shallow water. It doesn't take long to realize our team efforts aren't enough to budge the boat. But we don't sulk on the lower outer deck for long before spotting the Coast Guard. There are three on duty aboard the small craft. It takes under an hour to rouse the slumbering *Silver Lady*. We now know our houseboat's too large for us to free by ourselves.

"The water level in this part of the river is a lot lower than it once was," a big mustached Coast Guard official informs us. I can't stop thanking him until he finally says, "Lady, we're just doing our job." I can't help but salute our rescuers as they drive away.

We high-five each other once we are cruising the river again. It is a great bonding moment, but I'm worried it won't be long before we get stuck again. No warning signs are letting us know about the large rocks and there is nothing on the navigation map.

"What if those trees tore a hole in the hull?" I ask, thinking aloud.

"It would be one hull-of-a-mess!" responds the witty Leon. The rest of us groan.

RIVER VOICES

Zona

I keep reminding myself why I'm taking this river trip. If I don't, it feels like a fucking waste of time. Cassie, our gray-haired captain, thinks she's my mother one moment, and BFF the next. One of these days, I'm going to lose my shit and be all over her ass. Still, being here is better than life behind bars. There is that. But does this old lady have to keep yelling "Ship, Ahoy!" at other boats going by?

That private investigator didn't impress me much—he kept obsessing over that warrant for my arrest. Like I told him, it was just for a little shoplifting, but he said he had a problem working for a thief. I'll bet he's got a steady income.

I'm here on this boat for a couple of reasons. For starters, I wanted to get away and take a break from actively searching for my parents, and, because of that tip-off from the PI about my parents' disappearance. If it's a good one, it might turn into a lead. Also, I'm hoping I get more restful sleeps.

Although he doesn't yet know, it turns out Vincent lived in the same town as my parents a few years back, at the time of their disappearance. The PI added how Vincent left town, around the same time, never to return. Now, it may have coincided with his father's death. Still...

The authorities said my parents were kidnapped because of their leftist activism. There've been a few leads as to their whereabouts, but so far, the only real one was a note from my mother stating they were in a jail in the South. It may or may not have been her handwriting. She didn't state where, though the postmark was from Appling, Georgia. When I got there, they weren't in the local jail and officials said they'd never heard of them. Maybe they're both dead. I don't hold out much hope. If my lead doesn't pan out, maybe I'll find a town to my liking and take off without even saying goodbye. I mean, I owe these people nothing.

Too bad Leon is Kali's man. She's too upbeat and laughs like a hyena. Being around her too much would drive me bat-shit crazy. There's something bougie about her. I get his anger at white society and the injustices of the completely rigged system. Older people are always talking about a past when there was hope for equality, though now it doesn't matter since even the rich can't escape the burning building we're all in.

I've been sleeping a little better, but then when I'm rested, I get restless just sitting around. I even joined Cassie's Qi-ging group (or something like that) yesterday before the boat got stuck. Guess being on the River Road will keep me from getting another tattoo, at least for now. The only times I used to sleep well were the night after getting one. Probably my body's response to the pain.

Leon

Glad Kales and I got some time to ourselves back in that bar in Byron. Didn't like all the stares from the white folks when we first walked in, but after we were seated, they were at least chill enough to mind their own business. Probably won't be able to do this when we get further south. It did my heart some good to see the crew could work together trying to free the boat. Made me feel a little less dubious about them. Vincent suggested I record my poetry on my phone video. While I have lost none of my printed poems, I guess it could happen. This would be another way to save it. So far, phone pics and videos aren't disappearing like printed works. Simple idea, my man, and I'm grateful. Why hadn't my homies told me about this? Shit. From now on, I'm going to work this way.

Kali

I told Leon we should think about saying our goodbyes to the others. Not now, but after we reach the next town. The boat seemed large enough at first, but now we're all getting in each other's way. I have my doubts about us all winding up as friends. I like Cassie well enough—she acts more youthful than most her age—but she talks too much and acts nervous. Margot's so mysterious because she doesn't talk. Her boyfriend, Vincent, is a little too old-school for me to relate to. Worst of all is Zona the Interrupter. Why is she so hostile? It's clear she doesn't like me, and likes Leon a little too much. She's hiding something, and if I wind up staying here, I'll make it my mission to find out what. I'll soon let Cassie know, though it wouldn't surprise if she had her own doubts about her.

What were Leon and I thinking, taking this sort of vacation? I know his doctor thought it would be a good way for him to manage his anger, but a trip like this might end up making it worse. Still, we needed to get away from the city and the craziness that became our lives. I just hope we can be alone together more often. I so want to become a decent poet and for him to see I've got potential enough to get a little name recognition.

Margot

They think I'm strange since I don't talk. At least that's the vibe I pick up. Vincent's been a sweetheart and has done his best to explain why, at least for the time being, I'm unable to converse. I hope that one day during this trip, I'll find my voice again, though who knows? It's not like I've ever lost my voice before, so how do I know it can be found? Every morning, I practice vocalizing. So far, I've only been able to emit strange, little scratchy sounds. It's like my throat is not only parched, but clogged with sandpaper. It's not a pretty sound, not one I'd want to irritate others with.

Cassie asks too many questions, or she did at first. She seems to understand why it's not a matter of choice for me. Kali seems sweet, but she's so chatty. Also, I wish she'd stop staring at me. I don't think Zona cares two figs about what's up with me, or anyone, besides Leon. Vincent and Leon have sort of connected; they both laugh at each other's dumb jokes. I'm glad about that, especially since I'm not great company these days.

I hadn't given much forethought as to the boat's available space for me to practice my dances. Late at night, when everyone's asleep, I rehearse one or two of the five dances I've choreographed. Last night, I seemed to have forgotten some of the moves. Could this be part of the Collapse? Maybe I should have recorded them on my phone, but I've promised myself to use the internet only when necessary. At least I have my flute, though I've been a little shy about playing it around the others.

Vincent

Does no one else find this river spectacular? The others don't seem to enjoy watching her like I do. She's moody one moment, and serene the next. Sometimes she's hard to read because her brownish waters are churning, but then she'll settle down and her blue water will fool you into thinking she's always been calm and unruffled. Am I being politically incorrect to refer to it as a she? Frankly, my dears, I don't give a rat's ass. I'm admittedly obsessed. But why aren't the others? Maybe Cassie is, but she talks so damn much and asks too many questions. Why did she want to be captain of this craft in the first place? Someday, I'll ask her. I love the bluffs, the herons. The birds look primordial; otherworldly, or at least like an earlier world before humankind screwed it up. My phone pics will probably last longer than my sketches, so I've got to remember to use it more.

Leon's a cool guy. First time I've bonded with another guy in a long time. I think the last time was before my dad's death. The only one I'm uncomfortable around is Zona. Wonder what her deal is.

I haven't been this curious about what's around the next bend in a long time. Such a perfect get-away from those immigration people trying to track us down…I miss the kids, though, and I know Margot must be having a hard time. It's been weeks since we last saw them.

Margot and I are both worried that the End Times are nigh. I've tried to reassure her humankind will be around for at least another century or two, but who knows? It's a topic I haven't brought up with the others. At first, I'd hoped she'd talk to me in private, but so far, she hasn't. A couple of times she tried, but nothing came out. No one likes the dry heaves, so I don't blame her for not trying, at least for now.

DAY 5

The world's oddness has intensified, despite the unseasonably warm weather, blue skies, and little wind. Being on the water may have little to do with keeping the artwork from vanishing. The theory may not be correct. Some sketches and handwritten pages have vanished. Could it be they were exposed to a small but intense hot spot? Maybe that would account for it. Yet the water in this part of the river is fairly cold, so water temperature must not have a whole lot to do with it.

Vincent didn't bring paints, but a few drawings in his sketchbook are gone. Also, last night, one of Leon's handwritten poems, penned in his beautiful, tiny script, kept fading right before our eyes. It faded until we could barely make out the words, and then, quick as a blink, disappeared entirely. Leon furiously tried to rewrite the faded words but could only recall the first few lines. The same thing happened on his laptop. Maybe entries in my captain's log haven't vanished because they aren't true art. The others know nothing about the kind of writing I do in the log

We're all upset, save Zona, who doesn't see it as a big deal. She's clearly never spent time on a creative project. I'll bet she was the sort who never spent much time on homework when she was in school.

Leon remarks that soon he'll begin recording his poetry on his phone.

Why is this happening? We're all mystified.

Kali, who only recently began to write poetry, says she lost none of the rough drafts she's written since boarding *Silver Lady*. However, she left a thumb drive containing her finished poems with a friend for safekeeping.

I tell her I'd love to either read or listen to her work, adding how I've always loved poetry—especially when it's recited. Not that I understand it well. She seems delighted to hear this and tells me not to worry about 'getting it' right away, as few people do.

"Margot's not only a choreographer and dancer but also a flutist," says Vincent.

We argue about whether a flute player is called a 'flutist' or a 'flautist.' The internet claims Americans prefer 'flutist,' but not me, so 'flautist' she is.

"Zona and I will be a captive audience for the rest of you!" I say to the four others. "How about an occasional evening performance? If you don't want to dance on the boat, Margot, how does a park in a riverside town sound?"

Margot takes a small bow and smiles. Everyone smiles, except Zona, who smirks at my suggestion.

"It sounds like you're encouraging children to play Show and Tell. Yuck."

"That's not what I intended, Zona. I'm truly excited to be around so many creative people. Aren't you?"

She side-eyes me but doesn't answer.

The conversation switches to the Vanishing. We try to recall how long we've been hearing about it. The consensus is that it's been going on for a couple of months now, though, like the original coronavirus back in 2019, it's probably been around a lot longer than first thought. What hasn't vanished are artwork in museums and published books. At least not yet, they haven't. It seems to be a problem mostly affecting new creative works.

Zona rolls her eyes and remarks, "Why do we even need more art or books, anyway?"

We have to physically restrain ourselves from taking a swing at her. Zona is met with a barrage of unwelcome invectives and words. I won't repeat them here. Then, trying to defend herself, she falls asleep. Her head falls forward like a top-heavy flower. A bonding moment for the rest of us, weirdly.

I share what she'd revealed to me: she suffers from a condition—a mild form of narcolepsy that comes on under stress. Will this help them view her differently? Give her a pass? No one seems sad to have this bitchy and sarcastic person unconscious for a while.

Then we all fall silent and gaze at the riverbank.

Zona wakes up after several minutes. A helicopter flying overhead welcomes her back from the realm of sleep. At first, we think the pilot is trying to get our attention. We give up trying to talk about what he is possibly pursuing because of the racket of the helicopter's blades. It gets ahead of us and traces the River Road for about a mile before turning inland toward the smoke. Then we hear the popping of gunfire. The Collapse is no longer confined to cities. My throat feels dry and for the first time, I question my sanity in trying to enjoy a vacation during such a time.

There are fewer bluffs along this section. We pass by areas covered in reeds and rushes, and some of the tallest cattails I've ever seen. I'm tired of driving the boat, but don't want to put anyone out by asking for a break at the wheel. Next, we encounter small sandy beaches followed by foamy inlets. No sooner do I think that Nature has donned a simple evening gown, when we spot some unusual sights. At least they aren't violent.

First, a woman singing the Joni Mitchell song "River." She doesn't seem to notice us. Her rendition isn't all that great, but she looks like she's enjoying sitting on a branch of an oak tree singing her heart out. She has long straw-colored hair and wears a red flower tucked behind an ear. Her super-short blue-jean shorts show off her long, lean legs. Her feet are bare and her legs sway as she sings.

No sooner have we passed her before coming across a man standing at the end of a dock. An older guy with white hair wearing a mask—not like the kind we wore during the pandemic, but a clown mask. He is delivering a monologue to no one in particular, but his mask garbles his words. Something about the End Times. He paces up and down the dock with his hands behind his back.

I get so swept up in the scene that I almost steer the boat into the dock. Even then, he seems oblivious to *Silver Lady*.

Next, we notice a lone cow on one side of the water's edge staring across at the other side. The cow doesn't even blink as we glide by. Is she fixated on something that caught her eye? Hypnotized? At last, we hear her moo and then a long, mournful echo of the moo. It would be heartbreaking, were it not so strange.

What's going on? Will we keep encountering the unexpected? I hope so, but then again...

I need a break. We pull up to dock at a small, abandoned marina. While I can't help but enjoy the surreal riverbank, a Qigong practice with a few of the others helps settle my somewhat frayed nerves. I guess I enjoy having some sense of control. I tell my small class, "Rotate your wrists one way a few times...now, the other way. Lift one foot off the ground and rotate your ankle. First one way, and then the other way. Now, as you inhale, pivot and raise your arms as if you are reaching toward the sun. Exhale as you lower them."

It's then I lose my balance and fall off the lowest, most outer deck and into the drink. Must have been when I was pivoting. So much for my sense of control! Then comes laughter from my students, though mainly from Zona. I'm surprised she's joined us, as she's taken little interest in the exercise.

Wouldn't you know—it is Kali who reaches out her hand for me to grab after I climb up the boat's side ladder. The others are too busy laughing their asses off.

As I towel off, I tell them how it isn't the first time I've had two left feet.

While I don't know for sure, I think the others might like me a little better now. Human nature sure is odd.

. . .

This has been my first chance to travel more than a couple of hours away from home. As a working stiff, I had neither the time nor the money for grand adventures. I saw more students graduate than I ever did babies being born, as I was a teacher for twenty-five years and a doula for only ten. While both careers were rewarding, I wish I'd been born a free spirit like my folksinger parents.

My fairly famous musician parents—Phil and Pat Navrone, otherwise known as The Navrones—are now in a nursing home. My mother doesn't know who her husband is, but he sings to her whenever she's agitated and she immediately calms down.

I wish I could tell my crewmates what I've just written, but no one's expressed much interest, at least so far. Might have something to do with the invisibility of being an older woman.

During the year of the pandemic, I couldn't visit my parents. It gave me some comfort knowing they were there together. I called them weekly—first talking to one and then the other. They put me on speakerphone. The problem was, my mother only chimed in now and then. And as the months went by, she rarely spoke at all. When I'd ask how she was doing, her standard line was, "Fine, dear, don't you worry about me." Dad revealed little about how she really was. When the nursing home at last allowed visitors, I ran to them in the large dining area. After hugging them both, I looked into my mother's face and saw that she almost knew me, but not quite. It broke my heart.

. . .

Back to my doula days. Audrey was my first client who invited me to remain in her life after she no longer needed me, following a couple of weeks after giving birth. But for a couple of months, every time I stopped by to check on her and little Pearl, they'd both be sobbing—especially Audrey. Her crying jags kept getting worse, and I realized my emotional support wasn't working. Not only did I feel embarrassed, but that I was somehow at fault. I consulted my class notes and even called two other doulas, both of whom told me Audrey's post-partum depression wasn't at all my doing. All I could do was refer her to professional counseling.

I kept stopping by to see her at no charge. On my first day off the clock, Audrey served coffeecake and coffee. She teared up, but smiled through her tears, saying how the routine was getting easier and she wasn't so afraid of not being up for the job. And by the last day of the week, she hugged me, and even admitted she simply needed a friend.

I began singing made-up lullabies to Pearl as I rocked her in her nursery, musing over what she'd be like as a girl and teenager. Audrey would always nap at this time. Then one day, she walked in on us. Pearl was smiling up at me, making cooing sounds, like little delighted squeals. Audrey wasn't pleased. Maybe she'd never gotten a response like this. I'd never know as she dismissed me on the spot. She changed her phone number and wouldn't respond to my emails. I still occasionally have dreams about Audrey. They're rarely good ones.

• • •

After we docked for the night, I noticed I'd received several voice messages from Melanie. The first was a sweet, but imploring one. "Mom, I miss you!" Yet the ones that followed were insistent, petulant, and commanding me to "Turn the boat around right now!" followed by, "What have you done with your life?" and finally, "Oh, my God, I don't believe your drama!" In the last one, she threatened to have the authorities pull the boat over and take me into custody. I'm sure she will tell them I'm unfit to be a captain, that I'm delusional, and that I'm endangering the passengers, as well as myself.

My feelings are beyond hurt. Hard to believe how much a child can turn the tables on a parent. This one sure has.

I phoned her back. She didn't pick up, so I left a voicemail: "Don't you think the police will have better things to do, especially during these times? You're the one always saying we're in a civil war!" I can well-imagine what she'd say. Something like: "That's precisely why I'm worried about you. You've really gone off the deep end this time, Mother!"

I'm heartbroken over how ashamed she is of me. Nothing would matter more to me than to have my daughter look up to me. I know that's never going to happen, so I have no choice but to deal with it. I wish there was someone here I could talk to about this. Maybe Margot?

• • •

I became a doula soon after grown-up Melanie informed me she would never have children. While I never wanted a big family, I sure wanted her. I wouldn't want her to have a child if she didn't have the longing for one. Soon afterward, a friend told me how pleased her daughter was with a doula she'd hired for the first few weeks after she'd given birth. I took the necessary childbirth education courses, followed by training, during the last couple of summers of my teaching career. I quit teaching and became a certified post-partum doula. One way or another, I was going to get my fix at being a grandmother! I hoped at least one of the new mothers would want me to stay on in both her and her baby's lives. They would become my adopted daughter and grandchild.

Melanie laughed until she cried when I told her my plans.

"Mom, do you really think you'll find this fulfilling? Why not just volunteer at a pre-school and become one of those smiling grannies who bring homemade cookies to the classroom? You'll get those hugs! Isn't that really what you're after?"

Melanie didn't get it. At least I hoped not.

DAY 6

Yesterday's delightful oddities led to a sense of unreality unlike any other. Maybe these more creative individuals are used to unusual perceptions, but not a mostly grounded person like me. I'm afraid to stand up since my head's whirling. While I love dreaming, I hope I'll soon slip into a dreamless snooze. Am I imagining that the boat deck is rocking or is the river itself churned up and causing everything to be off kilter? I doubt my morning meditation or a Qigong session will help calm me down. Even Zona seems rattled. I'm glad I'm not the only one feeling strange. The tattoos of butterflies and ladybugs on her left arm look so agitated, it wouldn't surprise me if they flew away. Mind you, this is a girl who could be deemed Queen of the Poker-Face.

· · ·

Vincent's at the wheel. As mentioned earlier, one of my crewmates takes it over whenever I need a break.

After a two-hour dreamless snooze, I join a few of the others on the upper deck. I'm grateful for the silence. We are together, but alone. The river atmosphere has changed since earlier. The opposing banks now look closer, a lot closer than before.

Lately, I haven't received any threatening texts from Melanie. So far, she hasn't responded to my voicemail.

I go inside to the driver's cab.

"Could you have taken a wrong branch of the river? It's much narrower here, though still fairly deep." I try to be gentle and non-accusatory with Vincent.

He denies having done so and gives me a hostile sneer, which I pretend not to see. Why can't men ever admit mistakes?

"Well, it won't be a problem so long as it meets up with the main branch. Keep your fingers crossed we don't get stuck."

Vincent pretends he doesn't hear me. He gives an exaggerated sigh and gestures toward the wheel like he is giving me a present. Without so much as a nod, he vanishes down the steps to the lower deck. My face burns and it's hard to swallow. Just when I'd begun to think of them as my crew, this happens.

I pull up to a short dock and turn off the engine. We need to talk.

"Anyone else notice that we took a different branch of the river?" I ask the others, except for Vincent and Zona, who is in her cabin, no doubt asleep.

"It seems like it narrowed down some in the past half hour, but Vincent kept us on River Road. I'd almost swear by it," says Leon. The women either have no opinion on the matter, or they don't want to offend Vincent. There's a general sense of uneasiness.

"Do any of you realize how easy it would be to get lost if we stray from the main branch? That is, unless we're supposed to. I checked the chart, and it didn't show the branch we're on, but it didn't show the river narrowing either. I know it's hard to be constantly alert, but I don't want to backtrack."

My remarks get stonewalled. Now they perceive me as a dictator. Wonderful.

"Cassie, do what you think is best. You're the captain, so you get to make the call. Just don't expect us to do any better than how we're doing when we're filling in for you behind the wheel," says Vincent, with arms crossed in front of his chest.

"Yeah, but everyone agreed to take shifts before the trip. It doesn't mean falling asleep behind the wheel!" Do I sound as irate as I feel?

"That didn't happen on my watch. Maybe you don't want us taking turns playing captain. You could do all the driving and we'd just have shorter days on the river. How's that sound?"

"Forget I said anything."

After my semi-rant, I hastily make my way back to the driver's seat, feeling more anxious about the journey than ever before. If anyone gets in my way, they better watch out!

. . .

The riverside trees and small beaches all look the same here, but we haven't passed a single boat for several miles. Bird song is near riotous and the birds themselves have colorful plumage, almost tropical. You'd expect to see palm trees and steamy weather, but no, it's still springtime in the upper Midwest. The breeze is cool and we need to wear jackets on the outer decks. The river's churned up from recent rains and smells, at times, like rotten eggs or skunk spray. Right now it's musky and more tolerable, but for how long?

We pass a young teenage girl taking selfies and acting oblivious to her surroundings. Her long blond hair reaches her waist. She's dressed in a short skirt and a puffy-sleeved white blouse. She doesn't notice us, even though we wave and call out to her. How strange!

Next, in view, is a table for two at the end of a pier. Definitely romantic, until I notice a lizard beneath a glass covered lid. Is it the main course or an appetizer?

I almost put the boat in reverse. Did anyone else see it?

Kali and Leon both nod, and Leon's about to say something when the head of a dolphin-like fish emerges from the water. It's much smaller than the sort you see in salt water, but the exact miniature. Maybe it is anadromous and returns to spawn in freshwater. I explain in my best teacher's voice how the term applies to fish that swim up rivers from the sea. For the first time in a while, they look at me like I know what I am talking about.

The fish seems to smile at us, making seal-like sounds, trying hard to tell us something. But then the smile disappears, and its voice is sad, though still plaintive. I feel stupid for not understanding. Next, its entire body leaps from the water, then disappears. Maybe it's trying to explain how sad it feels, how it longs to be with dolphin cousins splashing about in a salt-water sea.

And then we see the cow again. A different cow, no doubt, but it sure looks like the same one from before. She's now sitting beneath a tree, but still staring out at the river, oblivious to us.

It's always bothered me to think of a non-human animal an 'it.' Regarding, the dolphin-like fish, it is a little easier—if in fact, it was a fish and not a mammal. Yet this one was clearly more intelligent than most of its brethren.

I would simply dismiss this as being a dream, if not for the group sitting in a circle around a campfire on a small beach. Three couples and several young children. They wave at us like we are long-lost friends and we wave back with equal enthusiasm. Despite the interest each group has in the other one, no one calls out greetings of any sort. No one from the other group suggests we stop and join in the festivities. Frankly, I'm relieved.

Silver Lady is suddenly conscious of the sound of her engine. She sounds like someone clearing their throat, the way her engine revs up then sputters, before revving up again. Why not turn it off and let her drift downstream? Maybe she doesn't want to pass by the oddities too slowly because she doesn't want to be seen. No, it's better not to dillydally.

A campground, a short distance away, convinces me the group must be campers.

How good it feels to know we exist! There is nothing worse than to doubt one's existence—to wonder if you're in a dream...

After some discussion, we agree that we had gone down a different branch of the river. Vincent, who has rejoined us, replaced at the wheel by Kali, concludes the same. Looking at a map, we note the fork we probably took. With any luck, we should soon meet up with the main branch. Relief surges through me like a mighty river, as I certainly don't want to make our trip longer than necessary. Something tells me even if this trip is merely a vacation, I'll feel better knowing we haven't gone too far astray. Will this happen again? Winding up on another branch happened all too easily, so maybe it's more than simply a matter of not paying close enough attention.

Maybe there are mysterious currents we can't control? No, that's superstitious hogwash! I won't succumb to that sort of mystical silliness.

We're about to pull up to a dock near a small town. Once we find out its name, I'm sure I'll be able to locate it on my map. Still, I don't know exactly where we are. If we're where I think, there's no town shown on the map. Maybe the town was recently built. I don't want the others to lose faith in me, so I will not let on that I don't know. Also, I won't admit to not knowing which state, or soon-to-be former state, we're in.

What I know for sure is that we're still in the northern part of the river and headed southeast.

As a little girl, I had a repeating nightmare about being lost in unfamiliar neighborhoods. One street would take me to the next. I kept getting more and more lost in the suburban jungle. If I had been brave enough to knock on someone's door, I could have asked to use their phone and called home. I knew my phone number, but not my address. Since I didn't know the landmarks and hadn't left breadcrumbs on the sidewalks, I couldn't even retrace my steps. After every nightmare, I'd wake in a panic. My parents would tell me I became much calmer after I learned my address and phone number.

Maybe I should tell the others about this, but no one cares. And why should they? They'd definitely have doubts about their captain.

. . .

We've moored at a small marina next to a deserted park. Like the last one, this marina is just outside a small town. It's clearly marked on my map, but the town is not. Could the marina have been moved to this location? As I don't want to appear as the addled captain, I will not ask my passengers. Any sniff of uncertainty could make them feel uneasy. I've got to bear this in mind. It is my job to appear both knowledgeable and cucumber-cool.

The marina is pretty rundown, and there are only a few boats in the slips. It's obvious we're all feeling uncomfortable; some of us are even leery. It would be different if we at least knew the town's name.

Since none of us want to walk around hungry on unknown streets, we decide to dine on our pre-made sandwiches. While it's late for lunch, it's too early for dinner. I can tell the others, like me, feel safe sitting at the picnic table. Even after quietly munching cheese or peanut butter on soggy bread, no one's exactly eager to explore the area. We couldn't be more hesitant than if we'd landed on another planet.

"It's a jacaranda," Leon says, pointing at a purple flowered tree in the center of the park. His voice is reverent and his outstretched hand shakes. I've never seen this sort of tree before. It takes the jacaranda to get us off our butts. He leads the rest of us over to it like a proud tour guide. Once again, I'm clad in my purple caftan and feel almost glamorous.

A spicy aroma braided with honey greets our nostrils.

"When I sniff the flowers, the fragrance disappears," I complain.

Leon says it's because the scent's coming from last year's dried blossoms, many of which are still beneath the tree. We whisper as we slowly approach this veritable goddess of flower trees. Even Zona looks gob-smacked.

The blonde who'd been taking selfies on the riverbank now stands nearby, taking another one. She's pretty like a Barbie-doll, and like Barbie, she seems stuck on herself. I no longer feel glamorous...She doesn't notice the tree or us, and we are the only ones in the park! Her oblivious manner becomes less disconcerting as almost everything seems off, almost otherworldly. The others, except Margot, look like dreamers struggling to wake up. Margot, in her long, flowy skirts, appears to be living a waking dream. She's the only one of us enjoying the moment, including our tree expert.

I call out to my stumbling, bumbling crew, "What if we just go with the flow?"

I begin to sing loudly, "'Row, row, row your boat, gently down the stream. Merrily, merrily, merrily, merrily, life is but a dream!' Anyone want to join me in singing it in rounds?" We might as well accept this air of unreality, right?

"No, thanks, Cassie," says Leon, who has donned his mirrored aviator sunglasses. They bug me because I can't see his eyes—just the reflection of a crazy, old, hippie-lady. Startled, I don't recognize myself in the mirror image.

"Think I'll pass, too. Maybe once we're back on the boat," Vincent adds, his long fingers combing back his unkempt hair. At least he'll consider my proposition, which suggests he's got an open mind. Still, there's something secretive about him, but maybe it's just his aloofness that makes him seem so. Why are some people such unsolvable puzzles?

The two younger women act agitated, like they are having difficulty breathing. Could they be having panic attacks? Is there a way I can help them? Seeing their discomfort helps calm me down.

This has happened to me before, when I'd be somewhere with my daughter. Even before the pandemic, she hated crowded places—much like me, though because I was her mother, I put on a brave face.

I suggest to the nervous duo to try some deep breathing before we walk into town. The area looks peaceful enough, but I know remarking about it will do little to alter their anxiety. None of us know exactly what we'll encounter here.

Margot smiles and hums 'Row, row, row, your boat...' She prods me to join her.

"Oh, c'mon, Margot, sing along with me!" I prod her in response, not expecting her to chime in. I worry she'll be mad at me for asking. She isn't. Instead, she laughs and shakes her head. Her calmness is soothing; it allows me to shift my focus back to Zona and Kali.

"I think it's the cumulative effect of the strange sights we've been seeing. Let's check out the town and see what mischief we can get in, shall we?"

With improved moods, the six of us stroll down a curvy little path through the park, then down a couple of residential streets until we reach the town. It is clean and has a freshly painted look. Not much foot traffic. Where are the townsfolk on this pleasant late afternoon? The attached buildings on both sides of the street are two-storied, and plain—typical of a town that doesn't have much history or is trying to whitewash its history. Many of the storefronts stand empty. This explains why there are so few people out-and-about.

The two younger women accompany me into Tony's Market while the others stroll down Main Street. The store's seen better times, but several cars are in its lot. An older man, I assume to be Tony, greets us in a friendly manner. It's obvious we aren't from the area.

"This is going to sound crazy, but could you tell us where we are?"

My question causes Tony to double over in laughter. Tears run down the corners of his eyes. His face and rather bulbous nose turns beet red as he continued to guffaw. I tell him if he will not tell me the town's name, we'll simply find someone else who would. We'll take our business elsewhere or ask strangers on the street.

At last, he catches his breath. After pinching his nostrils, he apologizes for his outburst. We aren't the only boaters who've asked this question, and he doubts we'll be the last. I refrain from asking him why he found it so funny.

"What you really need to know, ladies, is that you did indeed take the wrong fork, but no worries: you'll meet up with the main River Road in a couple of days. But pay close attention, as there's another junction you'll arrive at several hours downstream. Take the channel on your left. It should have a fairly flat and sandy beach. You'll know if you accidentally took the wrong one, as the current there is much faster. There've been many accidents, some of them fatal. Either way, you're in for some surprises and should take precautions."

After I thank him for the advice, Tony advises us to stock up on provisions, as well as gas.

"At one point, you'll come across a circus. Sorry to spoil your surprise, but I promise you'll still be surprised and more than a little amused."

"A circus? On the river?" I ask him.

Kali and Zona remain quiet, but listen with growing interest.

"No, it'll be set up on the riverbank. You should be able to watch it from your boat, or if a slip's available, you could watch it from there, or from makeshift seating. The setting makes it more fun than usual, as some of the performers do some incredible water tricks."

Despite his earlier rudeness, I thank Tony for the information. He has been most helpful. I next asked about the Vanishing. Is it getting any worse?

He shrugs.

If he knows anything, he isn't about to let on. He then quietly mentions the Land of Doze and how we'll like it there. As an afterthought, he adds, "Some folks find it strange. Mighty strange...but since you're on the artsy-side, it should suit you."

"Then what about the Collapse? Any talk of civil war?"

Again, he hunches his shoulders. If either has made its presence known here, he's not about to give us any information.

I tell him how I've heard about the Land of Doze, but so far haven't been able to locate it on a map.

"No surprise, it's not on a map." He then provides a rough description about how we'll know it when we get there.

Oddly, I don't think he has a clue about the Vanishing or the Great Collapse. I've been taking it for granted that everyone knows about how things are disappearing, like everyone knows there's no longer a united USA. Have I always made so many assumptions?

Once again, I thank him again for the information. Before the girls and I set off to do some shopping, Tony adds for us to be on the lookout for pirates.

Pirates on this stretch of the river? I haven't considered the probability, but due to all the violence occurring on land, certainly there's looting, or worse, along the river road. He also tells us to be especially on the lookout for pairs of men pretending to be friendly area locals. They may offer beers from their coolers and then suggest—even insist—on bringing the beverages aboard.

"They especially like houseboats. Beware of them," Tony further warns. "They're not only known for pilfering belongings, but they're often hunting for cash."

Next, he divulges another rumor about a group of five women in a patrol boat. They dress in stolen coastguard uniforms. It's said they'll pretend to search boats after forcing passengers onto shore. After doing so, they steal the craft, which usually winds up downstream—stripped down like an abandoned car.

"At least none of the victims get harmed. Not that I know of, anyway," Tony hastens to add.

This time, I don't bother thanking him for the new information, as my anxiety level is now dangerously high.

We load up two grocery carts with food. After adding bananas and grapes to the cart (though they aren't on our list), Kali asks me: Should we check once more with Tony about our whereabouts? I reply that based on his reaction, we should find someone else to ask. She readily agrees.

After the isolation experienced during the pandemic, it's disconcerting to be on a river trip with strangers and not know where you are.

The rest of the crew couldn't find out the name of the town either, but had also heard murmurings about the Land of Doze from residents.

I guess we'll just refer to this locale as the Town-Before-Doze. Doze sounds like a perfect stop for houseboaters. If luck remains, we'll reach it in the next couple of days.

Leon and Vincent listen attentively to the information Tony gave us. Vincent jots down the directions, lest we forget. No one's particularly surprised to hear about the circus or the pirates.

Vincent spoke with a guy, who, he says, looked like a public official in a shirt and tie. He got another scoop, too: a couple of miles inland there were definite signs of the Collapse, as formerly wealthy people were caught looting in stores and even rioting.

• • •

Leon and Kali fish from the pier and bring back four or five bass in a bucket. After staring at them for a while, I decide to forego having my share of the grill. Still bothered by the miniature porpoise we saw swimming alongside *Silver Lady*. Who wouldn't be?

Since Margot and Vincent don't eat meat, it's only Zona, Kali, and Leon who enjoy the fish fry.

We discuss one of Vincent and Margot's preoccupations, the End Times. Maybe we all feel it looming a little too close for comfort these days. Kali is the only one who doesn't want to discuss it. She protests so vehemently we soon change the topic.

We must have entered the right channel, as the water here is calm—presuming Tony gave us accurate information. But why wouldn't he have? We pass by a sandy beach, though I've been expecting a larger one based on his description. I don't want to worry the others unnecessarily, so I won't express my concern about the possibility of Tony's misinformation.

Everyone's curious about the circus. I wish I'd asked Tony for an approximate distance to reach it. I'm assuming it won't be along this branch of the river. There I go again, making assumptions.

DAY 7

The day began early, practicing peaceful Qigong movements with a few of the crew. It's now late morning. A couple of my crewmates have joined me on the upper deck as I motor slowly down the waterway. We piece together what we now know about the Land of Doze. It's no doubt a sleepy area where little happened, as its name suggests. The scenery is supposedly as placid and boring as its inhabitants. We guess that those who live there haven't yet heard of the Collapse. It makes us long for simpler times.

There isn't much to observe on this leg of the river, but we've seen water-fowl, a couple of locks, and a few barges. A woman's floppy-brimmed hat, a red scarf, and a yellow flip-flop float by. Could they be from a shipwreck or careless boaters? A strong skunk scent makes us plug our noses.

We decide to take a break near another sandy beach.

"Ship, Ahoy!" I cry out to a couple of canoers, who, like us, have stopped to stretch their legs. Zona again shoots me a menacing look. An available slip makes it a perfect place to give *Silver Lady* a brief rest. I wonder if the others heard her sigh—not that I dare to ask.

The canoers turn out to be a friendly older couple. The man is short, slight, and mostly bald. He rises from a picnic table holding a coffee mug. "Join us for some coffee?" he calls out with the lungs of a younger man. His female companion remains seated, but waves. She has short, silver curls that don't match her kittenish face. There are four extra mugs on the table. It's as if they've been waiting for us.

The girls dawdle by the river, but the rest of us join them.

Jim and Doris tell us about the town of Doze. Evidently, they're on their way there, too. They've been renting a cabin outside of town for the past several springs.

"It's lovely to shop in town, and they have some cute little eateries. There's a pink hotel and a boutique, but no swinging hot spots," Doris says, then laughs in a high-pitched, girlish voice. I am the only one who laughs, as no one else gets her reference to a Joni Mitchell song.

People named the entire area the Land of Doze because of its sleepy character—a relaxed lethargy is said to immediately affect you. Jim tells us how some folks doze the entire time they are in the area. "Bad as the land of poppies," he adds.

It doesn't sound like somewhere I need to visit, but the others are now curious.

Our bluebird mascot lands on a nearby tree branch. Have I mentioned him before? He's blue with a red breast. All morning, he could be found on one of the decks. I'm sure I also saw him on a tree branch a little downstream. We've seen a lot of him ever since Byron. I hope Blue—that's what I named him—continues with us on our entire journey. While I don't think he will, maybe I'll invite him.

Blue's presence means we're in for good luck, I tell the group.

Zona tells us she's read bluebirds stand for a connection between the world of the living and the dead. Maybe Blue is simply a friendly bird with blue feathers. No more or less. As Zona isn't one to tangle with, I refrain from saying so. Instead, I ask if anyone can recall the name of the lovely purple tree we saw in the Town-Before-Doze. Puzzled expressions tell me all I need to know. It's on the tip of my tongue, but never rolls off it.

We wish Jim and Doris safe travels and they tell us the same. If it weren't for Blue, the tedium of the scenery—or lack thereof—would really get to us. Maybe it already has. I feel grouchier than usual since I'm unable to locate a page from DAY 5 of my captain's Log. Someone probably tore it out of the log-book.

Since we're all together out on the top deck, I ask if anyone has noticed a loose sheet of paper. Either no one has seen it, or will admit having seen it. I explain in as non-accusatory a fashion as I can muster that I could have lost it—though how, I don't know.

"On that specific page, I'd written the tree's name, so if anyone comes across it, please let me know," I state in as neutral a tone as possible.

Instead of dwelling on the possible culprit who ripped the page from my captain's log, I decide to never leave the log out for anyone to read. There's a cabinet below the steering wheel where I'll be sure to lock it up. I'm the only one with the key.

I'm upset with myself, as I'm the supposed captain of this cruise. No point in getting paranoid or dwelling on the matter. Still, I can't help but wonder if one or more of the others have built up some resentment toward me. Maybe I've come on too strong, but I am the one in charge, after all. The social complexity's beginning to tire me out. Had I been able to persuade Melanie to take this river adventure with me, maybe I wouldn't have needed all these others. Yet there was no way I could have persuaded her. Maybe it's for the best she didn't come along. I don't know how anyone could turn up the chance for this sort of adventure: for never knowing what's beyond the bend.

If Tony was correct, tomorrow we should meet up with the river's main channel.

Several of the larger streams we've passed aren't showing up on my navigation maps. Odd, as I thought I'd bought the best ones available. We still can't get the electronic navigator to work. The underwater rock piles closer to the shores are on the maps, so why not all the channels? Not wanting to alarm the others, I keep this to myself.

Zona trumpets her boredom for the tenth time in the last hour, and then smacks her gum while absent-mindedly twirling a small section of her spiky, dark hair. The other two women bite their lips to keep from letting loose on her.

Who does Zona think she is? Why is she even on this trip? Will she be complaining the entire time? I've felt restless myself now and then, so I see why she's bored, but why complain about it? It only makes things worse. She's no doubt taking this trip because she wanted more drama in her life after the isolation of the pandemic, but this isn't exactly the high seas.

I commiserate with her over the plainness of the riverside, but remind her we've certainly seen some unusual scenery, and no doubt, we'll be seeing more.

Zona purses her full lips in response. "I wouldn't be complaining if my phone was working, right? How about you, Kali? Aren't you bored?"

Kali shrugs her scrawny shoulders and smiles widely. "Guess not as much as you, but I have my poetry. When I'm not chatting with others, I'm jotting stuff down."

"But you know it's just going to disappear, so why bother?" asks Zona, rolling her eyes.

"None of my poems got erased unless I was the one doing the erasing."

Zona's mouth falls open in exaggerated surprise.

"It's true," says Leon. "My theory is it's because she crosses out so much, anyway. Whatever the invisible force is that takes away what should be indelible, it can't quite keep up with her. I call her the Cross-Out Queen."

He's wearing his mirrored sunglasses, making it difficult to tell who he's looking at. If it's Zona, why is he wasting his words?

"I'm your queen, you mean," teases Kali.

"You know you are, Kales. All hail Queen Kales!"

Zona rolls her eyes again, blowing a gum bubble and then popping it with a finger.

"Maybe I'll just sleep the days away once we're in that supposed Doze Land."

Two things occur to me. First, the tree we saw in the Town-Before-Doze was called a jacaranda. The others congratulate me for remembering it. Second, I realize what had become of the page from the captain's Log. Zona stole it. I have no proof, but I suspect her more than the others. No mention needs to be made, nor will I directly accuse the girl. However, I'll take notes following scrupulous scrutiny. I should seriously think about buying a pair of mirrored sunglasses.

The sun on the top deck slips behind a cloud, making it chilly, so everyone but Zona and Kali decide to return inside. Leon takes over at the wheel, giving me time to mull over Margot's muteness. She gives Vincent a nod, which I see as permission to give me at least somewhat of an explanation. Her large blue eyes blink and then look away. She plays with her thick black braid, masking her mouth before flicking it like a horse's tail, trying to get rid of pesky flies. My two braids combined aren't as thick as her one. Even when I was younger, my hair was never so thick and lustrous.

"You sure it's okay to tell Cassie?"

Margot, sighing, smooths her skirts, nods, and drops her heavy braid.

Vincent begins the tale. About a year ago they'd met at a riverside park. She'd been flying kites with several children of various ages. He knew she couldn't be their mother, as there were simply too many. "Ten of them, in fact, right, Margot?"

She nods again.

While he'd been curious about her, he hadn't introduced himself to her that first day. Instead, he'd sat at a picnic table sketching. She hadn't noticed him then, or in the next few days, for that matter.

At this, Margot shakes her head. It looks like she wants to say something, but doesn't.

After a good hour of kite flying, they'd had a picnic, and then Margot enchanted the children, and him, with her sonorous flute playing.

"A Jethro Tull tune, right?" he asks. Margot nods again, smiling at the memory. Her smile reveals a small gap between her two front teeth.

"It was truly sonorous. So-nor-ous." Vincent repeats the word slowly, incorrectly sounding out its syllables.

Vincent began sketching her in one of her long, gypsy skirts while she played the flute. And then he began drawing the large, dark-eyed children of various ages. They still hadn't spoken to each other, but he knew she'd show up with her kids at the park on Tuesday afternoons. Each week, there were fewer children with her than the week before. So, on a Tuesday, a couple of weeks later, he walked over to her picnic table. Only three children were playing on the swings. He figured she must be an after-school teacher.

After they'd at last introduced themselves, Vincent showed Margot his sketches, hoping she'd tell him why she hadn't brought all the children.

Instead, she told him how she'd once been a dancer, but now worked in a drugstore. Also, her father had been a conductor of a small city orchestra but now had dementia.

Vincent was amazed at how readily she offered the information. Were the children members of her dance troupe?

"It's nice to finally meet you!" Margot had called out, not answering his last question, as she and the three kids made their way to an old mini-van in the parking lot.

When they next met in the park, she was by herself. Margot spoke breathlessly about how she'd gotten fired from her job at the drugstore. Her boss thought she should be friendlier with customers. This struck Vincent as strange, since she'd certainly been friendly enough with him.

It was on that day when she finally asked him about himself.

Presently, on the houseboat, Vincent winks at Margot after saying he hadn't known at the time if she'd been truly interested in him, or if she had been redirecting the conversation so she wouldn't have to tell him where the children were.

Why is he so slow in telling the tale of how they met? Who were those kids? Still, after hearing the story, I can't help but feel better about both of them. While Vincent is artistic and intriguing, he doesn't strike me as trustworthy. This isn't the first time I've had this thought. I don't know why, except it could have something to do with Margot's silence. Maybe it makes him nervous. Also, I'll bet he's on the secretive side because of those children. Maybe the children have something to do with her muteness? Being on the boat, they can better hide out from authorities.

I have some concerns about concealing my attraction to Vincent. There's something about his beard, the dimple in his cheek, his receding reddish blond hair, as well as his lankiness that would've made me swoon as a younger woman. I'll bet he was born looking like Van Gogh, and that's why his parents named him Vincent. Maybe I'll ask him. Unlike the famous artist, this Vincent is a portrait painter, though he claims to enjoy dabbling in other sorts of art forms, too. Somehow he's eked out a living at it. Also, he doesn't seem to see himself as an artist with a capital 'A,' and even calls himself a lowly artist.

I can't help but feel interested in him, though I'm well-aware that not only is he in a relationship with a woman, but I'm old enough to be his mother. I used to laugh at women I saw as cougars and here I am now, running with the pack. Never did I think I'd be attracted to a younger man, at least not at my current age. For Margot's sake, I'll conceal it as best I can.

Apart from Peter and Giles, I've always found myself attracted to the wrong sorts of men. Those bad boy types who are usually married but don't want to be. A therapist once told me my fear of loss keeps me from committing. An obvious explanation, but at least I found out I wasn't interested in the men strictly out of lust.

After Margot goes below deck to get something, Vincent tells me—his words, first trickling, then gushing out, unlike before—how he lost his wife and little girl to the plague five years ago. The vaccine hadn't been tested long enough for them to trust the science. It had nothing to do with politics, he said. After their deaths, he changed his mind and got vaccinated.

And then, three years ago, his father died from a massive heart attack. Vincent had recently moved back to his hometown, where his dad had just lost his job as mayor. After the funeral, there'd been little point for Vincent to continue living there, as he had no other family or friends. The deaths of loved ones drained him of all vitality. "Although," he said, "meeting Margot and seeing her with the children ignited my tired old soul."

"I guess that gives you an almost sunny disposition," he recalls Margot once teasing him. They'd had a good laugh together. Then he'd asked Margot, "So, what happened to all those kids you used to bring to the park?" Again, she said nothing. Already smitten by her looks and talent, Vincent was now taken by her mysterious nature. Who was this woman? He fell for her hard, and they began going out. Their relationship quickly developed.

My feelings of being excluded diminish. I feel honored Vincent has confided in me. A couple of my questions are answered. Still, there's something mysterious about him, not exactly sinister, but like he's hiding something. Do the others, except Margot, see him this way? Could that explain why Zona acts skittish around him, and sometimes even recoils?

I asked what happened to the children. What was Margot's role with them in the first place?

It is then we both realize the boat is stuck again. This time it's a sandbar. Since we aren't snagged on jagged rocks, it should be a simple matter of all of us pushing—giving a simultaneous heave-ho. To call *Silver Lady* stubborn will only worsen the situation. Even Zona knows to keep quiet. The water is colder than the first time we were stuck. The problem, I think, is that although we are closer to shore than before, it's more difficult to get a firm footing on the river bottom. Our feet keep sinking in the sand. Not like it was back in the headwaters. There is nothing we can do but get back aboard and wait for a larger boat to come and free us. While I'm the one responsible, Leon has been the one driving the houseboat.

Back on board, I scold Leon for not paying attention to the channel guides, but he reminds me that our navigation charts don't show this channel. He, clearly, wants to tell me to take a flying leap off the boat. He doesn't. For a minute, I thought of apologizing, but why should I?

I was hoping to hear more from Vincent about Margot, but the two of them disappear into their cabin. What exactly had happened to the children she'd cared for? Is the couple here to hide out from someone? I wish I could express my suspicions, but hopefully, the rest of their story will come out.

The rest of us sit around the living room trying to warm up.

Leon and I usually get along pretty well, though I wouldn't describe him as the easiest person on the boat. He's in his early forties, wears glasses that enlarge his already enormous eyes, and has an afro. Not as tall as Vincent, but still well over six feet. If it weren't for his anger, I'd find him just as attractive as Vincent. The others don't seem as bothered by his temper. Kali's able to defuse him and turn him into a teddy bear. Leon is not only a poet, but two years ago he became a local-level leader of Black Lives Matter. He mostly talks about his fears that the fight for equality will be unrealized because of all the civil unrest around the country. Not only is it intensifying, he says, but soon we'll wind up in a civil war. While we're all concerned about the possibility, he acts like he's the only one aware of it. It's become his mission to wake us up, and to keep us all awake.

His doctor had advised him to take a trip, thinking it would help lower his blood pressure.

Earlier today, after Zona and Kali had left the room, Leon confided in me about a premonition he had about Zona.

"I told Kali this morning what I'm about to tell you: Zona won't be with us for the entire trip," he said, pushing his glasses up the bridge of his nose.

"And what makes you think that?"

"I guess you'd call it a premonition," he replied. "Yesterday, I had a vivid dream that we were all looking for her and couldn't find her."

"Have you always been able to see things before they happen?"

"Not always, but often enough. And I'm not always right."

"Let's hope you're wrong about Zona."

"Amen to that."

RIVER VOICES

Leon

So now there's no choice but to wait to be rescued. What the hell was I thinking when I signed up for this long boat trip to nowhere? Doc Bennington thought it would be a great way to lower my blood pressure, but I've got my doubts. I've already lost a few poems. It's supposed to happen less on water than on land. Then there is that theory about hot and cold spots. Will this strange scenery on the riverbanks just vanish, too? Now, that I wouldn't mind. Okay, I guess Vincent could turn into a brother from another mother, and Cassie's alright for a silver-haired lady, but that strange woman, Margot, who doesn't say shit—who can figure her out? Vincent needs to clue me in on her, but as of now, I'm just keeping my distance. I could easily ignore her, but she's got this stare that won't quit. When I stare back, she'll look away, but it takes a good while.

My real problem is Zona. She's sexy as hell—if not somewhat hostile, and if it weren't for Kali, she'd really mess me up. I thought I had anger issues. That girl needs an extra-strength chill pill. She sure doesn't like Vincent much. I'll try to ask her why if I get the opportunity. But then she'll fall asleep right in the middle of saying something. Got to admit she has a sweet, angelic look—when asleep. She's into me, a little too deeply, but I'm sure Kales won't let her get away with it. While I can get away by myself, it's harder than I thought.

The boat is plenty big, but I find myself anticipating all the stops. Now we're stuck on some rock pile and who knows how long it's going to be before that old current carries us again. Got to admit, I love sleeping on board the *Silver Lady,* and I'm looking forward to seeing the circus Cassie and Kali heard about. Just so long as we don't end up like Gilligan and his crew, and wind up on some island, forever, when it was supposed to be a three-hour tour.

Zona

Here we are stuck on this stupid boat and I'm almost out of gum. If I don't get some more soon, I'm gonna take up smoking again. I shouldn't have bought that carton of cigarettes with me—I know Cassie would throw me off the boat if she knew I had them. Still, I've only smoked a few cigs since we set sail. Maybe I'll switch to e-cigs. Guess I better remind her that we all have our little bad habits. Late at night, Cassie takes a swig or two from a silver flask she tries to hide in her jacket pocket. I'm more than a little bored by the drama here.

Kali's a little fly I could easily squish. That other couple—Vincent and his weird-ass lady friend, Margot, give me the creeps. I feel like he's watching me, suspicious of my every move. Well, I'm suspicious of them for good reason. I think he sees that and lately, he's been acting paranoid. It could be for a good reason.

My parents once lived in the same town where Vincent's father was a mayor. This was around three years ago. For a short while, they contributed articles to the local newspaper. My PI gave me some background info about everyone here. Vincent is the only one who might know something. I don't think the article my parents wrote about his conservative and creepy father was the reason his father lost his job as mayor, but maybe Vincent blamed them and wanted revenge. I'm not saying he's a murderer, as he doesn't fit the profile, but he could have had them kidnapped or killed. When I get the chance, I'll ask him what he knows and watch how he reacts.

I really need some more gum. Maybe I'll have a smoke in my cabin.

Old girl, Cassie, means well, but if she ever gets into my shit, that's it. Game over. She suggested I take pics with my phone of anything I find halfway interesting and maybe that's not a bad idea. So far, the only good thing about this trip has been Leon. I didn't know I could feel so crazy-hot about someone. If it weren't for him, I'd have bailed from this boat days ago. He's too cool, that Leon. Maybe I could accidentally but on purpose, get rid of his little girlfriend, though. If I wasn't afraid of getting caught! Don't need to become jailbait now, do I? But she's so sickeningly sweet. Can't stand that bitch. How can Leon? Oh, I know. She builds up his rather large ego, and no doubt gives him enough blow jobs to keep him in his happy place. A dude like that won't last long with a little fool like Kali. She thinks she's so superior, but I know she's gonna wind up getting in his way. I got to make him see my energy and willingness to fight for the cause. Sure, I'm white, but not on the inside. I just got to figure out a way for him to see that. I know she knows I'm into her man. Too bad, so sad! I can't be too obvious, though. If I fall asleep when I'm trying to give her the stink eye, though, I'll shoot myself. That's why I got to get some gum and soon. Chewing gum and downing caffeine are my only weapons against losing consciousness these days.

Kali

I don't understand why we all can't get along. What's wrong with Zona, anyway? Clearly, she can see that I'm with Leon. I'd never do that to another woman. She has issues. And it's also obvious that Leon's attracted to her. I guess I can see why. She's got that all tough and can-do superhero attitude. But I'll bet she's never read a poem in her life, except for school. It wouldn't surprise me if she's a dropout. But is her tough girl persona all an act? I'll bet it is. Maybe if I had lots of tats, Leon would be more attracted to me. Someone like her could never understand Leon. After her blatant display today, I've got to talk to Cassie in private and get her advice.

While I know little about Cassie's past with men, I'll bet she could give me some good motherly advice. I know Zona thinks I'm thin-skinned and maybe I am. Leon wrote a beautiful love poem for me the other night. He's memorized it, too, just in case it vanishes like the other two he wrote for me back on the mainland.

Vincent

At first, I only wanted to be on this river cruise with Margot, but with her not talking at all, it's nice to be around others. Hope her silence doesn't last the entire trip. Leon's a cool guy and Kali is a sweetheart, though naive. I like Cassie well enough, but she's a little nosy. One of these days, I'm going to put her in her place. One of my reasons for taking this journey is to fly under the radar, so I don't need others probing into my life. Why are women like that? But the only one I really mistrust is Zona—the girl's a bruiser. I can't stand to be around anyone who doesn't like art.

Is the chip on her shoulder over her famous parents' disappearance? Maybe she's trying to solve the case. I put two-and-two together the other day after realizing she was the daughter of the couple who forced my dad to resign. She must know who I am. I'll bet she's here to solve the case. Why hasn't she said anything? Does she think I'm somehow responsible? Guess I better watch my back. Do the others know about her parents? I better not say anything. At least not yet.

She's always interrupting and smacking her gum, but it's her defensive attitude that is the real problem. I'm not sure why, but Leon's attracted to her, though he's old enough to be her father. Something tells me that more than one person is going to get hurt before this trip is over. That is going to be a long way off if we keep getting stuck on rocks or sandbars.

I've been trying to sketch some of the scenery on the riverbanks: the lone cow, the table for two set for a romantic dinner, the woman singing in a tree, and that man on the dock in the clown mask. Some sketches have already disappeared, but I've written notes in my journal in case they completely vanish from my sketchbook. Feeling impatient for the river to roll by again; there's little of interest on either bank here—just greenery and occasional birds flying by.

It's good to be away from the worries Margot and I had about the children. She was so worried about the legal consequences of finding homes for illegal immigrants. I tried to convince her there are way too many of them in the country now for the legal system to handle—we're doing it a favor by keeping it on the down-low. Plus, the country's in shambles. Still, she was eager for us to keep a low profile by taking this trip.

Margot

They don't know how much I long to speak to them, to express my thoughts aloud. At first they seemed sympathetic, but lately it's been like everyone's avoiding me—all except for Vincent, of course. I growl and hum to make sure my vocal cords are still working. They are. When I first tried to speak after I fell silent, I could feel the words get caught and tangled in my throat. It happened right after the children were gone. At least it happened after Vincent and I got to know each other. At least someone knows my story. And, I have my choreography and music. Maybe I could make up a dance about a woman who can't talk. I'm especially glad I have my flute. It makes me worry less about the children and about the world ending. It can speak for me these days. I'll communicate my feelings through sound. After all, that is why we make music. Words are clumsy, inadequate things, anyway. If we don't get rescued soon, maybe I'll let loose a scream to end all screams.

DAY 8

It took two hours and forty-seven minutes for help to arrive yesterday. Once freed, *Silver Lady's* engine sounded re-energized, and she seemed to have picked up her usual pace of ten miles-per-hour. She can go faster, as she is a luxury vessel, but we need to conserve gas. Everyone cheered except for Margot, who showed her thanks by smiling and waving at the two men on the battered-looking tug boat. They were much friendlier than our earlier rescuers from the Coast Guard. Alan and his son, Josh, were happy to assist us and said they often helped boats like ours that wound up beached in shallow waters. Alan wondered if we had an underwater GPS. I told him how ours was on the fritz.

"Those pesky rock piles don't always show up on the navigation charts. In the future, whenever you take a smaller channel, be sure to stay as far away from the shore as possible," Alan said.

As captain, I took their words to heart and accepted full responsibility. I should have realized this back when we were stuck on the sandbar.

"Perhaps you've also been warned about the more unusual aspects of the river that you're soon to see?" he asked. He had a long salt-and-pepper beard, was heavy-set, and had laughing eyes framed by thick, dark eyebrows.

"Do you mean the Land of Doze? We've heard a little about it."

"Yes, I'd definitely say it's one of the stranger locales, but it's not the only one. My best advice is to not remain there long—in the town of Doze, that is—and to keep conversations with locals to a minimum. Also, don't be surprised if those you pass on the banks act like they don't see you. I could tell you more, but I don't want to spoil your adventure. Hope everything turns out well for you folks, but Josh and I can't dawdle. Just got word there's another houseboat that got upended downstream a ways and we don't know if there are any survivors. Strange, as we haven't had a storm recently, though there is one in the forecast."

I thanked them for their help, and then Alan for his helpful information. He gave me a shy look and turned away. Had he thought I was flirting with him? I pulled the brim of my captain's hat down a little lower. I didn't have to look in a mirror to see the flush on my cheeks.

We hadn't thought about the possibility of capsizing until then.

The mood was a little more subdued as we rode down the river to the next small marina. I'm sure the others wonder, like I do, about what lies ahead.

. . .

After a long and sluggish afternoon, slowly traversing muddy waters beneath a sunless sky, we dock near a book boat. On its side, in large, but faded script, is written the *River Reads*. It must be the floating bookstore we'd heard about. The monotony has gotten to me and I am grateful for a break. I can't wait to hop aboard and chat with the owner. Maybe he's a scholar, or a poet. An older man with wise, well-read eyes who will tell me about his private collection, as I stroke his sweet but sassy Tabby cat, curled up on a broken but plushy rocking chair. How fitting if he calls her Ernestine.

The door leading into the wooden boat's cabin is half off its hinges. The paint is faded and chipped. On shore, an older man is holding a spray bottle up to an open book. Why is he doing that? He stops what he is doing when he notices *Silver Lady*. He looks familiar, but I can't place him. There is something about his graying goatee...

As we pull closer, it's hard to tell if the boat is wooden, as spines of hundreds of books make up its ribs.

"Permission to come aboard?" I call out. No answer. We wait, but hear only the soft knocking of the boat against its moorings, and the creaking of rotten wood. The only greeting we receive is the smell of old books. As the door is open, a few of us decide to check it out. Something tells me there will be no elderly bookish gent, no well-loved Tabby mouser.

The man on the shore has vanished. Could he be the owner of the boat?

At first, it is exciting to see so many books. We can't tell if the boat is abandoned or if the owner is running errands or possibly having a meal in a nearby town.

River Reads doesn't have much space to move around in. I open one book and then another. Not only are the pages blank, but they are also damp. In many instances, pages are stuck together, not that it matters, since they are all blank.

I continue opening books, but with mounting fury. The others flip through pages, but soon give up. I keep up the task, the foolish optimist that I am.

"There's little point in looking further, Cassie," says Leon, putting his hand on my shoulder. I suppose he's right. Is it our collective sighs that cause a few empty pages to flutter in some books we've cast aside?

The only intact items are comic books. There are two large stacks on a counter.

It is then we notice the cobwebs everywhere, as well as the mold in a couple of coffee mugs. Most likely, the owner abandoned the ship weeks ago.

Little point absconding with any of the books since they are all blank. However, we decide to take one stack of comic books—out of nostalgia, I suppose. At least we wind up with a bounty, small as it is. The faces of Archie, Batman, and Spiderman haven't yet yellowed. Even Gotham doesn't look menacing, but somehow innocent—pleasantly unreal juxtaposed with the all-too-real Collapse occurring in actual cities and towns.

Why hadn't Alan mentioned the *River Reads*? We speculate about the whereabouts of the owner, but it isn't long before a bend in the river turns into another bend, and the memory of being aboard the book boat becomes as indistinct as last night's dreams.

. . .

I just received a text from Melanie. Her tone was a little less nasty and a bit more resigned. She told me to take care of myself but to come home soon. I wrote her back, telling her my plan to head home within the next couple weeks. She didn't ask me to keep in touch, but I promised I would.

. . .

I've been dreaming about fish almost nightly. I see them when I close my eyes in morning meditations. It amazes me to think there is a whole other world not on the river, but *in* the river. How fish have this whole other consciousness. Their world exists below our boat, which is gliding through *their* waters. People are merely visitors to this *fishdom* that empties into the sea. At first, I didn't think they were aware of us, but now I do. They swim about in my subconscious.

I ask the others if they've been dreaming about fish, but no one else has, or not that they'll admit.

. . .

Good news! Vincent's sketches have not been disappearing from his sketchbook. He claims they are as fresh as the day he rendered them. He's shared a few, but not all. Maybe he doesn't think the rest are good enough to share. The ones we've seen are mostly of the riverbank, though a few are of Margot. He's captured her almost as well as a photo could, though I wish he'd render her in motion with both her black braid and flowing skirt in mid-twirl.

Also, according to Leon and Kali, their recent poem drafts haven't faded from their notebooks either. Neither poet has shared their recent work, though Leon recited a few of his favorite memorized poems—both of his and others' work. Could the artwork and poems still be here simply because we haven't yet passed through any hot spots?

• • •

Alan was right: the river road sure is showing us the unexpected. Shortly after our exchange with Alan and Josh, we pass by them once again. They are among several others pulling a capsized houseboat to shore. It's a lot smaller than this one. It's hard to tell if there are any survivors. Had there not been so many helpers, we would stop to assist. Not wanting to get in the way, we motor by. Alan waves, but his somber expression suggests grim news.

We journey for hours by some most unusual spectacles and odd places. It might be best to call them partial-places, for they are gone in a blink—replaced by something, someone, or somewhere else equally strange. It isn't the first time we felt like we'd entered an alternate reality. On Day 5, there was the woman in a tree singing the Joni Mitchell song, the guy in the clown mask, and the cow. On Day 6, we saw the romantic table for two at the end of the dock—not that this was especially odd, but there had been that lizard under the glass lid—as if it was going to be a dinner course. Not to mention the dolphin-fish who tried so earnestly to tell us something. And then, today, on Day 8, *River Reads*, an abandoned book boat.

We pass someone singing in an enormous willow tree. This time it's a teenage boy, sitting on a branch. His long, thin legs appear pink in the twilight. His voice must have recently changed, as at first it is low, then breaks and becomes high-pitched. It's almost like there are two people on the tree branch singing: "Row, row, row your boat, gently down the stream..."

Is his song a warning? If we don't row gently, will there be problems? Or does it simply mean that life is a dream and not to take it too seriously? We discuss this without coming to a conclusion.

It's hard to tell whether the boy notices us. I don't think he does. A hush falls over us and no one stirs.

Next, we see several elderly people bathing in the river. On shore are a couple of picnic tables covered by red checked cloths and plastic food containers. Most of the bathers look pretty frail—their limbs pale and wobbly.

We have no sooner noticed them before the river carries them downstream.

The current isn't swift, but it is fast enough to prevent them from anchoring their fragile-boned feet in the river bottom. The old-timers laugh as they give in to the insistent river. You would think they are children riding on an amusement park ride in a water theme park!

All that we can see that remains of them are their smiling faces and bobbing gray and white heads. Only two of them struggle against the current.

Then there is only one head above the water.

Leon dives in and helps a man up the *Silver Lady's* ladder. Bone-thin and blue veins trellis his limbs like ivy.

After we warm up Edward with towels and a cup of hot tea, the bushy-browed man tells us if we are lucky, we'll be safe in the town of Doze before the storm reaches us. After the next sputtered breath, he says his wife had been next to him in the water. "She was there one moment, but was gone the next." He repeats this a few times.

Before we get the chance to commiserate with him or thank him for the information about reaching Doze, he dives off the boat. For a moment, his frail body is strong and young again. But he lets the current take him. His sweet acceptance brings tears to our eyes.

How I wish he hadn't told us his name.

Our bluebird mascot is no longer around. I'm a little worried, but remain hopeful that we'll see Blue again.

I feel drowsy, and a few of the others report feeling the same. I hate feeling out-of-it, especially when I feel like I should feel rested. But then it hits me: we are in the Land of Doze! Drowsiness will have its way with us. We better pinch ourselves or we will all be dozing in no time. While my eyelids feel a little scratchy and heavy, it's more of a general lethargy. Will sleep help? Will we become immune to it after we've been here awhile?

We spot a long, worn, wooden dock that extends into this wide expanse of the river. Nothing's on it, or so we first think, but as we get closer, there's a curious sight at the end of the dock: four old-fashioned dolls having a tea party at a little table. Vincent thinks the one with brown curls waved at us. No one else saw it, but he remains adamant.

There isn't a path leading to a house; in fact, there are no dwellings of any sort along this stretch of the river.

When we look for the strange or expect it, it's like a trick is being played on us, because then we don't see it.

Where is the circus? The one that Tony, the man from the store, had mentioned. Will it be around the next bend? Maybe it has moved on to somewhere else. The oddities we've been seeing will make a circus seem less than extraordinary.

While I've written about the river's sights, I haven't written about its sounds. For this last stretch of the river, as if in accompaniment to the strange visuals, we hear loud laughter coming from clumps of trees, and though not as often, the howling of wolves. A slow, steady drumbeat follows this, and then, as if serving a sound-dessert comes tinkling wind chimes. And from deep below the water's surface, we hear a pulsating noise followed by garbled human voices. We can't tell what they are saying.

These sounds, combined with the curiosities along the riverbanks, lead to a sense of being disembodied, as if life truly was little more than a vivid dream.

What abruptly brings me into full awareness is one of the most pungent odors I've ever smelled. Worse than shit or rotten eggs. It must be like the way corpses smell when rotting beneath a noonday sun. We cover our noses and flee from the outer deck into the main cabin. Hard to believe a single burp from the river could so pollute the air.

After the surreal scenery and din, comes a feeling of blankness. Maybe not total blankness or emptiness, but something close to it. Drowsiness intensifies, and an extreme sleepiness overcomes us all. At first, we struggle against it but there is little point. Time seems to have stopped. We haven't passed another boat in what feels like forever. I can't get anyone to take a shift as captain, as everyone's afraid of falling asleep at the wheel. Well, I am, too.

I tell them the best way is if we each take shorter shifts—a half hour to an hour, and no longer. Everyone nods in half-hearted agreement.

We decide to sleep in shifts, too. Those fighting to remain awake need to splash cold water on themselves if necessary. Maybe we should find somewhere to dock, but I'm certain we'll feel more alert in the town of Doze. But the closer we get, the further away it feels.

The inlet we've taken has little current, and the light is dim in the moonless sky with an occasional tree or bush near the river. Without mentioning it, we realize we must be in the heart of the Land of Doze.

As we drift through this near-barren and birdless land, we are dulled and barely conscious. I bring up the supposed oncoming storm, but everyone acts like they could care less.

Leon then reports that two more of his poems have disappeared, but that it happened before entering the strangely empty Land of Doze.

· · ·

From My Hotel Room in Doze

Thinking back to our collective mood from earlier, we hadn't just felt sleepy after entering the Land of Doze, we were apathetic. This was most likely a result of sensory deprivation, as well as because of the long day we'd had. I'm sure my sleep tonight will be dreamless. The air is still and humid like a summer night. Maybe the old man's warning was correct and a storm is headed our way.

The hotel clerk—Fred Simon, according to his badge—looked surprised when the six of us straggled into the hotel lobby. Fred's a short, mostly bald man with large owlish eyes.

"You're sure lucky to get here before that storm. Sounds like we're in for a bad one."

I nodded and told him we needed four rooms for the next couple of nights.

"You're again in luck, as we only have four left. Are you sure you don't want to stay an additional night? The storm should've come and gone by then." Fred smiled for the first time. He is one of those people whose appearance completely changed when grinning. His dimples add charm to his already handsome, middle-aged face.

I told him we'd think about it because we were delivering a houseboat to its owner and needed to get it back to him. Fred gave me a confused expression. I further explained how we weren't simply travelers on a cruise. He laughed so hard he shook the dusty chandelier on the ceiling.

"My dear, we're all travelers on the cruise of life. You'll definitely want to make sure you've secured your boat as well as possible."

DAY 9

The storm still hasn't started. It's almost noon on the following day and we've just eaten a hearty breakfast of eggs and pancakes, the largest breakfast of the trip. While the food was overcooked, we were all hungry after a long, but dreamless night's sleep. I slept for twelve hours, though my travel companions topped me by an extra hour or more.

I'm now sitting alone in the formal dining room. The others just left to explore the town, which I did on my own last night. Not only did I want to make sure we had the boat secure in its slip, but I wanted to get the lay-of-the-land, or in this case, the town. I was the only one on the streets. It feels wonderful, though strange, to be off of the *Silver Lady*. I hadn't realized how small and confining it had become. Hard to believe it first felt so roomy.

The dining room looks like something out of Victorian England with high ceilings and chandeliers, and musty, pulled-back, rose-colored velvet curtains. They are a few shades deeper than the pale pink façade of the hotel. The tables, covered with faded linens, exude a touch of elegance, similar to well-bred dowagers.

Our server, Claude, with a white serving cloth over his forearm, attended us at breakfast. We were all rather surprised by how quick Claude was in serving us. It felt strange to be waited on.

Margot told us about the magnificent magnolia trees in town. You heard me right—Margot is now speaking a little.

"It's marvelous to hear your voice!" I exclaimed.

Margot's voice was soft and husky. "Oh? Why is that?" she asked.

"Because you never spoke on the boat."

Then Vincent shut me down: "Let's not dredge up the past, shall we?" I wondered if she'd revert to her former muteness once we were back on the boat. I kept this thought to myself.

"We're off to stroll the gardens," Vincent informed us, as he protectively escorted her from the room. He looked eager to get away from us. Everyone stared down at their plates or out the window.

The gardens are almost as lovely as the flowering magnolias. The pink faces of the blossoms are all turned up toward the sun.

Claude just returned to ask if I would like more coffee. Not only do I shake my head, I cover my cup with my hand. He laughs and scurries from the room. Claude has a handlebar mustache and little darting eyes.

So far, we haven't seen other guests. Was Fred Simon being truthful when he told us he had only four rooms left? While it's a fairly small hotel, I rather doubt it. But why would he lie? Maybe there had been only four *available* rooms. The guest rooms have the same old-fashioned formality as the dining room: four-poster brass beds and pitchers in bowls atop old wooden dressers; creaky floors and mattresses; velvet-covered fainting couches; oil paintings of still life fruits and flowers. While I enjoy mine, something tells me not all the others feel the same.

I've never felt so far away from my daughter. It's like Melanie is in another world. I haven't been able to reach her lately, so that's partly why I feel so estranged. But this new place seems otherworldly, too, and is definitely contributing to my missing her.

Ever since we registered yesterday, I've been feeling like I'm being watched—both at the hotel and when I went out walking. I'd planned on mentioning it to the others at breakfast, but was too paranoid to bring it up. Thankfully, it didn't keep me awake, but I wonder if it will tonight. As oddly charming as the hotel is, I'm glad we didn't reserve the rooms for a third night. If the expected storm hasn't let up, of course, we'll tack on an extra night. But I have a few other reasons for not wanting to remain here longer than necessary:

Reason #1: The friendships that were forming on the boat seem to have all but vanished. It's like we hardly know each other. There's this stiff formality usually seen between strangers. You'd think we all just met yesterday. How can that be? The two couples still seem close.

Reason #2: If I try hard enough, I can recall the days we've spent together aboard *Silver Lady*, but it's almost like revisiting memories from long ago. The strange scenery we have passed is like something from a dream. And I can't seem to recall any conversations with the five others, though I know that we've had them. It makes me shudder. From their polite but curt behavior, I can only surmise they feel likewise.

Reason #3: Despite my lengthy slumber last night, I'm still sleepy, though not as bad as I felt when we first arrived. If I weren't writing my thoughts down, I would've nodded off by now.

. . .

I'm still seated at the table, not quite knowing what to do with myself. Claude returns to my table once more and asks if there is anything more he can bring me from the kitchen. "How about a sense of reality?" I almost ask, but instead shake my head. He sits sideways in a chair next to me and describes the town. Strange, as I hadn't asked.

"As you travel down Main Street, you'll pass the pink hotel, a gift store, a rundown tavern, and an art gallery. Plus, there's a hardware store and a general store, but little else. I guess the restaurant in the hotel is the only one in town. A small street of houses line the town square, but otherwise, there are no other visible buildings, though we were told there's a gas station a little way out of town. Surrounding the town square are the most beautiful flowering trees I have ever seen. The pink petals are as delicate as they are large. I should know the name of the tree, but I've never been good at names of anything growing in gardens, except the most obvious varieties. You won't pass many people on your tour. When you do, you'll be lucky to get a nod. Most act as though you're not there. It's a disconcerting feeling, and only slightly better than being treated poorly."

I thank Claude for his description.

He stands up, nods in stiff formality, and exits the room into the hallway off the kitchen.

For the first time since arriving in the town, I'm overcome by an overwhelming drowsiness. It's hard to keep my eyes open. Should I join the others in town? No, lying down in my room sounds best. Maybe it was the big breakfast coupled with the sticky breezes coming in off the river, but a wee nap sounds delightful. I'll put my head down and try to recall the Before. There must have been one, right? I know their names, not as well as my own, but at least I know who-is-who. Leon, Vincent, Margot, Zena—I mean Zona—and one more. Oh, yeah, Kali. Suddenly, I feel eighty instead of sixty-two. I am tired, so tired.

. . .

Later the same day...

The others have also been experiencing extreme sleepiness. We should have considered what it would do to us before we docked in Doze. Its very name should have been warning enough. Now all I want to do is doze in Doze.

. . .

Again, at dinner in the hotel restaurant, 'The Rose Room,' there is a ridiculous formality, or more aptly—impersonality—between us. I mention it to the others. At first, a few of them shrug it off. Vincent faults the oppressive decorum of the room. Who wouldn't feel stiff here? Then Leon remarks, as he pushes his glasses up to the bridge of his nose, that maybe it's because we've all been so sleepy—that it's all we can do to stay awake, and therefore it's not like we've been distant with each other on purpose.

It's beginning to add up, but we're missing something. Shouldn't the sleepiness make us feel less inhibited? I feel surrounded by strangers.

Has anyone else noticed their memories fading? Even my recent ones from the trip are sketchy. No one else has, or at least not that they're willing to admit. Maybe they are afraid to deal with their own faulty wiring. I refuse to believe I'm the only one with memory fog. There is no way I could have developed a sudden onset of Alzheimer's. Little point in harping about it, but I once again feel isolated from the others.

Then Vincent changes the subject and informs us: "Since we've arrived, none of my sketches have disappeared from the page. Karen Logan, owner of the art gallery, let me in on Doze's little secret—artwork here is safe, so far, anyway. She said she doesn't tell everyone, or else artists from everywhere would want to move here."

The others finally awaken from their stupor.

"I wondered about the last two drafts of poems I wrote," says Leon. "Luckily, both are still on the page. Before we entered Doze, I looked through a folder of my finished work and the pages were blank. Good thing I'd saved them to several places on and off the internet. After hearing about how fast they've been disappearing, I made voice recordings, too."

"I vote we stay here a little longer," announces Margot. She turns to me, her long lashes sweeping her high cheekbones. "Though, of course, Cassie, it's entirely your decision." Her smile reveals the slight gap between her front teeth. She glances around at the others for support. Since she's only just recovered her voice, I can see why she feels this way. The rest wait for my response.

I weigh my words before responding, something I don't often do. "It will help my decision after we get an update about the oncoming storm. I mean, it's great about you getting your voice back, Margot, and certainly it's a plus that creative works aren't vanishing here, but it's countered by memory issues and sleepiness. Think about it. Leon, how satisfied have you been with your writing since we've been here? Vincent, were your sketches of the same caliber as before?"

While both men reluctantly agree the sleepiness has made their work a little sub-par, neither admits to memory fog. Maybe this is only my issue since I'm at least twenty years older than the others. Margot adds how she sure hopes that once we leave Doze she'll still have her voice.

From the Hotel Basement

The storm is going to be a nasty one, according to Fred who has just heard the latest weather report. He adds how there is a beneficial aspect to the storms in Doze: the sleepiness we've been feeling will go away. We'll have loads more energy and a newfound zest. He no sooner tells us this than the town siren blasts our ears. The roar wakes us from our stupors.

"Everyone, please follow me," Fred commands, escorting us courteously but quickly from the room, along with Claude.

As luck has it, the lights remain on for over an hour after we move downstairs. We're all grateful, as it's like we've descended into the Paris catacombs.

Fred conducts a brief tour of several dank and windowless rooms, most of which are filled with broken furniture and tons of unlabeled boxes. Neatly stacked and sealed boxes fill several large shelving units. A potent smell of mothballs makes my nose twitch. After several sneezes, I notice a rancid, foul odor. Everyone does. In the middle of Fred telling us something—who knows what—we lose our composure. He raises his voice as mayhem breaks out when we all try to squeeze through a narrow doorway at the same time. What's that hideous smell? No one seems to know. Lucky for everyone, it doesn't follow us into the next room.

While Fred is right about our energy returning, it's become frenzied and uncomfortable. The deeper we descend into the bowels of the basement, the more unnerving it becomes. I feel so wired and out-of-body that I panic and almost forget about the raging storm.

Small, bronze sculptures of children fill one of the larger rooms. The sculptor froze several of them as they were running. What were they fleeing from? They remind me of the ruins of Pompeii. A few gazed upward, kneeling with their hands folded in prayer. All of them frozen in time.

The server, Claude, pinching one side of his handlebar mustache, tells us that back in the 1990s, the Pink Hotel was an orphanage. He hadn't been living in Doze then, but heard it was more populated back then.

The story goes that one night, all the orphans ran away, never to be seen again. Many of the townsfolk dismissed this version and believe that the orphans were poisoned with arsenic and buried beneath the basement of the hotel. The only body discovered was the skeleton of a dog. Only a sensitive few have heard the plaintive crying of the orphan ghosts, which led to the belief that the hotel is haunted. The locals swear on their mothers' graves that on the anniversary of the orphans' disappearance—the orphans walk the hallways sobbing.

A few years back, the hotel owner designated an entire floor for them. He brought in beds, bedding, and even a few children's books and toys. To make the ghosts feel more at home is certainly a clever idea. But can an orphan-ghost ever feel at home? Some say that occasionally, indentations have been noticed on the pillows.

After hearing all this, we examine the sculptures more closely. No one speaks. Then the lights go out. A high-pitched scream shatters the silence. Was it Zona or Kali?

Almost simultaneously, we turn on our flashlights. I refrain from shining mine into the faces I suspect responsible. Then, I drop my flashlight to the floor with a loud thud, causing everyone to jump—even Claude and Fred. At least this time, no one screams.

Once calm is reestablished, the two hotel workers tell us they need to investigate if the power outage is limited to the basement. Before ditching us, they escort us to another room by the stairwell. There is a large table and rickety chairs that are, thankfully, still functional. It reminds me of an old farmhouse kitchen, minus the stove and fridge. Even the most anxious amongst us—Leon, Kali, and Zona have no problem staying put. I thank Claude for putting a few battery-powered lamps on the table.

We discuss our renewed energy and what a jolt it is to our systems. Margot is paler than usual. Her skirt has faded but is still lovely and her matted braid remains strangely attractive. I think her skirt is the same one she has been wearing since the trip began. Doesn't she own a single pair of blue jeans? I rather doubt it, but I don't ask. Instead, I ask her how she is feeling.

After claiming Margot feels fine, Vincent adds how the orphan story must have reminded her of the children she'd cared for.

Margot tries to silence him with an angry glance.

I try my best to change the subject, but he attempts to clarify. While I know about the children, I'm guessing the others don't.

"When I met Margot, she had about ten kids in her care. I thought she was their teacher since there was no way she could've been their mother—not with a body like hers!"

Margot shoots him dagger-eyes. "How about we don't get into that now, Vincent? And by the way, I've seen plenty of mothers who are in decent shape despite having lots of kids."

"Yeah, man, that wasn't a cool thing to say," Leon adds. He pushes his glasses up, looking sternly at Vincent.

Vincent reddens, and changes the topic by asking me if I think *Silver Lady* will be in decent shape to take us further on our journey tomorrow. It's anyone's guess, I reply, knowing better than to ask Margot anything further about the children.

I'd hate to have instigated any discord between them, but now that she's speaking, it's only natural that complexities arise—at least for Vincent. Does he wish she'd remained mute? If so, I would lose all respect for him. It's the second time he's mentioned the children, so I can't help but be curious. Had she done something underhanded, even criminal? Why does talking about them upset her? I know better than to ask for now.

Since Claude and Fred haven't yet returned and we are stuck together in this dreary but safe locale, I ask the others if their families knew about this journey. Most do, though not the specifics. We discuss what our parents do, or once did, for a living. It's then we discover something we all have in common.

Talk about coincidences! Vincent's father was a former mayor of Hamilton, Ohio. Margot's mother played cello for the Chicago Symphony Orchestra for several years, and her father was the conductor of a small city orchestra. Leon's mother was once a Broadway star, and Kali's is currently a president of Eden Glen, a small, private university. As mentioned, my parents, The Navrones, were folk singers from the 1960s. They produced four albums during that time and even became well known in Europe.

The real surprise comes from Zona. It seems her parents are journalists—both missing for the past few years. Presumably, someone kidnapped them. Some of the crew already knew about this, but I'm surprised.

Right in the middle of Zona telling us about it, Vincent gets up abruptly. She furrows her brows, causing him to almost trip over his enormous feet before leaving the room.

If a few in the group weren't fully conscious before, they are now.

What are the odds we all have somewhat famous parents, though none of us have big followings? While Vincent is a decent portrait painter, and Leon's published a few poems, they aren't well known. The rest of us are mainly known by family and friends. Plus, here we are on this strange river journey together—a trip we're taking for neither fame nor fortune.

Had it not been for the civil unrest and general breakdown of society, Leon's mother and Margot's parents would still be in the public eye. It's good to know Kali's mother's university didn't close, like so many of them.

Zona's mention of her parents being missing must have increased Leon's attraction for her, as they play footsie under the table. Is Kali aware of it? I hope not. As if there wasn't enough going on already, both with the storm and not knowing whether *Silver Lady* will be able to take us further downstream tomorrow.

The revelation about our parents allows us to feel an even stronger bond between us than before. I just hope we can keep this connection going, even if it can't be classified as friendship.

· · ·

We remain in the chilly and damp hotel basement for another hour.

"Who's up for a little Qigong?" I ask, feeling much like a camp counselor having to entertain kids on a rainy day.

Sighs and grumbles are audible, but soon my shipmates are facing me as I lead them in a short practice.

"Remember to breathe as you do the moves. Sink your feet into the floor with a slight bend in your knees. Be like a tree, planted but agile enough to sway in a gentle breeze."

While the graceful stretching of our limbs and the controlled breathing makes us forget our circumstances, it's only a ten-minute session. Afterward, the basement still feels chilly and damp.

At long last, Claude and Fred return for us.

DAY 10

Gone is last night's energy, and exhaustion has replaced our former sleepiness. None of us got much sleep in our hotel beds due to the constant thunder and lightning that lit up the sky like a strobe light show.

The backup generators are working, but only with the refrigerators and some of the lights. After a simple fare of fruit and stale pastries for breakfast, we don't know what else to do with ourselves, so we stumble around town in a daze. We walk in silence, though we are careful to be on the lookout for downed power lines. The world has gone belly up.

Branches were scattered everywhere like kindling for a giant's bonfire, and the storm completely uprooted many trees. The weight of fallen trees caused several rooftops to sag and even collapse. No surprise if a tornado had touched down. It sure looks like it did.

Fred, having little better to do, catches up to us. He continues to be apologetic, as if the entire storm was his fault. The sad part, he informs us, is the town's population is small and cut off from other towns, so the clean-up and reconstruction will take a long time.

We hold our breath at the marina, but release it when we see that the *Silver Lady* appears undamaged. The bow lines had only loosened somewhat. There are a couple of small tears in the canvas side covers that Vincent and Leon are now securing on the top deck. Some water leaked through, so several of us do our best to bail it out, along with twigs and river weeds on the lower decks. Also, there's no apparent inside water damage.

As we're attending her, I can't help but feel like the *Silver Lady's* slipping in and out of consciousness. She's a poor injured patient and we are her medical team. I know better than to ask the others, but I pose another question to the group: Do we stay and help the Dozers, or thank them for their hospitality and continue our journey? While not everything we do calls for a vote, this time it does.

Here are their votes and the reasoning behind them:

Margot: Stay, at least for a few days. It's the right thing to do. These people need our help.

Vincent: Leave. The town functioned before our arrival and will do its best after we depart. We sure as hell don't need these people to become dependent on us—not that they even know we're here.

Kali: Stay. What Margot said. But wait, I kind of see what Vincent is saying, too. Do I have to vote? I do? Okay, stay.

Leon: Stay. They need our help.

Zona: Leave. We don't owe them a damn thing.

Me: Stay, but for only the next couple of days.

Looks like the 'stays' have it! Still, the vote-winners don't jump up and down in victory. It would be all too easy to slip away downstream, but most of us would feel guilty doing so. We know it's going to be tough work. Since the Dozers will have plenty more to do after we leave, we'll derive little satisfaction, but at least we'll know we did what we could.

Is it my imagination or is Vincent particularly bent out of shape since he wasn't able to persuade us to leave? I'm sure he'd like to be our fearless leader. Now that Margot rediscovered her voice, he's less in control than before. If I were a therapist, I'd be having a field day—seeing as I'm not, maybe I should simply observe the way events unfold.

When I tell Fred and Claude about our decision, they become overjoyed.

Claude prepares a grand spread of assorted cheeses and tea sandwiches. His cucumber and cream cheese ones are my favorite. As we are finishing up, we receive our marching orders from the mayor, Gabrielle Goodie.

She's about my age with short platinum-blond hair, a commanding voice, and an Angela Merkel charm. I can't help but think she looks way older, but what do I know? Since there are six of us, she suggests we work in teams of two, mainly in downtown Doze, and one or two of the side streets. Makes sense, but I almost laugh when she tells us to be sure to take breaks. As if we wouldn't! She clearly doesn't know who she was dealing with. Gabrielle adds she will also assist in the clean-up. Moved by our willingness alone, she extends an invitation for us to become permanent residents. Following your river trip, she adds.

"I can tell you folks are artsy types and I'm sure you know by now that artwork here is—if not eternal, it's surely lasting. We're a small but caring community. What better venue for artists to work and thrive in?"

Leon, Kali, and Margot quickly agree, though Vincent doesn't—no surprise. Is it because he thinks the town's using us for free labor? On the side, I whisper to him how I'm hoping Fred will give at least one free night's stay.

Gabrielle provides trash bags, work gloves, and hard hats, and then tells us to join the other townsfolk who have also agreed to help. I sure wish I had the zippy energy of the others, but I've got to remember I'm way older than the rest.

It's been a few days now since we were on the water, and I long to return. I especially miss being on the boat at night. Not only to gaze up at the moon and stars, but to be rocked gently to sleep. It's one of the most pleasant sensations I've ever known—reliving cradle day memories, no doubt.

I am stuck with Zona as my clean-up partner. She doesn't look any more pleased by the prospect of being with me than I am to be with her, but at least I try to mask it.

"Tomorrow we'll be back on our river adventure," I say, as we set off down the muddy walk, wearing hardhats and carrying garbage bags.

"River adventure? Seriously? If that's what you want to call it." She swats at a fly that has landed on one of her many tattoos—a butterfly.

"I think it's exciting the way the scenery is always shifting. Don't you love how we have no idea what's around the next bend?"

"All the same, it's been mostly a boring boat ride, lady. Sorry if this offends you, but then again, you seem to get offended pretty easily." Zona is back to calling me lady. Talk about salt in an open wound.

"Not true, but I'm sure there's no convincing you. You say it's been mostly boring, implying that some of it's been okay?"

"Some of the people are alright, I guess. Especially Leon."

"It's pretty clear you have a thing for him. You do know he's involved with Kali?"

"Not like it's any of your business! Look, you don't need to point out the nose on my face. Yeah, I know about Kali, but she's too young and naïve for someone like him. It won't last."

"You're hardly much older than she is." I feel bad making the judgement, but I can't help myself.

"My soul is way older."

"I'm kind of surprised you believe in a soul."

Before she gets the chance to respond, I slip into a puddle and fall on my side. The part of me that believes in a Higher Power fears this is my punishment for judging the girl.

Zona doubles over in a fit of laughter.

Not funny, Zona. Still, I am almost glad to have amused this standoffish, taciturn person. There's no point returning to the Pink Hotel to change my clothes, as the outdoor work will make me grubby in no time. At least she helps me up.

It is then that I notice the storm has shredded almost all the lovely pink magnolia blossoms. They now mingle on the ground with branches, broken glass, and litter. When we first arrived, I'd noticed it was such a tidy little town. The trash must have blown out of the toppled-over garbage containers.

We aren't the only group out trying to contend with Mother Nature's mess: several Dozers are out here with trash bags, too. Some act bewildered as they search for their lost pets. Once again, most never acknowledge us.

Zona and I decide to head over to Orphan Park, which we'd heard about from Claude. I am limping a bit from my earlier spill, but otherwise I am okay. In our earlier quick tour of the town, we hadn't really noticed the orphan statues that were said to be much like the ones in the hotel basement.

Zona asks me a strange question: Do I think Vincent looks capable of kidnapping or murder?

I burst out laughing, and then Zona does, too. Certainly he can be a man of mystery, but a killer? What could make her think so?

He seems shifty and untrustworthy, she explains. It made her wonder about those children Margot had cared for and who they supposedly found homes for. Had I noticed the weird look on his face in the hotel basement after she mentioned her parents were missing?

Not especially.

Zona repeats what she had said in the hotel basement about why Vincent's father had lost his job. It was due to a particular newspaper article written by a socialist couple. He had said there was no way his father was a thief—he was a man of integrity, if not incorrect political positions.

"Come to think of it, they had your same last name. Workes, am I right?" Vincent had asked.

"They had bigger fish to fry than small-town mayors! Too bad your dad lost his job, but I'm sure they weren't the only ones who knew about his dealings. Do you have the article?" Zona answered his question with a question.

He didn't have it with him, he'd said, but he'd always had a gift for recalling names. And since that time, he's never had much use for socialists, particularly socialist journalists. And hadn't she admitted her parents were socialists?

So, Zona thinks Vincent was responsible for their disappearance? Is that what this comes down to?

I tell her how her idea, while not out of the realm of possibility, seems a bit of a reach. The nation has been divided for a long time. Why would Vincent have any more of a vendetta than anyone else? While he had his nervous tics, he hardly seems like a criminal.

Zona claims she is looking for any possible kind of connection to her missing parents. And this could be a big one.

"I don't blame you," I say, in a feeble attempt to console her. It must be frustrating, for sure. We agree not to mention her conjecture to the others.

Could her parents have been among those who disappeared in the early days of the Vanishing? It must have occurred to her, even though it wasn't common for people to disappear. I have only heard of a few instances.

By the time we get there, Margot and Vincent are already in Orphan Park, busy righting the knocked over statues. It's a small park on the corner of Main Street. They are taking their work as caretakers seriously.

"There should be ten orphan statues here, but we only see six. The mayor wanted us to check to see if we saw the scattered remains of the rest. Don't these orphans just break your heart?" Margot asks in her velvety voice as she gestures toward the statues and wipes off a little mud from my cheek.

The statues appear to be in the process of escaping. But from what? A storm like the one we just had, or something else? Their worried expressions make their faces look old, though clearly, the small bodies were those of children. Had the storm scattered the limbs of the other four? If so, the heavy, bronze body parts should still be in the vicinity, right? We don't see any.

Since there is so much work to be done, it doesn't matter if there are four of us working together in the park. Vincent keeps his distance from both Zona and me. He acts like he barely knows us. I can tell his attitude has changed, and that he is giving his all to the clean-up. Since we are all busy, the timing for asking him why he'd changed his mind about the place—about staying here—doesn't seem right. If I were a serious artist, maybe I would think about living here, too. It can't be simply the storm alone that changed his mind.

As I help an orphan up from the wet ground, her expression seems to change, and I'm almost certain she looks a little happier. I recall being at a statuary store when I was a child. My mother was taking forever to decide on a birdbath, when I accidentally tripped over one and broke it. I felt so humiliated, but when my mother tried to pay for it, the store owner assured us it wasn't necessary. The memory has always remained.

Zona sits on a park bench to rest and promptly falls asleep. After a few minutes, I try shaking her awake, but it is pointless. Recalling my earlier drowsiness makes me more sympathetic to my narcoleptic companion. If I plunked down next to her, I too would be in danger of entering the Land of Dreams via the town of Doze. There is little point hanging around and waiting for her to wake up, so I leave her there. I doubt the townsfolk will give her a backward glance, since few seem to be aware of the strangers in their town.

. . .

(Evening)

It feels more like a July summer night rather than early May. We worked for most of the day, taking only occasional breaks. Between our effort and that of the inhabitants, we made progress clearing up, though the toppled-over and uprooted trees will undoubtedly be there for a long time. The day got increasingly warm, so resting up with the others on the hotel verandah feels well-deserved. I'm bone-tired but relaxed. Speaking in drowsy voices, we speculate about what lies ahead of us on the journey.

Turning toward Vincent, I ask, "Have you changed your mind about this town?"

He sighs. "After seeing the mess made by the storm, for sure I want to help, but I still don't want to stay here longer than necessary."

"I thought you'd never want to leave once you'd found out that paintings weren't vanishing from canvases."

"You're right about the paintings, Cassie, but it seems people are."

"What?" While we have all heard stories about people having gone missing since the Vanishing began, no one knows if it was coincidental or part of the Vanishing.

Everyone turns their attention to Vincent, who leans in as he explains in a whisper.

"It seems the townsfolk have been vanishing. The population is only a third of what it once was. It's anyone's guess about what happens to the bodies. There are a few cases in which entire families have disappeared. I'm told—and sorry I can't reveal my source—that it often happens at night."

"Could it be the Rapture?" asks Kali, saucer-eyed.

"I doubt it, as the mean and ornery folks get taken just as often as the good ones," Vincent says with a guffaw. "Just as importantly, it seems to happen only to residents, so I don't think we have too much to worry about."

We shift about uncomfortably in our rocking chairs. Had it not been for this reassurance, I would insist we leave immediately. I want to press him about the source of his information, but decide it would be futile. I feel sad for the town. Why are Fred, Claude, and the others we've met, still here? Who would want to stay, knowing they might not be here tomorrow? Home is that important to some, I guess. I make a snap decision: we'll sleep on the boat tomorrow night. To my relief, the others immediately approve. It's not like I would change my mind had they not agreed, but it sure is nice when we can reach a consensus.

Margot tells us how the orphan statues reminded her of her children—the migrant kids she had cared for. At long last, her side of the story gets told as Margot starts talking. Ten young children lived with her for nearly a year. They went from being frightened and barely speaking a word, to being lively, healthy kids—if not exactly joyous. But they were in the country illegally. If discovered, they would be deported. She and Vincent found homes for them with acquaintances who were living off the grid. Sadly, the children, even those with siblings—had to split up. Immigration officials kept getting hotter on the trail. She explains how she and Vincent would have visited the children and would have become like their aunt and uncle—but the situation got too risky, and they had to leave town.

The boat trip could well be their way to go 'underground.' At least the children hadn't simply vanished.

A few of us remain on the verandah, enjoying the warm evening, listening to the hooting of owls and the scolding of mockingbirds. Leon and Zona have been gone for over an hour. Kali asks if any of us know where they went. How can she be so naïve? Hadn't she noticed them staring at each other and playing footsie every chance they could get? C'mon, Kali.

"It's just I need to talk to Leon about something. I'm not jealous. I mean, shit, we're not married. We're both free to do as we please, but I thought...oh, why am I telling you guys? Guess I'll take a walk. Tell him that's what I'm doing if you see him."

Vincent, Margot, and I nod but say nothing.

"Better yet, please don't. I will not give him the satisfaction!" With that, Kali stomps off into the fading light, away from town.

Poor girl. While my heart goes out to her, there is little anyone can do for her. I hope the romantic entanglement will have worked itself out a little by the time we leave, but I'm doubtful. Messy episodes in life last longer than those involved would like.

Margot and I make predictions about how it is going to turn out for the three of them. The best one, though the most unrealistic, is the one she put forth in which they all agreed to be platonic friends.

Vincent is working on a scene of the verandah in his sketchbook, occasionally shaking his head and looking amused one moment, then furious the next. Earlier, in the hotel lobby, I was glancing through a hotel brochure when I happened to overhear an angry exchange between Vincent and Leon. I didn't think they saw me there.

Vincent was letting Leon know his thoughts about being involved with Zona. I couldn't help but listen in. "It's not cool, man. I mean, you're on this trip with your girlfriend, but you're doing the wild thing with someone else when Kali's back is turned. Why not do the decent thing and break up with Kali, or tell Zona you'd made a mistake?"

"Who put you in the role of advisor-in-chief? No one's asked for your take, my man."

"I thought we were friends. Don't friends try to open each other's eyes about what's going down?" asked Vincent.

"Little big ears, Cassie, is listening in, bro. Let's talk about this later."

"Sure thing."

Recalling Zona's question from earlier about Vincent possibly being a kidnapper or even a murderer, I almost tell him just to see his reaction. I don't, as it would only cause more friction between them. If it was just the two of us on the verandah, I would. Curious, if I were half my age, I would probably be accused of flirting with him. Nothing wrong with being a friendly older woman. It's one of the better aspects of being my age.

A few dim lights come on in the windows of the orphans' floor. Since it is now dark outside, I wouldn't think much of it since it—except for the fact the power hasn't returned.

. . .

Margot and I decide to investigate and climb the rickety stairs to the third floor.

She's the first real friend I've made in a long time. When I was younger, it was sure easier. I know I'm difficult to get to know. I'm crusty and more than a little jaded from worries and woes.

Margot hears giggling, but I don't. The door-knob is stuck. We both hear a faint sound, possibly coming from the third-floor hallway. Then muted, but unmistakable laughter.

I twist the knob several times, making our presence known.

As no one else is staying in the hotel but us, who could it be? Zona and Leon? But why would they want to find a room on the third floor when there are five other unoccupied floors? They both know about the orphans. Could some locals who'd supposedly disappeared be living here? But that doesn't make sense. I must admit, there's been much on this journey that isn't adding up.

DAY 11

It is a foggy, warm morning, and *Silver Lady* once again heads downstream. I wasn't successful at locating this branch of the river on the navigation map. I hadn't been able to find our location before we'd entered Doze, so what makes me think I can now? The town is about five miles behind us, but based on the flat and relatively treeless scenery, we are still in the Land of Doze. Another tip-off: we are all sleepy, and the one cup of coffee isn't kicking in.

Thinking back over our days in Doze, some events have already blurred. What I best remember, besides certain moments in the hotel basement during the storm and helping to clean up afterward, is how formal and distant we were with each other that first night as we dined in the restaurant of the Pink Hotel. The more I strain to recall specific moments, the fuzzier my mind feels. I feel dazed and almost disembodied. Do the others feel like this, too? Maybe it's the fog and the atmosphere causing this effect. Whatever the reason, I don't like it.

I ask Vincent to relieve me at the wheel. His grin could charm the pants off any woman. I wouldn't doubt if he was thinking I've come to my senses by turning over my role to him. If so, he doesn't let on and simply asks if I am feeling okay.

"I'll be fine. Just need to do some deep breathing in my cabin. Are you feeling sort of out of it, like me?"

"No, I'm doing alright, but go for it, Cassie! Let me know if you need anything."

Why does he look so concerned? My hands are trembling and numb. Could it be my heart or a stroke? My left arm feels fine. But when I stand up, everything starts to go dark. Am I about to disappear? Can it be people are disappearing from anywhere in the Land of Doze and not only from the town?

I steady myself against the top rail before going down the steps.

During my college years, I had one particularly nasty hangover, and felt like I was going to pass out. My vision went dark and voices slowed to a near halt; I thought I was dying. Now, a small voice from deep within snaps at me to get a grip: *You are the captain, and under no circumstances do you let the others see you're not in control. They all paid good money to join you on this trip, so you owe them as safe a journey as possible!*

There were other times I felt physically numb. Peter enjoyed being on the water even more than I did. Getting the canoe had been his idea. We bought one when Melanie was little, before the second Gulf War. The three of us had been having a grand time paddling down a river on a cool but sunny summer day. We sang silly songs to keep Melanie from getting too restless. He was a big guy and usually fairly well-coordinated. Not on that day. I'm not sure how he'd caused our canoe to capsize, but it had to have been from shifting his body weight. One moment, we were singing, and the next we were all in the water, and the boat was upside down. The river was shallow, but still over Melanie's head. He immediately grabbed her while I chased after the paddles. After handing her over to me so he could flip the boat back over, I noticed a warm patch in the water. Later, we laughed our heads off when we realized the experience had scared the pee right out of our little girl.

The icy river water also caused my hands to go numb. Back in our rented cabin's bathroom, I had to run warm water over them for several minutes to get rid of the numbness. My hands turned an ashy gray. Then, I experienced a different sort of numbness that spread from my fingers deep into my soul following Peter's death. It was about a year after the river trip. Except for the love I felt for our daughter, I felt nothing but desolation and a great sadness over my marriage, cut short by a stupid war.

Had Peter been more of a people-person, he would've enjoyed a trip like this. When mulling over applying for the job of houseboat captain, there were moments when I'd felt his breath on my neck—his spirit coaxing me to do so. I've idealized his image over the years, but he did have a pushy side. In my more nostalgic moods, I miss him, but other times, there's that all-too-familiar numbness.

My instincts tell me I'd feel better if our little bluebird mascot flew back to us. I have a feeling we'll see him again.

. . .

Melanie never needed my help with homework. When she was little, she had a couple of good friends. She claimed she didn't need them, though they needed her. Whenever they visited, she always shut her bedroom door. Sometimes I would knock, offering snacks or giving reminders. We probably spent our closest times together watching movies on the couch or going to the library. She loved informing me of the latest small scale town she was creating. When she became too old for wooden blocks, she'd fashion her buildings from whatever small material she could get hold of— from wood scraps to tinfoil. Then, she learned how to design them on her computer. Over the years, she 'built' several Utopian towns and cities. I told her one day she would become an actual architect. She looked at me like I was nuts. Didn't I realize planning them was enough? Not being all that creative, I didn't understand.

. . .

Six months after Peter returned from the war, he committed suicide. Melanie was only three, but I told her the truth: he was very sick and died. When she was older, I told her more about his illness. My bonds with Sasha and Janet helped sustain me through some dark times. They were both war widows whose husbands had also died of suicide. But grief is a solitary animal. Talking about it eased some of the pain, but it was only the passing of time that truly helped.

I taught for twenty years. My students meant a lot to me, but none remained in my life, though a few stayed in touch before slipping away. After becoming a doula, Giles entered my life, and I thought I could finally put Peter in the past. Giles and I had some great times, but he left me for another woman shortly after I proposed to him. He married her within months of leaving me. Her name was Cassandra, like mine. She wasn't a Cassie. I loathed her and plotted her death. I often fantasized about slow ways of torturing her and shocked myself—though I knew I'd never be capable of carrying out such evil acts. The visuals I once imagined have blurred, so I won't try to specify them. Bitter feelings toward Giles replaced my earlier ones.

So, you see, I have a vested interest in making friends with all the passengers—except for Zona. I need friendship as much as a change in scenery in a life that is beyond half-over. The bonds that tied me to Sasha and Janet are no longer as strong as they once were. My love for Melanie is tiger-mother strong, but if our relationship were closer, maybe I wouldn't crave the closeness of others, or at least not as much.

While I've told my fellow travelers about my careers, I haven't yet mentioned Peter's suicide. Maybe I will and maybe I won't. But if I reveal little about my past, will I ever be able to feel close to them? The trip has connected us, but there is still a lot we do not know about each other.

• • •

Before the river trip, I'd given up trying to coax Melanie to meet me for lunch or a shopping trip. She didn't want to risk it. She began stopping by my apartment once a month during the warmer weather, when we could sit outside on my balcony. But even then, she'd keep her mask on the entire time. I tried offering her a glass of wine. She refused. I sure needed one and pled my case.

"I could turn the other way when I take a sip," I'd told her.

"No way, Mom. I'm not going to risk it."

"But I haven't been anywhere in weeks."

"Didn't you just meet Sasha for lunch last week?"

"Yes, but Sasha's fine. We were about the only ones in the restaurant."

"About the only ones? Sorry, Mom, but I just can't risk it. I'm surprised you're so 'c'est la vie' about the plague. Haven't you heard about what can happen to your vital organs, including your brain? Frankly, your risky behavior puts me at risk."

"But the numbers, at least locally, have been pretty low."

Melanie sighed after my last comment. I should have known better. I did know better. She wouldn't change her mind about her self-imposed rules of conduct any more than I was going to alter what she perceived as recklessness. My daughter is one of the cautious minority who rarely leaves home. Her standard line is, "It's still out there, so why take chances?"

When I announced my decision to become the captain of a houseboat, it must have shocked her. I'm still holding out the hope that I can lure her to take a break from her isolation and join us. She's young and single. This trip should be hers, not mine. To reduce my guilt, I remind myself that it is her decision to live like a cloistered nun is her choice. She's not pining away for a different life. I enjoy solitude; she thrives on it. If I thought otherwise, I couldn't carry on as a captain of this river journey.

• • •

Soon after turning down a river bend, we see hundreds of white balloons in the sky. There is no sign of the person or people responsible for launching them. I can't recall the last time I saw such a large balloon flock. We all feel joyful, staring up, pointing and exclaiming—except for you know who: Zona. She looks at them for a moment before rolling her eyes.

"People, it's no big deal."

"Oh, but it is, Zona. It's like watching souls ascend."

"Did you just say what I think you said, Cassie?"

"Hey, back off gritty girl," says Margot, coming to my rescue. "I think Cassie's right and that's why we're all feeling a giddy joy—with you being the exception. You should try to lighten up some."

"Yeah, right." Zona sneers and then furrows her brow in a manner accomplished by only the most cynical and jaded. She no sooner makes the comment when the white balloons vanish without a trace of them ever having been in the sky.

. . .

Last night, we all slept deeply, lulled by the slight rocking of the craft, and comforted by knowing our chances of disappearing were smaller on the water than on land. I remind myself about it now as I lie on my bunk. Vincent has the wheel. My breathing slows and evens out. My inhales are no longer snagged by fearful thoughts.

. . .

The river cold spots must be outnumbering the hot spots, as artwork and written words are still completely intact.

. . .

Last night's dream returns unbidden: the crew and I were circus performers. I was the ringmaster; Margot and Kali were trapeze artists; Leon and Vincent were clowns; and Zona was The Lady with Three Eyes. The third eye, in the center of her forehead, was lidless and seemed to take in the world without being able to process it. I almost didn't recognize Zona, but then I did because of the tattoos along her arms. Scorpions, black widows, ladybugs, and hummingbirds came alive and flew into the air. She tried to snatch them before they flew off, but couldn't. The skin on her arms was raw. It was like the tattoos were being ripped off and stripped of their former glory, demoted and unworthy of their permanent status.

. . .

Back to reality. Something strange occurs after I rejoin a few of the others on the top outer deck. Margot mentions her throat feels scratchy, and she's worried about losing her voice again. She whispers that this was the way her muteness began the first time.

"No, Margot! Don't let it happen!" I implore, putting a hand on her shoulder. "Tell me more about your kids...how they came to live with you and how you felt after saying goodbye."

"It's still difficult for me to talk about, even with Vincent. Well, if I do lose my voice again, just ask him."

I give a resigned nod, but a feeling comes over me that something more than a little odd is about to happen.

Then Kali emerges from below deck, exclaiming, "Zona is not only trying to steal my man, she's a thief!"

"And you're a liar! Maybe you should be the one to walk the gangplank! We need to stop at the next town so you can get your head read, Kali," Zona replies.

"I'm a liar, eh? Where did you get these little trinkets? I found them tucked in the bottom of your backpack." Kali is holding a small pipe in one hand and a copper ashtray in another. She claims they belong to her.

"What the fuck were you doing in my backpack in the first place?"

"Just answer the question!"

We all look at Zona.

"Who are you, my judge and jury, Miss Kali?" she asks before stomping off and disappearing below deck.

Everyone wonders how she could do such a thing. Everyone thinks maybe we should have a gangplank.

RIVER VOICES

Margot

Could this possibly be the weirdest, yet most enriching, experience of my life? We've just left the town of Doze. Even before arriving there, the river had become dream-like. Do the ghosts of the orphans truly haunt the Pink Hotel? The only time I felt grounded was following the storm when we helped pick up the fallen branches. Even then, the people there seemed strange. It was like they saw us, but didn't. And when we heard about how people were disappearing, we realized it was time for us to leave. But now, I'm worried. The magical properties of the town allowed me to recover my voice, but what if I become mute once again when we're back on the water? My throat feels like sandpaper. The same feeling I recall before losing my voice the first time. And yet when we were in Doze, Vincent and I actually fell in love all over again.

To lose one's voice has got to be one of the worst things, especially when you're around others. While Vincent and I had used other ways to communicate, the others ignored me. Because I couldn't verbally express myself, they had little use for me—except for Cassie, who gently tried to persuade me to talk. It was kind of funny because she acted like it was a matter of will; as if I could simply decide to speak and start jabbering away. At first, it was helpful for Vincent to do the talking for me. He became presumptuous about my thoughts, but who wouldn't? So, yes, now I'm afraid I'll lose my voice again. I'm going to play my flute more often, hoping I can help calm myself down. Perhaps it will help others as well.

Vincent

While I've mentioned to the others how I lost my wife and daughter to the plague, they don't need to hear the details of their deaths. To talk about the dead is to dig them up from their graves. The others don't need to know that my grief continues to this day, despite my relationship with Margot. They wouldn't understand how the idea of remaining in a town where people were vanishing was a little much for me. I should be a hardened SOB right now, but I'm not. I was so relieved when Margot recovered her voice, but now she's afraid she's going to lose it again. And I was happy as hell to leave Doze. Now, there are other concerns, and who knows what is ahead on this river road? Waves of feelings for her are about to knock me over, and I've never been the romantic type. Not really.

Got to admit that after hearing how paintings weren't disappearing in Doze, I was ready to become a resident. It would've been easy to say goodbye to Cassie and the others, provided Margot stayed with me. She had also seemed enchanted by the town.

My memories of Monica and little Tara are sometimes fuzzy, though my love for them remains. Some thought I was an anti-vaxxer for political reasons, but no, Monica and I had been living off the grid at the time she fell ill.

I'm kind of disappointed in Leon. I really thought he and Kali had a good thing going, but since he's been fooling around with Zona, I guess they don't. Since I wasn't faithful to Monica, so who am I to judge? He must not be ready to settle down, but nothing good is going to come of this, and I sure as hell don't want to be there when the fireworks turn into bombs. Like I've thought since the beginning of the trip, Zona is this side of evil.

Zona

Maybe it's for the best we left that town. No sad goodbyes, though I'll miss sneaking off to empty rooms with Leon. It was nice not to have to share him with Vincent or Kali for a short while. He said he loved all my tats. I told him how I thought he looked like Jimi Hendrix, returned from the grave. I'll bet we could get it on all day and never get tired—were it not for that little bitch, Kali. She needs to let him go. Why can't she see Leon doesn't belong to any woman? He's a wild and wonderful poet-man who shouldn't let someone like Kali domesticate him. I was happy to hear that he'll tell her when it's over. I kinda wish he'd let me do the honors, but I need to stay on his good side. Then again, maybe she'll end it, though I'm guessing she won't.

I also got into taking phone pics in Doze. The aftermath of the storm was pretty cool, so I snapped a lot of shots. I wanted to take ones of Leon and me, but he said he didn't want to risk Kali's over-the-top reaction. He said my pics are pretty good, and maybe I could turn into a freelancer or some shit. Maybe I will.

My insomnia got worse in Doze. Were my occasional memory lapses because of brain fog from the virus I had a few years ago—not from the Strangler Virus, but an earlier Corona strain, or were they just from a lack of sleep? So, yeah, I guess it was time we got the fuck out of Doze. I wonder what we are in for down the river. Where's that circus Cassie mentioned days ago?

I don't regret swiping that old-fashioned ash-tray and the wooden pipe, as they're my souvenirs from that crazy place.

I overheard Vincent talking to Margot when I was sitting in the living room area on the opposite side of the thin wall. For once, I was the only one in the room. I heard them talking about the End Times. He was trying to persuade her that the world wasn't about to end. His voice was quiet, but then I could hear him saying something about my parents and how his father had them followed. I've got to say something—maybe I'll mention it to Cassie first. If Vincent didn't murder them, he more than likely knew someone who did. At any rate, his father was obviously more than just a right-wing asshole.

Leon

Guess I'm the only one who wanted to remain in Doze to help, but I get why we left when we did. Also, I would've liked a little more time with Zona, too. That girl takes my breath away, but I'm afraid she won't give it back. Lately, she's been jumpy, and since she's not the type to wear her heart on her sleeve, I doubt I'll find out why. I need to come clean with Kali, but I'll do so when I'm good and ready. Two women—especially those two, would be too much to handle. Maybe I should break-up with Kali. She deserves better. But I've got an uneasy feeling about Zona. I meant to tell her that knowing Vincent like I do, there's no way he could have gotten rid of her parents. When I get the chance, I'll say something to Zona. But it's like she's about to get into some shit. I don't know how or when, but I've always been good at knowing things ahead of time. At least sometimes, I am, and most folks don't know this about me. I don't know if I should call Zona out on it. She doesn't scare easily, but if I tell her, maybe she'll take some precautions. No point in breaking-up with her since we're not really together.

I wish I could talk to Vincent about my problems with women, but I know he doesn't see what I do in Zona. He'd judge me before hearing me out. Maybe I'm wrong. Men don't talk to each other about relationship issues. Not the ones I've known. Sometimes, I sure do envy women and their ability to figure things out with each other.

I'm going to pull out my harmonica, play some blues, and think about it. Going to do some deep breathing and shut my eyes, as I don't need to see the scenery—unless we pass by that purported riverside circus, which I know is going to get strange again. I just know these things. My methods will calm me down, as well as the rock-a-bye rhythm of the boat.

Kali

I've never been more upset than I am at this very moment. Just overheard Leon and Zona talking about trying to find another time they could hook up. ANOTHER time? I know they've been flirting like crazy, but when were they first together? I've got to tell Leon that I know. If he gives me some lame excuse, I'll get off at the next town we stop at, and I won't look back. I don't need this. Life is crazy enough right now! The truth is I'm intrigued by Zona. Alright, I admit it: maybe I am somewhat attracted to her. I can see what Leon sees in her. Still, it doesn't make them having their little affair behind my back, okay. But maybe I should stay and steal her back from Leon. I'll do it right under his very nose! That will shock the shit out of him, to borrow a Zona phrase. But something tells me he'd say it was cool and ask if he might watch Zona and me in bed together. That's what irks me about the man. He's angry about some shit, but cool about other stuff. I'm so glad we left Doze. Everything was spinning out of control there. Here on the boat, at least I can monitor on the situation.

DAY 12

For a long stretch, the water levels are so low I have to steer down the exact middle of the river or a close approximation, so we won't get stuck. We can see hulls of several small boats that people must have been abandoned and left for scrap. Some are older, but many look to still be in good condition. Why didn't the owners have them towed? It makes me think we might see skeletons—and then we do.

And then, we see our first bona fide shipwreck: The Amphora.

I'm not the only one who, at first, thinks it a hokey tourist-trap. It gives us something to do for an hour, as well as a chance to stretch our legs.

According to our tour guide, Captain John, the Amphora was a steamboat built back in 1885. Close to five-hundred people had been aboard, though capacity should have allowed for only a hundred.

Before giving us more details, the captain tells us it won't be long before the river will flood, as it does every year. This is the last day he will conduct tours until summer. Only part of this whale-of-a-boat will be visible.

We climb aboard, and Captain John gives us the tour and informs us how most passengers had perished.

The Amphora had been on a weekend cruise. Dinner was being served, and a band was playing banjo music when the boat smashed into a gigantic boulder.

Before he allows us to peer inside, Captain John shows us the smashed up hull.

"Oooh," and "Oh, my!" we exclaim in unison. This made 'Captain' John grin. He next escorts us to portals covered by drawn shades. Outside the first portal, he presses a button, and the shades go up and banjo music plays.

What we next behold makes us gasp. Most of the skeletons wear nothing but their bones. Only a few of them sport shocks of hair and wear threadbare garments. The former musicians still hold wood-rotten, broken-stringed banjos. Through another portal, you can see a very bony server in a bowtie with a platter, broken plates and splintered glasses lying next to him. Another portal reveals small groups of skeletons on top of each other.

Then we gaze through a blurry glass window at a couple lying in each other's arms in bed. It almost feels like we are disturbing their privacy.

The last portal reveals a baby's skeleton laying on top of a larger one—probably its mother.

Our guide tells us that a flood had occurred, as if out of nowhere. Swirling water swallowed entire trees on the banks. After the steamship hit the boulder, one boiler exploded, immediately killing all those nearby. Some passengers became trapped when the upper deck had collapsed into the middle one, while others were thrown into the water. Then the boat sank. There hadn't been a chance to lower the lifeboats, and only a few had made it safely to shore. The paint-chipped boat had been listing on its side on a flood plain ever since the tragedy occurred.

"Almost a river version of the Titanic," I remark, and the captain nods. "Why did the boiler explode?"

He explains how they never determined how it happened, but assumed the swift impact of the boulder had somehow caused it. Certainly, a sad and memorable tale.

Captain John takes his time posing us for a group photo. We stand somberly in front of the remains of the steamship and found it impossible to smile.

. . .

Zona keeps trying to tell me something when we return to the houseboat, but every time she does, someone else joins us. It's obvious that something is bothering her. But then something's always annoying or upsetting her. I rap at her cabin door after everyone else is sleeping, but she, too, must be asleep. Sleeping on the river sure takes you down deep into slumberland. I'll have to check with her tomorrow.

DAY 13

There is reason to believe *Silver Lady* is a ghost ship. While we're here in the flesh and are fairly certain we exist, I don't believe those we pass by know we're here. It's been this way for the last several miles.

I try to start up a round of "Row, row, row your boat…", but none of the others feel much like singing this beloved but well-worn little song. Why didn't I choose a more like-minded crew that could laugh at the absurd? Like any good captain, I try to assure them this uncomfortable situation is temporary. I feel their frustration over feeling invisible. A little too reminiscent of how I felt during the last pandemic and the following two years of my self-imposed isolation. Maybe I hadn't been the only one hiding out during that time.

I suggest a group meditation, but no one shows interest.

I'm not completely sure, but based on our experiences, there is every reason to believe that we'll soon be visible again. Maybe it's because I'm an older woman and I know all about the condition of being invisible. It isn't pleasant, but you get used to it. It can be great fun to spy on others without being seen. You can lurk, pick your nose, say and do outrageous things and others won't pay much attention.

But the unfolding scenes also spellbind us. This morning we've seen three distinct moments from three separate time periods. Despite being disconcerted, it's a relief to be more alert than we were in the town of Doze or in the Land of Doze. We've been almost as lively as we were in the first few days of our trip. The only difference is an accompanying anxiousness, if not exactly dread.

I'm feeling more relaxed now that everyone has been pitching in at playing captain—except Zona, of course.

We are somewhere else in time when we pass by two people working on a raft: a tall dark-skinned man and a white, scrawny looking teenage boy. We immediately recognize Jim and Huck, as everyone aboard *Silver Lady* has read the once-banned classic, now banned again in many parts of the soon-to-be former USA.

Huck is handing Jim a cord of some sort. We call to them, but neither glances up from their work. At first, we assume they are simply engrossed in what they were doing, so it never occurs to us that they can't see us. Does this mean *Silver Lady* has traveled back in time? They could be look-alikes, or actors in a play, couldn't they?

Shortly after seeing Jim and Huck, we encounter a tribe of Native Americans erecting teepees. A couple of boys are swimming in the buff. Could be early in the 19th Century, but it's hard to say. Neither the boys nor the others from the tribe look in our direction. But this time, we don't call out to them, fearing we won't be welcome. Why would we be?

"It's like we're watching scenes from various plays," I say. The others nod, speechless by the two scenes.

"Think we're having a collective dream?" asks Leon. He removes his large-framed glasses and rubs his eyes.

"I don't think so. Pinch yourself to know for sure. No, I'm beginning to think we went through a time slip while we slept last night," I reply.

Even Zona looks mystified. For once, she isn't smacking her gum from boredom.

Two figures on a raft come into view. Huck and Jim again? As we get closer, we see an older white woman and a younger black teenage girl. They are both in blue jeans and T-shirts, so they must be from the recent past or present. At first, they seem to notice us, and the girl raises her hand like she is going to wave, but doesn't. Then they sit cross-legged, side by side, both lost in thought. Who are they? Should we know them?

A fourth scene unfolds after we round a bend in the river that is unmarked on my chart. No chance to tell the others, but I think these are movie scenes. The actors can see *Silver Lady* and her passengers perfectly well. We must be in their film. It makes a kind-of sense, right? Especially given the need for reasonable explanations.

Next, a bunch of blue-jeaned hippies are dancing and singing Pink Floyd's song *Comfortably Numb*. The song blasts from the radio of a yellow car. Leon, who knows old cars, says it's a 1968 Mustang. While at least thirty flower children are dancing on the shore and in the water, only a few cars are in the parking lot. No doubt most of them are probably too high to notice us, but one young woman, who looks a lot like Janis Joplin, calls out, "Hey, do you guys see that boat? A houseboat on the water and those people staring at us?"

"Blues lady, you're blowing my mind. There's no boat out there," says a guy who could have been Kris Kristofferson's twin circa 1970.

But Janis (or her double) sees us. My latest theory must be correct. We collectively heave a sigh of relief. Most of the crew agrees: we haven't entered other time periods. It is still somewhat of a rational world.

Silver Lady comes to another bend. She seems as alert as the rest of us as we gaze at the passing scenery, wondering what lies ahead.

First, we eye a tall oak tree and then a child sitting on one of its branches, a boy of about ten. He is sobbing. We think he sees us, too, because he seems to stop crying. But then he vanishes. We rub our eyes and scan the various branches. There is no trace of him, not even a rustling in the branches.

Will we, too, simply disappear?

Once we believed it could only happen to artworks and written works but rarely to people, until we'd heard about it happening in Doze. Why wouldn't the river's cold spots have kept him safe? Would the boy have been safer on the boat? Maybe consciousness is one big Etch-A-Sketch. Why is this happening when, throughout human history, death occurred naturally or violently—and even then, the body remained behind?

With a new urgency, I try to corral my memories, to rein them in before they vanish, as well. I can still picture my first-grade teacher, Mrs. Sutherland. She was from Australia and smiled a lot. She taught my class some really cool Australian songs. One was about the bird, a laughing kookaburra, also known as a kingfisher. Another memory: that Christmas morning when I gave my seven-year-old Melanie moon boots and a long, pink boa. She sashay-thumped through the house, occasionally tossing the scarf over her shoulder before marching on. Another memory of kissing a man in the middle of a city sidewalk—my late husband. But is it the photo I'm recalling or an actual memory? No one took a picture of me kissing him, so it's got to be a real one. But some I'm unsure about...Memories of my parents or photo memories?

I ask the others, and now they're concerned about their memories, too.

Margot's voice cuts out completely for a few minutes, but then returns. The rest of us stare at her in wonder. Her voice is like a flickering lightbulb. Vincent holds her hand, but she snatches it away.

For a few more miles downstream, all is calm. A red baseball cap followed by a blue beach ball floats by, and then a few white feathers, and a Styrofoam box. The day feels summery, and dragonflies wage war on mosquitoes. Mosquitoes, left to their own devices, would wage war on us. Last night, a few got inside my cabin and buzzed around my ears, so I wound up joining Zona for a game of cards at the kitchen table. I'd hoped she would confide about what's been bothering her. But no, we lost the opportunity, as a couple of others joined us in the game.

Two fish reveal their faces above the water. They immediately try to talk to us, bobbing their heads about. One is especially excited and seems to interrupt the other; the latter looks none too pleased to be upstaged. But like the few other fish we've seen, they are gone in a flash to the river depths.

Conversation resumes among the crew. It's like the talking fish have motivated us.

We talk about the hoped-for circus. With all we've experienced on the trip, most of us are no longer expecting it. It's become a mythical place, an El Dorado of sorts. Even if we find it around a river-bend, I'm sure it'll be a big disappointment.

I mention my circus dream in which Zona had three eyes and how her tattoos came alive and flew away.

Zona snorts and guffaws, saying her next tat will be an eye on the back of her neck. Ignoring her comment, Vincent chimes in how he's also had circus dreams lately, though he can't recall any details. Zona eye-rolls us both and smacks her gum. It isn't easy, but I resist the urge to put it on her nose.

We talk about our well-known parents and what it had been like to be in their shadows. For some of us, living up to their expectations has been a challenge, though we discovered Zona and I both had parents who did everything in their power to keep their children from experiencing performance anxiety.

"I know my parents aren't just missing. They were murdered. It took me a fucking long time, but I get it now. I'll never see them again. A couple of months back, I hired a detective, but the leads turned into dead ends. Vincent, you wouldn't know anything about them being followed, would you?"

All eyes are on him. No one says anything. His fingers comb through his bushy beard. Everyone fidgets, shifting about from one foot to another. He finally breaks the silence.

"What makes you think I'd know about your parents being followed, Zona? I thought we'd cleared the air back in Doze. Like I said, I only knew my father wasn't wild about their leftist writing. That article sure hurt him, but I know others had it in for him, too. If I knew anything more, I'd tell you, but that's it. End of story."

"I heard you telling Margot that he had them followed."

"Well, you heard wrong, girl. I'm sorry they've been missing for so long, but you're barking up the wrong tree."

"I heard what I heard." Zona gets the last word in, but seems to realize the pointlessness of trying to get Vincent to admit anything. She gives Margot a questioning look.

Margot shakes her head and shrugs.

Has she lost her voice again? Strange that Zona doesn't press her further, though maybe it's because she, too, realizes the couple never contradict each other.

I embarrass Zona by hugging her. My spontaneity startles me more than the others. Has she now planted doubt in their minds about Vincent? In everyone's except Margot's, that is. I'll bet that's why Zona brought the subject up.

After an awkward silence, I try to steer the conversation back to the discussion we'd been having about our parents. Although addressing the entire group, I pointedly look at Zona when I remark how my parents never expected their first folk-rock album to have made such a splash. The Navrones toured the world and made a few more albums for over fifteen years. I stayed with my grandmother whenever they were away. When they played at local places, they'd often take me with them. I still play their music, which I'm sure I would've loved, even had The Navrones not been my parents.

"Awww," says Zona, without a hint of sarcasm. I think it's the first time she's given me a genuine smile. Am I seeing things? Did her eyes actually well up with tears?

Then an owl lands on our boat and, once again, the mood shifts. It's a barn owl, claims Vincent, the knower-of-many-species. You can tell because of his ghostly face. He adds how they don't hoot like other owls, but hiss and scream.

His relief that there is an opening to discuss something less personal is obvious.

The owl stares at us with his all-knowing eyes. Like the fish, he seems to be trying to convey a message.

We shrug and shake our heads. He is clearly agitated.

A boat dock is just ahead. If there is a town nearby, we need to pick up a few provisions we forgot to get in Doze. We go through bread, coffee, and wine a lot faster than I've expected.

Then we hear not only one owl hooting, but several. Pendulous clouds darken and seem to fall from their own weight.

Maybe the fish had been trying to warn us.

The sky darkens, and it's like night has descended, though it's only mid-afternoon.

The water artery of the river thins, making for such a narrow ride that we feel like we are going down a chute. I don't like my lack of control behind the wheel. It feels like a water ride at a macabre amusement park.

Next, we hear thunder from an approaching storm, but it isn't thunder. It is a loud hooting. It grows even louder and stranger. Then we see hundreds of owls watching us from both sides of the river. They are not only on the dock, but in the trees, and on the grassy banks. The sky further darkens, with many now airborne. They hoot and stare at us in a menacing, foreboding way. Strangely, I can't help but feel relieved to be seen by them.

We are all a bit too fascinated to hide below deck.

"This must be Owl Town. Remember, Kali, how the storekeeper in Doze, whose name I can't recall, told us about it? Was it George? I guess people used to live here, but the owls drove them out. They probably think we're invaders. Let's just hope they don't dive-bomb us as we pass by."

Four of us try to remain out on the upper deck, but the deafening sound soon drives us inside.

What if the owls find us worthy prey?

I take over the wheel and give the boat a little more gas. And, wouldn't you know, almost right after doing so, we get stuck on some rocks. Shit. This couldn't have happened at a more inopportune time.

For a few minutes, we sit there, motionless. Then I ask if owls are carnivores. No one knows. If so, hopefully, like buzzards, they'll wait until the animal died before tearing flesh from the bones. If we weren't already considered the best of the local cuisine, we could very well be now. I can imagine my daughter laughing at me—not that she longs for me to die this way. *This is serious, Mel...*I'm sure she never pictured this scenario to be my last, but it will further validate her quiet life. I'm only sorry there was no way for me to get in touch, to say a last goodbye.

While we all feel a little safer inside, a few of my fellow passengers are nearly hysterical. Are we actors in a remake of Hitchcock's movie, *The Birds*? I know better than to ask. The boat feels smaller than ever. Everyone's out-shouting each other about how to proceed.

The two men yell at me to floor the engine, and the women scream at the men to get out and push. Including Margot. I'm relieved she hasn't lost her voice. Then I hear my voice command. "Listen up, everyone! Put on your scuba gear for protection." None of us have yet worn our scuba gear. "There's no time to panic," I add.

Surprisingly, it isn't me who calms the crew—it is Margot. She stands on the outer top deck with flute in hand. I stop barking commands as she begins playing the sweetest strands of music I've ever heard. I'm not good at recalling song titles, but this one I know: a Mozart flute concerto. It helps us all relax. As pleasant as her velvety voice is, her sonorous flute music is her true voice.

Almost at once, the angry owls settle down, and the last few haters among them hush.

Zona's head drops forward and, within seconds, she's sound asleep. I'm surprised she doesn't fall off her chair. *Silver Lady* seems to rock in rhythm to the music. As she dances, she rocks herself free of the rocks below and glides effortlessly downriver.

Margot next plays, "Row, row, row your boat gently down the stream…" After a while, she stops and the two of us sing in rounds, "Merrily, merrily, merrily, merrily…Life is but a dream."

So long, Owl Town. While I'd hoped to garner some of your wisdom, it looks like—at least collectively, that you have little to offer. Not so different from humans, right? Put too many together and there is too much competition, which soon turns into the ugliness of selfish desires—if not outright blood-sport. I've always viewed owls as sacred. Maybe I still will, but I'll no longer wish to know the species any better than I do my own.

A silver moon rises and spotlights Margot. Her long black braid shimmers as she drapes it over a shoulder. I give her the last of the cheese and a bottle of champagne for her quick thinking. She pops the cork. We raise our glasses, and even Zona wakes up to toast the numinous flute player.

Then, as we all relax and process our near-death experience, there is a sudden chill in the air.

After returning from my room with a sweater, I notice chunks of ice ahead in the river. It's beginning to snow.

Here we are, on the thirteenth day of our journey south, and it has turned cold and snowy. How the hell could this be happening? We seem to go from one incredulous moment to the next. We laugh and rub our gooseflesh.

Vincent remarks how it felt jungle-like as we were passing through Owl Town and now this! Welcome to climate change, right?

Have I mentioned our fireplace? As we sit around its fake fire glow of the living room, Margot, with great care, pulls something from a skirt pocket. We stop yapping about the weather to observe a tiny owlet on her palm. Before we can ask whether it's hurt, she tells us the only problem with the little guy is his size.

"Seriously, Margot? After what we just went through…How could you?" asks Vincent, shaking his head, but looking somewhat amused.

Margot answers his question with a question. "How could I? How could we not allow him safe passage? My guess is that his life was endangered in Owl Town, that is, unless he simply likes my music."

"I don't see any reason he can't ride along with us. He sure isn't adding much weight to the boat now, is he?" I ask some of the more coldhearted crew members. No one dares to counter my position, so Ollie the Owlet may ride with us for as long as he likes. In no time, Kali and Leon are fawning all over him. Zona nods off once again to one of Margot's melodies. If there is such a thing as owl wisdom, maybe Ollie will gift us some of his. Maybe he'll somehow let me know the true nature of reality, so long as I don't press him for a definitive answer.

RIVER VOICES

Zona

I'm so awake right now—too awake. Maybe it's preferable to sleeping. That fucking storm! I've seen some pretty scary shit in my life, but never something like this. Never will I be able to forget it. The town could've been easily blown off the map. It turned us all into a bunch of zombies. Once we were back on the river, everyone on the boat acted like it never happened. Then there was that weird place, Owl Town, with all those damn owls. I admit Margot playing her flute lulled me into a sweet stupor, but no one's even talked about what we went through back in Doze.

It still bothers me how I can't be online whenever I want. Mostly, to check for possible news about my parents, though Cassie probably thinks I'm just missing my social media fix. Lately, my phone's only good for taking pics. Two of the others have said I'm getting pretty good at it. Weird, how my shots from other time periods never showed up on my phone. Has this happened to the others, too? Glad I could replenish my gum supply in Doze since I'd begun smoking more. Cassie almost caught me a few times. Maybe when I'm good and ready to say au revoir, I'll smoke right in front of her. That'll show her...if only I didn't have a major crush on Leon. I swear to God, he is the only reason I'm still here.

Leon

I can't seem to locate my harmonica, but I know I brought it on the trip. Not to compete with Margot and her flute playing, but I've been told my bittersweet blues can make a rock cry. Right now, I'd sure as hell enjoy playing a riff or two on my mouth harp, if only to calm me down some about that crazy vision I had about Zona. Granny used to say I had her ability to see things before they happened, but unlike her, sometimes I've been wrong. Sure hope I'm wrong this time, as I'm crushing on that girl in a major way. I know Kali suspects Zona and me of having sex, but I'll deny it to my dying day. I'll tell her again how Zona won't be around much longer. Man, I could use my harp right now. Too many dreamlike places we've seen—from Doze to Owl Town, to those time-slip scenes on the riverbank. I need something which will return me to a sense of the real. My homies would get what I mean. They'd help me get me off this weird visual high. They'd find some rhythms for my words. Our commonalities would see me through. Yeah, I'm missing them, though not all the time. And I sure don't miss the city crime or daily fears of being pulled over by the cops.

Kali

I feel so bad about sometimes wanting Leon's premonition to come true. While Zona is bad news, I don't wish she'd leave. Or do I? Women will always want to steal him from me, so I better get used to it. I could've gone for a plainer guy, a simpler soul, but I'd get bored pretty fast. Leon's intelligence and his sexiness about put me about over the treetops, if not the moon. He's my poetry man. But if we ever had children, I bet he'd leave me. I don't know how I feel about the whole becoming-a-mother-thing, anyway. If the world were less crazy, maybe I would.

Little owl, what are you looking at? Ollie's been escaping Margot's pocket every chance he gets. He is on the cute side. Maybe she'll let me borrow him.

Shouldn't people be wild about kids and wanting kids—if they decide to have a family? Like Leon always says, "We've got plenty of time to figure that part out, Kales." I love how he calls me Kales. I drank too much champagne last night on an empty stomach, and my head is throbbing. Maybe I'll go below deck and sleep it off. I need to get away from this little owl staring at me, or I'll start making him little hats and scarves. Not a good use of my time.

Margot

I never thought the river cruise would be so enjoyable. Things sure turned better after getting my voice back, finding sweet little Ollie, and seeing the effect playing my flute had on the owls and the crew. My song-dreams seem to go straight from my soul to my flute. I surprised myself when I began riffing after the Mozart piece. I don't know if I'll remember tomorrow what I played today, but that's okay. Not like I'm going to record an album. I truly enjoy getting to know the others, especially Captain Cassie. I hope I always remember seeing those riverside sights: Huck Finn and Jim, the unknown woman and girl, Janis Joplin, and those hippies. Then, the boy in the tree and how he vanished right before our very eyes! What vibrant and electrifying colors—this is such a strange and magical place! Colors are vibrant, even electrified. Could it be because Vincent and I are so deeply in love, or has the river cast a spell?

Vincent

Margot was beside herself when she realized her little friend, Ollie, had disappeared. After searching the entire boat, we found him perched next to Kali, asleep in her cabin. We burst out laughing, as the little owl looked like he was guarding her. Kali glowered at us after being awoken abruptly. She then shooed us from her cabin. I was surprised Zona hadn't absconded with him—it would've been in keeping with what we know about her.

I haven't said anything to Cassie, but I'm a little concerned about how *Silver Lady* will stand up to the next storm. Leon and I agreed we could be in for some real trouble. Sure storms are typical at this time of year, but since climate change has messed with the intensity of storms, the damage they cause is no longer predictable. While the boat is a newer one, made of fiberglass, I doubt even the most top-of-the-line models could escape the potential damage wrought by the extreme weather we've been having lately.

Margot asked if something was wrong. I tried to deny it, but she can read me like a book and knows when I'm preoccupied. Truth is, I've been thinking about Monica and our sweet little Tara more than usual. They've been on my mind because I haven't dreamt about them as much as before. Hard to say if this is because of the trip or my love for Margot. I must admit to having gotten used to the role of talking for her. I do love caring for those I love. Now that she doesn't need me as much, I hope my feelings don't diminish. Does the thought itself mean they already have? No fucking way I'm going to allow it.

Plus, Zona's accusation has been on my mind. Do the others now think my father had Zona's parents followed? I guess it doesn't matter if they do, as long as I keep the truth away—even from Margot. Maybe one day I'll be able to tell her. For now, I've got to keep the others thinking that Zona is one messed up and paranoid girl.

DAY 14

We pass by a cove where the water is so pristine and glassy—it sparkles. If not for the many clusters of lily pads, we could see the bottom. The air is sticky and summerlike with whiffs of a lemony-clean scent. I'm almost certain the serenity this provides will allow us to get through whatever happens next. A good thing I've learned to expect the unexpected.

No sooner are we back on the turgid water of the main channel when two double kayaks pull up alongside us. A single kayak trails behind. I'm about to yell out, "Ship, Ahoy!" but stop myself. Next thing we know, five women have climbed aboard the bottom outer deck of the *Silver Lady*.

Pirates.

The tallest one has long brown hair, which falls well below her waist. It's snarled and greasy—like it hasn't been washed in weeks. Well over six-feet, she towers over her minions, and stands with hands on hips, scowling at us. She is clearly the leader. No one says anything or dares to move. After an uncomfortable silence, she swats at an army of flies that have followed the pirates aboard. Until now, we haven't noticed many insects.

She motions for me to pull over to a temporary mooring site just ahead.

I kill the engine, unable to speak or swallow.

"Well? Somebody going to welcome us aboard?" the leader asks, after we've docked.

Zona mumbles something, but gets cut off.

"Looks like we'll just have to make ourselves at home. What's for breakfast, Granny? We're a hungry lot and get mean if not fed."

Everyone looks at me. If breakfast is all they're after—well, okay. I try to smile my best old-lady grin.

"Sure. Uh...we've got cereal, muffins..."

"Bacon and eggs?"

"Eggs."

"I like mine fried. Ladies, what'll you have?" She turns to her pals.

I bite my lip to keep from exploding in nervous laughter. For a few minutes, I am relieved to be inside preparing breakfast and away from the smelly pirates, but it isn't long before a couple of them join me, along with Zona. Bulls in a china shop would be more careful than they are, the way they rifle through things, tossing a quartz crystal, a screwdriver, and a small paperweight into a canvas bag. The paperweight is Margot's. Nothing particularly interesting about it, but it is clearly of sentimental value. She's often held it, staring at the little flowers inside. She will be upset to find out it's become part of the booty.

Then Zona addresses one of the pirate 'ladies':

"Hey there, Cheyenne. Don't you remember me?"

Cheyenne is short and has a sweeter face than the others. Black leather pants emphasize her stocky legs. She pushes back her long, greasy bangs to better see who is addressing her.

"Zona?"

I am dumbfounded to witness the two hug. After a quick catch-up, Cheyenne says she will talk to their leader, Foxy Lady, who is anxiously awaiting eggs. As it turns out, Zona and Cheyenne are friends from way back. Foxy Lady, after minutes of insisted silence, decides breakfast should suffice and commands Cheyenne and her partners-in-crime to return the almost-pilfered items.

Foxy Lady chews with her mouth open, though she doesn't speak. A fly lands on her eggs, but she doesn't seem to notice.

Following breakfast, Foxy Lady warns us of another pirate gang, the Coast Guard Pirates. Supposedly, they are ten times more vicious than her pirate band, the Ladies in Waiting.

Before they disembark, Foxy Lady winks at me after telling us how she has a plan for dealing with them. Then the crew of *Silver Lady* and the Ladies in Waiting bid each other a good day. I swat several flies they've left behind.

DAY 15

At last, we see the circus. A good thing, too, as after today it'll be all but invisible. Bobo the Clown and two trapeze artists aren't shrinking as fast as the rest. Let me back up some...most likely, we wouldn't have noticed the riverside show, had we not seen the two normal sized trapeze artists walking from one side of the river to the other. At first, we thought they were walking on air, high above the water. Could the river be any more magical? But as the *Silver Lady* got closer, we saw the thin trapeze wire. It was a lovely sight, if not as magical as it first appeared.

When the tents come into view from the boat, I am sure they are further downstream, but realize they are part of a miniature circus. Next, we see several tiny clowns riding even tinier scooters, accompanied by an overpowering aroma of cotton-candy and peanuts.

Every feature of the circus is over half as small as a normal one—the performers, tents, animals, right down to the concession stands. There is no audience, save those of us in boats on the river. We see a couple of boats docked, but no regular-sized people on land. They must have remained in their boats for fear of the Vanishing.

It is then I exclaim over a chimpanzee driving a speedboat and a clown water skiing—the skis are his long red shoes. Curiously, they are normal-sized.

Margot points at a clown on a sinking raft only a few hundred feet from our boat. He is sputtering as he flails his limbs, trying to stay afloat. We laugh at first, thinking it is part of his act. Vincent, the honorary captain, steers the wheel in his direction.

Once we have him on board and he's dried himself off, the grateful Bobo gladly accepts a warm blanket and a hot cup of tea. His eyes grow large and he can't stop thanking us. He then removes his clown nose to blow his real one. No sooner has he stopped shivering when Bobo sees Dolly, one of the trapeze artists, slip from the wire into the water.

Bobo dives right in. Within a couple minutes, he's rescued Dolly and gotten her safely aboard *Silver Lady*. He keeps pulling his endlessly long handkerchief out of a pocket to dry her tears. It is then they tell us how the landlocked performers are all shrinking, and how soon they will, as well...better than suddenly vanishing.

I offer them both the opportunity to travel downstream with us, but neither will consider leaving their circus family, though they thank me for the invitation. Afterward, we say our goodbyes, leaving them on the dock, but not before noting the several dog-sized elephants, kitten-sized lions, and baby-sized adults. They shrink right before our eyes. Bobo and Dolly are, as well, though not as fast, possibly because of being with us.

Before parting ways, Bobo tells us how their fates are still more hopeful now than a few months ago when they'd been normal-sized and performing in small inland towns. For a time, they were chased and treated like low-life villains. And while never treated like royalty, this bewildered them, until they discovered three of the performers were KKK members using the circus as camouflage. They chased the entire circus to its present location at the riverside, and it was there that they gunned down the imposters.

Bobo continues: "We all spat from the boat into their watery graves. And it is here the circus pounded down the tent stakes permanently."

Bobo and Dolly share his handkerchief to wipe their angry tears. I wipe mine on my sleeve.

Soon it will be the size of a flea circus, praying not to be flattened by a human shoe. Yet, it will exist beneath a larger sun and moon, and alongside an enormous and fast-flowing river.

· · ·

Even if the trip takes another week, my five companions will have been with me for such a brief part of my life's journey. Something tells me I've invested way too much time trying to become friends. I need to think about what I'll do once the trip is over. What I now realize is that I can't return to the way I was living before. I've changed and outgrown that time. I once read that if snakes don't shed their skin, they can develop infections and die.

. . .

After not being able to get a proper nap, I pull my hoodie over my caftan and join Zona out on the deck.

"So you and Cheyenne go way back, eh?"

"Met her in juvie. She had my back and I had hers."

"At a juvenile detention center?"

"Must you always say the obvious? Let's just say I had a little problem with shoplifting. We were just kids. Then two years back, she helped me look for my parents. Went our separate ways after a bit. Doesn't surprise me she wound up a pirate. Shit, maybe I'll join the Ladies in Waiting."

I want to say, "Except you're no lady," but refrain.

Zona returns indoors without even saying good night. Typical. I don't call after her and instead gaze down into the inky water flowing by. First one fish, and then five others, poke their heads out of the water. Like the dolphin-fish we saw before, but larger. So much of the river has been fishless. They are staring right at me—checking me out, and wondering about me the way I wonder about them. There are six of them, as there are six humans aboard the *Silver Lady*. I rub the sudden goose-bumps on my arms.

Has it been naïve to think the Great Collapse will never reach us on the water? Are the Coast Guard Pirates waiting for us around the next bend? How can I keep my crew safe?

I'm in way over my pay grade.

DAY 16

Last night, we docked at a marina near the small city of Realidad. Its name was clearly printed on the map, unlike some of the other towns. I never thought being seen by others could be so gratifying. Two fishermen helped us with the moorings and other boaters stopped by the dock to admire *Silver Lady*.

Not only were we grateful to set foot on land once again, but before doing so, we'd found our way back to the main channel. I'm sure they could hear our hearty cheers for a mile. After raising our glasses in a joyful toast, I made an offering to the river goddess, Ganga, by pouring a bit of the cheap wine into the river. This is something Margot and I have done a few times now, though we have made offerings to different river goddesses.

Knowing an actual city is nearby helps make our quarters feel less cramped. Snarky moods have vanished. We even have Wi-Fi here, and the two girls are especially happy to once again be online. There is a slight chill in the air, but the jacket-weather feels good after the near tropical feel of the Owl Town area.

Except for our little buddy, Ollie, we have no concrete reminders of the strange scenes and situations we've witnessed. While there are many pics on several of our phone cameras, most of the details don't show up clearly, even when zooming in. Zona has become our resident photographer, but her phone's a cheap one, so the camera's not all that great. Vincent's phone camera is a decent one, like mine, but neither of us remembers to use it when we're passing by the more bizarre sights.

I love how the ordinary feels like sunlight on cold, bare skin. As a teenager, I once took a hallucinogen with a friend before attend a Leon Russell concert. One song Leon played was a blues rendition of "Somewhere, Over the Rainbow." While Louise's father drove us home,

Bing Crosby belted his rendition of the song on the car radio. Had her father realized how stoned we were? Later, Louise and I giggled over the irony, as we, too, were somewhere over the rainbow. My point is, the following morning while eating a breakfast of French toast at my friend's kitchen table, I marveled at being back in a familiar reality, but with all my senses reawakened.

While we've been told food prices are expensive here, the stores are well-stocked. Still, this isn't Utopia. While everyone here seems friendly enough, so far, most locals have been somber and downcast. Why? Only the other boaters—oblivious to the world on land, laugh or joke in a lighthearted manner.

The six of us decide to go out for breakfast together instead of splitting up the way we have before.

Carla's Café is busy and the customers appear to be composed of both locals and boaters. Sitting in the booth across from our table is a man I've seen before. The last time he was on shore when we had explored the abandoned book boat. He was spraying something from a bottle when we were exploring the boat. I hadn't realized it then, but this was the same older man who'd been playing the sax at our first port-of-call. What was the town's name? Byron, I think. Seeing him here is undoubtedly a coincidence, but all the same.

We now exchange glances and brief smiles. He scratches his goatee and then gazes down at his menu.

Our server, Diana, tells us the talk of an impending civil war has grown louder in the last couple of weeks. She is thin and slightly knock-kneed, with hair pulled back in a tight dishwater-blond ponytail.

I am sitting down, but upon hearing this, the room begins to spin. I grab the table ledge and take a deep breath. Biting my lip helps me refocus.

Diana whispers how protests have now turned into riots in several major cities. Not just random drive-by shootings or mass shootings in the shopping malls. The military could step in but hasn't, at least, not yet. Maybe the federal government has broken down, and there aren't enough National Guard reservists or state police to quell the violence. If so, the states really could actually turn into separate countries. And if this happens, it could well result in the complete dissolution of the United States. While I've known the country has been teetering for a while now, the reality smacks the wind from me. No wonder why the residents here in appear so grim.

I wonder where Diana got her information, but decide not to ask. At first, everyone at the table holds their breath. The tension is palpable. Following a long silence, we make the smallest of small-talk and squirm in our seats like restless kids at school. I long to discuss the situation, but feel too anxious and paranoid.

After refilling our coffee mugs, Diana tries to reassure us that Realidad has seen little trouble. Most of the violence has been occurring in more urban areas, she repeats, as if to convince herself, as well as us. Also, we should keep an eye out for the marauders—the Coast Guard Pirates. They're said to be in the area and way worse than most bandits.

Are my jitters from coffee or fear? I do my best to take a few deep breaths.

Several strands of hair have escaped the confines of Diana's ponytail holder. She leans in and whispers: "No one knows the exact number killed, but weekly deaths are now considered to be up in the thousands." For quite some time, they'd been in the hundreds.

I ask where she got her facts.

She murmurs how she'd heard it from her uncle, a former governor, who may soon become president of the country of Ohio.

I notice the familiar stranger—the man with the goatee, is paying the cashier. Why don't I walk up and introduce myself? I'll bet he remembers me. After thanking Diana for her info, I turn around, but he is gone. I feel a strange letdown. Something about seeing him makes me feel better—like the world's not about to end. Maybe it's because I recognize him.

Following breakfast, we decide to check up on our loved ones to see how they are doing, as well as to find out what they know about conditions in our various hometowns. According to our server, the South and Texas have, so far, suffered the most losses, though the East has been heating up, too, especially on the coast. The area we're returning *Silver Lady* to is a dicey one—both pretty far south and in a populated area.

I phone Melanie from a bench near the marina. Fully prepared to get her voicemail, I almost hang up when she actually answers. At first, it's wonderful to hear her voice. She is doing okay, and as far as she knows, there has been little destruction in our area. She sounds less upset about my river trip than before, though her tone is still icy. It almost crushes me. I prefer the angry Melanie, the imploring Melanie, but not this cold and distant person. Still, at least we have an actual conversation.

She tells me about her latest progress on her village. An architect by trade, she continues to work on the village she's creating on her former pool table. Now and then, she'll send pictures from her phone and I'm always amazed by the village's complexity and beauty. She claims she'll work on it until she takes her last breath.

I tell her about the shrinking circus we'd witnessed, but I'm met with silence. When I try to compare it to her village, I can tell she thinks I've lost my mind. Of course, her village isn't shrinking since it's a miniature! I stumble over my words. What I want to tell her is my absolute delight at witnessing another world and how I finally understand the enjoyment she derives from her omniscient role in her village. Maybe someday, I'll be able to explain it to her and we'll both be happy for each other.

For once, I am relieved by her extreme caution and am certainly not about to encourage her participation in any local political events.

Mel wonders if my travel plans have changed for the return trip, because of the uptick in violence. River travel should be okay, I inform her, adding how we haven't yet seen any rioting or chaos. Originally, I'd planned on renting a car for the return trip, but now there could be too much risk involved. I don't tell her about the pirates, or the occasional plumes of smoke and gunfire along the river.

She promises to do a little sleuthing and to let me know the safest mode of transportation. Air travel might be the way to go, even though it's become so expensive. As I'm about to tell her about some of the other sights along the river, we lose the connection.

• • •

A quick note: We won't be leaving Realidad until tomorrow, as Leon and Kali will perform their poetry tonight at Java Jim's, the town's coffee shop. It's an open mic event and they're both looking forward to it. Here, as elsewhere, poets have been memorizing their work and performing it more-and-more often, fearing that a hot spot will snatch their words from the page. While I've always liked poetry, I'll enjoy it even more this evening since I know two of the poets. I've read a few of Leon's poems, but none of Kali's. Something tells me hers will mainly be about romantic love and a little syrupy. Let's hope I'm wrong. Kali is nervous and claims she only knows two of them by heart.

Tonight, Kali also plans on giving her tip to the other poets tonight if they wish to preserve their poems—don't polish them and maybe they won't vanish. She'll likely add how she kept hers as rough drafts and none has gone AWOL or MIA. I told her not to mention that last bit. Leon has lost more than she has, but still relatively few. Being on the water has more than a little to do with this, but she won't tell the other poets. After all, we don't want the river too congested.

· · ·

I'm typing this on my laptop in the coffee shop at a table for two. While the coffee runs out fast in the mornings, they still have baked goods and some canned beverages for sale. No one has joined me yet. If they do, maybe they'll sit at another table. I hope this journal entry (not part of the captain's log) will remain on the page, though no big deal if it doesn't— unlike the word pearls of good poetry.

· · ·

It's now Intermission. Six poets have recited their poems. Leon and Kali have already recited a few of their pieces and are hanging out with some of the other poets. They're fun to watch. I've always thought poets were mostly wild and eccentric, but clearly that's not the case. Shame on me for making assumptions!

The woman and teenage girl are sitting at a nearby table—the ones we passed by on the river before going through Owl Town. I'm hoping one of them might recognize me, but neither does. After all, they are here to recite poems and appear a little nervous. Curiosity gets the best of me. I walk up to the woman and ask her if they'd been on a raft yesterday. "Did you see a houseboat go by called *Silver Lady*?"

Instead of answering my question, the older middle-aged woman asks, "You really don't know who we are, do you?"

"Should I? Are you famous?"

She doesn't answer, and instead turns back to her younger companion. The girl smiles apologetically, but then immediately gives the woman her full attention.

What's wrong with anonymity? Maybe a lot, especially if someone has something to give the world, and it's overlooked.

Vincent and Margot decided to return to the beach at Lake Realidad. They are supposedly going to be back for the second half of the poetry reading. Earlier, we'd all gone to the small lake together to check it out. It's close to the town. Vincent made a remarkable sand sculpture of *Silver Lady* and then one of Ollie and Margot. His sculpture of our vessel made her seem alive, which told me he perceived her the way I did. I wasn't the only one who viewed her as sentient. What a relief! He is planning to make one of himself. There are dozens of sculptures on the beach—everything from castles to sculptures of people and animals. Some are imaginary and of the two-headed variety. They're all solid structures, indestructible by the elements. According to our server, Diana, sand sculptures here immediately become solid.

What will Vincent do with his carvings? I hope he realizes they would add too much weight to the boat. Maybe he already plans to take them to Shifting Sands, the large gallery behind the city's art museum. You can find most sculptures on the large beach and they are stunning, genuine works of art. Diana asked us not to spread the word, as this is Realidad's little secret. Otherwise, they will have to build a larger museum, as well as deal with a rise in tourism. We promised her that *mum's the word*.

The real excitement over the sand sculptures is because almost all other newly made artistic creations these days, even here in Realidad, immediately crack, break, or even worse, dissolve. Word has it that sculptures and ceramics made more than a year ago seem to be spared, unlike paintings, which all seem to, partially if not fully, dissolve. I was recently told printed photos are fading, too. What's happening to this world? Nothing new will have any permanence, except the sand sculptures.

I wonder where Zona has gone. She'd stormed out of the coffee shop right after Kali's performance. Is she jealous? I found it a pleasant surprise that both Leon and Kali are fine poets. Two of Kali's poems were long and complicated—full of succinctly stated imagery. Wild haikus strung together in an exotic word vine. Leon's work is more political, but the ones he recited had to do with reconstructing a broken world with the last remaining shards of hope. Philosophical in their speculation, and thankfully, not dogmatic. Not being much of a poetry aficionado, I didn't grasp some of it.

My favorite poems of the evening have been Leon's and Kali's. The other ones didn't overly impress me. A couple of poems were about the times we're living in. They were pretty gritty. The last one was more upbeat and was about this delightful city. I really enjoyed that one.

• • •

I tried to get in touch with George Sherman, but he never answered. In a voicemail message, I reassured him of our progress, adding my apologies for not being able to be more exact about how long the rest of our trip would take. Certainly, he knows the mutability of the river: muddy one moment, surging the next.

• • •

(Back on the boat)
We stayed for the second half of the poetry event, which lasted close to another hour before heading back to *Silver Lady*. A man sitting a few

tables away was writing feverishly in a little notebook. He stopped for a moment to scratch his beard—a goatee. The mystery man I keep seeing. It had to be him! I gave him a brief nod, but his face remained burrowed into his notebook. Maybe after the reading was over, I'd muster the courage and introduce myself.

Vincent and Margot joined me at my little table. After telling them how well Leon and Kali performed, they seemed especially disappointed. Vincent told me there was one part of the beach the rest of us hadn't seen. It contained miniature sculptures of sphinxes and pyramids. Had it not been for their reduced size, they'd look like something straight out of Ancient Egypt.

I asked what they would do with his two life size sculptures of himself and Margot. If he asked to bring them aboard the boat, I planned on explaining how we simply couldn't take on much extra cargo, but he surprised me. Evidently, the solid forms simply return to sand again once they are immersed in water. From dust to dust; from sand to sand. He didn't seem at all sad about it.

"What happens if it rains?" I asked.

"Now that's the strange part. I've been told the sculptures stay intact unless they're completely submerged in water. About a year ago, Realidad experienced significant flooding, but the sculptures remained solid."

"I know, Cassie. Let's have a ceremony. We'll launch our forms into the water—give them a great sendoff. Margot could play her flute while the rest of us bid them our goodbyes from the beach."

I nodded, simultaneously sad and amused, but mostly amazed at his willingness to 'free' the sculptures.

The familiar stranger at the nearby table again vanished before I got the chance to meet him.

· · ·

When the five of us return from the city, Zona is waiting for us on the main floor outer deck, stretched out on a long bench with little Ollie on her shoulder. The many tattoos on her bare arms glow in eerie luminescence. She'd turned on the festive deck lighting and turned up the volume of a Caribbean jazz CD. Curiously, she'd traded her usual T-shirt and jeans for a long, slinky, and sleeveless gown. Like a just awakened Sleeping Beauty, she sits from her prone position and then rises slowly. She dances seductively with Ollie still on her shoulder. First a shimmy, then a little shake, a slight undulation. I'm surprised the owlet doesn't flutter away, but he looks as pleased to be there as she does with her appearance.

We join her for a drink, and since she's in a rare good mood, we take turns telling her about the rest of the poetry reading. She keeps eyeing Kali and Leon.

I mention how cool the sand sculptures are, but no one responds. I then ask Vincent how long it's taken for him to make his, but either he doesn't hear me or ignores me. That all too familiar feeling of being invisible comes roaring back. Mostly, I don't mind it, but tonight it hurts until it throbs. Why did I choose such young travel companions? There is only myself to blame.

Kali and Leon wander off without bidding the rest of us good night. Next, so does Zona. I'm surprised, as she's been acting like quite the party girl.

I try to ignore my invisibility and snap out of it. Charting our course for the Island of Lost Children should help me feel more pro-active. Before I retire to my quarters, I try to engage the others one more time.

"Think there'll be any lost children on the island? Will they be alive?"

"Much as I've enjoyed Realidad, I'm ready for a new adventure, Cassie," says Margot, smiling. I can't help but hug her. At last, a little validation.

Vincent, more irritated than usual, says we've been spending too much time in towns we found along the river, which, as he puts it, "does a lot of meandering, anyway." Another surprise, as he sure seems to be enjoying making sand sculptures here in Realidad.

I try once again. "Despite your misgivings about stops, the island is a place we've been hearing about for almost the entire journey."

"No one's given us much info about it except to say it's a strange place and we should avoid it." I don't know why he's being so contrary, as he's already agreed, along with the others, that we should check it out. We're hardly strangers of the unusual. True, we've heard that the few who have stopped there immediately returned to their boats and headed back to the main channel. No one has yet to describe what it is like, except it is like no other place you've ever been to—not so much due to the island's terrain, but the strange feeling you get once ashore. No one has exactly said that it is dangerous. It should take most of the following day to get there, but if my calculations are correct, we should dock well before nightfall.

"If it's too weird, we won't stay long."

Vincent and Margot both nod, but say nothing further. The couple yawns before retiring to their cabins. After we bid each other a good night, I am careful not to say anything further. I can't bear being further ignored.

I stop by Leon's room to ask him about his available times for manning the 'ship' tomorrow. Since Leon and Vincent signed up more regularly than the three women, I always turn to them first. His door is slightly ajar, so I push it open—not widely—but wide enough to see figures on the bed: Leon, Kali, and Zona. Zona is in the middle, stretched out on her back, with the two others stroking and kissing her—readying her for *the kill*.

I don't think they see me, but I sure see them. I don't linger in the doorway for long.

It now makes sense why they hadn't responded to my comments earlier, as well as what Zona was up to with the lights and music. My cheeks are burning and I want to hide. I'm too old to observe such nonsense. I guess it isn't nonsense when you're young and sexual. Go back in time, Cassie...You once played in the nude on many a bed. Yes, but never with more than one person. Had someone suggested it, I doubt I would have, but who knows? What do I do now? How will I be able to face them? What if they saw me standing there? Maybe I'll mention the event to Vincent and Margot. If I must know about the shenanigans on the boat, they should know, too. But then again, maybe telling them will just further complicate things which are already messy enough.

I'm in my cabin with the door shut. My cheeks are still warm, okay hot, but it's a little easier to breathe. I realize I'm not outraged or even much taken aback. The boat seemed so large when we first boarded, but now it feels cramped. Drama like this is like added ballast: too much for the vessel to hold. While it isn't enough to sink it, it sure slows us down. It's a shame those three couldn't have waited until they were somewhere on shore. Somewhere private.

I don't wonder who instigated it—I know it was Zona. She seduced the other two, and I'll bet it's because she wants one of them to herself. At first, I thought it was Leon, but it's more likely to have been her. Not my business, I know, but see, it becomes my business when it's practically thrown in my face. Will there be a repeat performance? If so, what do I do about it? Who are they harming? Only each other in the long run and they can't see it. Times have changed, old lady! While I worry that yesterday's ethical standards are no longer the same ones today, but threesomes and orgies have been going on forever. I can't help but feel further isolated and invisible. I wish there was someone I could talk to about this, but there's no one. You'd think they'd be more considerate, is all.

DAY 17

My captain's log went missing last night. At first, I wondered if it got nabbed by a hot spot, but then concluded that one of the participants in the ménage à trois must have stolen it. My last entry was around 11:00 p.m., so I knew I'd brought it back from Java Jim's. I found it late this morning, wedged between my bed and the cabin wall, which is strange as I never write in bed. While I missed it, it gave me a chance to observe the river last night and this morning, once I could forget last night's drama.

While my words aren't as significant as those of the two poets on board, I now realize the distress of having written words disappear. I sure don't want to go through that again. My initial panic was intense. It would've been hell trying to reconstruct my previous entries. I'm sure I wouldn't have been able to recall details freshly if I recalled them at all. Now, there's little choice but to be suspicious of my crew.

. . .

Last night, once our lights were dimmed, the thick, inky black of the water astonished me. While Realidad is close to the river, the marina is in a cove south of town. With Ollie perched on my shoulder, we gazed at the quarter moon—a fish hook dangling above the river at the end of the horizon.

. . .

Dreamed about wading in warm, clear water, and staring down at a sandy bottom. Something upsetting had occurred, and I was too afraid to look anywhere but down. I searched for life forms of any sort, but spotted none.

Upon waking, I realized the dream was the opposite of this mysterious, dark river water that until now, so often churns up living matter along with the dead.

• • •

This morning, the rippled water-skin of the river's murky body reminded me of goosebumps; it made me shiver thinking about it as a living being. Yoga stretches helped ground me.

• • •

Once again, *Silver Lady* traverses the smooth river road of this American Nile. Hard to believe it's been over two weeks since the journey began. According to my calculations, we are over halfway to her marina-home. However, I'm not exactly sure, as I thought we'd be roughly where we are now, several days ago.

Everyone sulks and fidgets like children waiting to see the principal. Except Margot, as she is now behind the wheel on the top deck. No one says much, apart from a few banal comments. We pass a floppy-brimmed hat bobbing along. Is it the same one I noticed days ago? Next, I can't tell if it's a long string or a water-snake skimming the surface.

Following an excruciating hour longer of passing only a few bird feathers, we stop to refuel.

I suggest doing some Qigong and standing stretches, but no one is interested. As I've about had it with this crew, I make a conscious decision to be silent. How tired I am of always trying to be entertainer-in-chief, and peacemaker, too! They'll view my silence as a punishing one, but I can't overlook what happened last night. Weirdly, I feel some anger, but mostly rejected. It's impossible to meet Zona's gaze. Did she know I'd been standing at the door? Maybe not. I've never had much eye contact with her. I hope none of those three realized my presence. Still, she is acting more secretive than usual.

Vincent tries making small talk—something he's not great at doing—but Zona turns away.

I'm glad to have my captain's log back, as the scenery's now dull and nondescript. I feel like I'm only half here, though I prefer dreamland to this. Except for an occasional bald eagle or white pelican flying through the sky, or a turtle or two, on small shoreline rocks, there is little else to observe. The river can be such a simple girl, but most lovely when she's unadorned. Gossipy birches and lonely-looking pines gaze at us as we pass by the nearly flat riverbanks. The air is still and silent. I'm sure glad it's too early in the season for bugs, particularly mosquitoes.

All of us river-riders are now lulled and dulled. Hoping to rouse myself from my stupor, I replace Margot behind the wheel. How did the *Silver Lady* shrink so much? She feels more confining than ever before. The increasingly blank landscape makes me feel barely conscious. I'd prefer a dreamless slumber, as at least there would be no awareness of time. Strange, but I don't feel sleepy. I'm alert but not. Once again, no one is talking, but silence is preferable to chatter. I can tell the others feel the same way. Some comfort, I suppose, but what about my memories? Are they still intact?

The last time I saw Melanie was following an attempt to visit her. She'd opened her apartment door, but only a couple of inches. Her frightened, but beautiful blue-gray eyes stared at me. She refused to let me in. I should have known better than to go there, but I had to try. I can picture her eyes so clearly. Despite knowing how her fears outweighed her interest in seeing me, why did I have such a need to see her? I still do. We met once in a park, wearing masks, but then violence lurked in the city, just like the plague. Fear that both would run rampant was not irrational.

Knowing I can't break down her fortress door, my attention shifts to Peter.

I've never talked about him to anyone except Melanie and a couple of friends, and I'm almost an old woman now. Maybe I am old and simply haven't woken up to the fact. Being old used to frighten me, but now I view it as another fact, as bland as this area. It provokes no feelings whatsoever.

Okay, so I can retrieve my memories here. Not like we are re-entering the Land of Doze. It's a relief that we are still continuing downstream.

A slight breeze picks up, though there is still not much to look at. Again, I notice Leon, Kali, and Zona observing each other, but not what is in front of them. Have any of them realized the change in the air? It is cooler and the current is faster. I know in my bones that the scenery is about to change.

"Do you guys feel it, too?" I ask, breaking my silence.

"Feel what?" asks Vincent. He is wearing a captain's hat. I've never seen it before. Some nerve he's got!

"It's soon going to be less boring. I can promise you that!"

"Good, as I was about to go under and snooze. Bring it on, River!" He must have noticed me looking at the hat and then tells me he bought it in Realidad. While it isn't easy to do, I compliment his taste. He grins widely. Such an attractive man...be still, my heart.

I whisper, "Careful what you wish for, Vincent!"

"Nothing seems any different," Kali says.

"Only because you're not paying attention!" Is it my voice that explodes? My tone is definitely more scolding than I intend.

"What's gotten into you?" Leon asks me.

Before I get the chance to respond, several bushes of sculpted green topiaries appear to be watching us from the riverside. There is an elephant, a pony, and a kangaroo. The kangaroo stares directly at us and calls out, "Turn around now!" When we don't, an enormous owl bobs its head on a tree branch, then breaks into song, "It's too late baby now, it's just too late, though we—"

Zona and Leon burst out laughing, but Kali screams out, "There's nothing funny, it's just weird. Unlike parrots, owls don't talk. At least they're not supposed to. A private joke between you two, eh?"

Before either of them can answer, the green sculptures are out of view.

Someone else laughs. No one aboard has a cackling laugh except for Zona after she's been drinking. But it isn't Zona, as she is pointing at a bird perching on a rail on the starboard side. It's the bird making the sound. Its feathers are brown, speckled with blue. The laughter continues like it is laughing at us. What is it doing here? Aren't they found only in Australia? It makes me recall my first grade teacher telling my class about a laughing bird, the kookaburra.

Then Vincent posits his opinion that the surreal images along the riverbanks are living paintings—paintings freed from frames and walls of houses, galleries, and museums.

What about the topiary sculptures? Aren't they simply what they are: bushes sculpted by lawn clippers and electric saws?

He mulls it over, then states his opinion that the sculptures had once been framed images—either by themselves or grouped. As for the singing owl, it is anyone's guess.

Vincent motions everyone over to the rail without saying a word. The crew tiptoes over, speechless. I remain behind the wheel, but have a pretty good view of the riverbank. There, watching us, are our doubles.

I almost don't recognize the older woman with long graying hair, but then, I do. It is me, a tired, haggard-looking-me. I've had laugh-lines around my eyes for years, except now they are further recessed; denying their status as wrinkles is silly and vain.

When we wave at our doubles, they wave back at us. When we call out to them, we hear our voices echo.

I slow the craft down, so we can have a better look and steer us closer to shore, then cut the engine.

There is no mistaking it. They are indeed our doppelgangers. The six of us stare at us-but-not-us in disbelief.

Zona's double speaks to us with an almost ear-piercing clarity.

"You think you've seen this before.

You think you know reactions to every situation—

How it's all going to go down.

NEWSFLASH: You don't—

And it's a long time, such a long time, going home."

After several minutes of staring and not knowing exactly what to do next, Vincent hurls a stone at them—an unusual one, shaped like a boomerang, which he'd picked up at one of our stops. The stone flies toward the group on shore. None of them get hit, but as soon as the stone lands on the small beach where they are standing, our doubles have doubled in size. They loom before us, casting shadows. None of the large, silly putty faces are attractive. The stone boomerangs back toward us, but instead of reaching the boat, lands on the river, and then sinks. Vincent is wise not to throw another stone.

Time slows down, and the sky darkens.

We stand frozen in place and speechless. We can no longer see them. Our doubles have disappeared.

The sun peeks hesitantly from behind a cloud. It takes a few minutes before we find our voices. What the hell?

Thankfully, there is the comforting familiarity of the blue sky. Blue herons stand in the shallows. Our breathing slows down. All is serene until we hear insipid waiting room music piped in from somewhere. An army of branches dip almost into the river. Margot carefully skirts them, as they are too low for the boat to glide beneath. A tabby cat pretends to be asleep on a dock but watches us with one eye open. They are as wary of this world as we are.

None of us call out, "Here, kitty, kitty." We know better.

The music ceases, and the sky darkens. Worry crosses our faces.

Objects float downstream: dish racks, hats, balls of various sizes, elbow gloves and a red satin evening gown. They bob along. I've never worn an evening gown or elbow gloves. Missed opportunities perhaps, but it's okay—no big deal.

What will we see next?

"I guess you never know. Maybe next it'll be the head of Orpheus," says Vincent, who describes the famous painting of the floating head by John William Waterhouse. "Poor guy, he was just trying to give joy to the dismal world."

I ask if he's talking about Orpheus or the painting. He ignores my comment and shows me an image of the painting on his phone. "Notice how it's the nymphs you see first, and not the head."

He sounds like a tour guide. He must be masking his worry or concern.

Let's hope it doesn't turn into a living painting, I'm about to say when lightning slices the sky, followed by the loudest clap of thunder I've ever heard. Even Vincent jumps. Still, we remain spellbound at the deck's rail. Then hundreds of fish fly from the water and sail overhead. It's as if their gills have sprouted wings. Hard to tell how long they are airborne, but they are all headed downstream.

Could Yamuna or Saraswati, or one of the other river goddesses, be angry with us?

DAY 18

The sleek sloop quiets its engine once it has pulled alongside *Silver Lady*. It flies a single white sail. Painted on it is a large black skull-and-crossbones. We are under attack by pirates. While the name on its side reads Coast Guard, we know exactly who they are, though not what they want. Frozen in place, we hold our breath and wait.

Ten people dressed in black diving suits hold us at gunpoint. They aren't wearing diving masks as you would expect, but white theater masks. Most mouths are downcast, but a few are grinning. All the masks are frightening as hell.

"We're from the Coast Guard," claims the leader, a man twice as tall as the others.

"If no one moves and you give us what we want, no one will get hurt."

I can't move if I tried. All I can do is nod.

Six of them point guns at the six of us. The other four pirates search for the booty. I hope they aren't after gold or gemstones, as we have none. We know these pirates are dangerous—way more so than the Ladies in Waiting, as circulating rumors claimed they've killed and ransacked many river cruisers over the past year.

I've never been held up at gunpoint. Is it moments or minutes that have gone by? Time stops but then fast-forwards the instant the four come running back with the booty in their canvas sacks.

"This time you were lucky," the low voice booms. "When we see you next, don't count on it going so well."

Their sloop is out of sight before our breathing regulates. Our supply of water and wine is gone, but most importantly, we are all okay. We hug, whirl each other around—laughing and crying as we do so. Even Zona joins in the communal wave of relief.

Before we can talk about it, we are again under attack. This time by the weather.

. . .

I'm at the wheel when the storm comes on suddenly. Within seconds day turns to night; the entire sky is an angry bruise. It doesn't seem real.

Leon replaces me so I can give directions to the crew. At first I'm clueless, but then yell out "Batten down the hatches!" Something I've always wanted to say, with little mind about the danger of what could happen next. Getting to one side of the river or the other won't be a problem...but then the engine dies and a gust of wind comes out of nowhere. The river man-handles the *Silver Lady*, making her sides seem paper-thin.

Everyone dons lifejackets. After we turn on the lights, I implore those inside to hunker down as low as possible mid-ship.

I take my place at the helm.

The storm rages for hours. I radio the Coast Guard. A scratchy voice says something about us dropping anchor. Lightning daggers the sky and thunder breaks and booms. It isn't long before a loud splattering of rain morphs into a deafening deluge. We ride the river rollercoaster—a thrill ride like no other. Our only thought is to try to survive.

I point *Silver Lady's* bow into the waves, trying to plow our way through them.

Dropping the anchor does little, as ours is too light to keep the current from having its way with us. Steering proves pointless, too. At separate times, Vincent, Leon, and I take turns at the wheel, trying our best, but the boat keeps listing. Vincent mainly handles the steering, as he seems to be the best navigator. Eventually, we realize the only one controlling *Silver Lady* is the storm. There is nothing we can do but try to keep her from capsizing. At least we're not out in the open sea.

The rest of us spread out in the living room, trying our best to distribute our weight evenly to keep the craft from taking on more water than it already has. Water sprays over the craft, and then sloshes over the sides. It is cold one second, and then warmer the next.

During the worst of it, we feel like a water bomb has gone off on top of us.

"How are we even still afloat?" I ask myself time and time again. Any second, the craft could flip onto its side.

I radio the Coast Guard again, but all I get is static.

The storm lets up for a few minutes, but not the rain. We get spells of wind along with the rain, but the most dangerous moments are when the winds would completely die down. Those of us inside wait uncomfortably for the next onslaught, much like soldiers in trenches waiting for the enemy's attack.

Then, a sudden gush slows to a trickle, and the steamy air doesn't stir. The quiet is especially eerie, and the sky remains dark. We eye each other warily and attempt to stand. Our legs are wobbly, and we are weak as newborn kittens.

Our breathing normalizes, but another rain bomb bursts directly overhead. Someone screams, but I don't know who.

I am so dizzy I can't keep my head up. It becomes hard to catch my breath. Little good is my effort to vomit into the river, since it flies back in my face and onto my already drenched clothing. At least the spray of water washes it off my face immediately. I don't lose my cookies indoors, though Margot and Kali do.

Margot, like me, has an especially hard time with dizziness; at least I'm not alone. We groan in unison below deck as we try in vain to get our bearings. Besides Margot, I don't know where the others are, nor do I care. This is a fight for survival like no other.

Several times, I pray for the entire crew, but mostly—sorry to say, I worry about my own survival.

This tells me I'll never be a true captain. Will my shame dog me for the rest of my days? There isn't time to contemplate it, as there's now another eerie calm.

Then it feels like the river is running backward. I lose my sense of direction, as the feeling came on suddenly. Everyone looks bewildered. I read somewhere about climate change or earthquakes causing this. Will we wind up seeing our doubles again or maybe find ourselves back in Realidad?

Following the storm, relief doesn't hit me all at once. The clouds finally part and I point out a double rainbow to the others. While lovely to see and certainly welcome to our weary eyes, we are all too exhausted to do much exclaiming. However, the cooler air keeps us more alert. Hard to imagine how storms at sea could be any worse, but I guess they must be, since the roiling waves are larger, and the gale force winds even stronger.

All of us are so tired we don't think to do a roll call. A worn-out *Silver Lady* has run a-ground.

DAY 19

The *Silver Lady* is stranded on a small, but sandy beach. She rests on her side, bedraggled like her crew, yet glad to be alive. Under different circumstances, her attire might be festive, as she's festooned in reeds, rushes, cattails, pickerelweed, and water lilies. The churned-up mud from the river bottom had not only splattered across her sides, but released a strong smell of raw sewage, and her engine still won't start.

Following a brief and dreamless slumber, I find myself sitting on the beach. Others soon join me. We hug and sigh in the dim, pre-dawn light. No one speaks for the longest time, marveling at the silence. Have we just stepped out of another living painting? There is no marina, or dock. No buildings are within sight. No trace of people or animals. All we can see is a grouping of reeds and larger rocks huddled together further down the beach.

The river is wider than we've ever seen it, making the opposing bank appear even further away. I know it's going to take a while to get our bearings, and to come up with a plan about how to get *Silver Lady* roused and ready to continue down the River Road.

There is consensus: it was a storm we'll never forget. At least we're now all seasoned sailors. We may look like a bunch of drenched and delirious rats, but it sure feels good to once again be on solid ground.

The ground, while solid, doesn't feel quite right. The greenery, and even the sky, has a feeling of being—if not artificial, different from the mainland. Almost like the way the world appears after retching your guts out. Is it from tiredness following the storm? No time to dwell on our fatigue and general discombobulation, as we realize one of us isn't here: Zona.

I call out to her several times, but no answer. Leon and Kali search *Silver Lady's* cabins and crawlspaces. Not a single trace. Since Zona often marches to her own drummer, we don't feel overly alarmed.

No one can recall when they'd last seen her.

I tell the others I remember her going off to her cabin and shutting the door before the storm began. Kali and Vincent both nod, as they remember seeing her then, too. Kali adds how early on, soon after the pelting rain began, she noticed how pale Zona looked sitting on the living room floor with her knees drawn to her chest. Leon and Margot can't recall seeing her at all.

Leon, Vincent, and Kali search for her further down the beach while Margot and I make breakfast sandwiches. Even making a simple breakfast is difficult. Is something wrong with the oxygen here? Everything seems slowed down, in slow motion. I ask Margot if she feels odd, almost like she is high. She laughs, but readily agrees. Her flowy skirt, damp and clingy on her limbs, has lost its flow. For the first time, she takes me up on my offer of a pair of jeans. I stop slicing cheese to retrieve them for her.

She's so thin, my jeans hang on her. I hug her without saying why.

. . .

The blue sky, along with the gentlest of breezes, makes it hard to believe there could ever have been a storm last night. If it had hit this area, it must not have been too bad, since the beach and surrounding area look undisturbed. Birch and cedar trees stand tall and proud, lining the back edges of the beach as far as the eye can see. But in one direction the beach continues, and in the other, the trees are closer to the water, as if they'd come down to get a better glimpse of the river.

I don't know for sure, but I believe we're on an island. Wherever we are, there are no obvious signs of human life. No houses or sign of a nearby town. Also, there are no roads visible from the slumbering *Silver Lady*. If we can't immediately rouse her, at least we've got enough food to last us a few days—if we ration it.

No one has yet received a phone signal. I don't know why, but I've begun feeling anxious not only about Zona, but Melanie, too. Not being able to call her whenever I want to is frustrating.

Margot and I take our mugs of instant coffee out to a large log on the beach. I haven't so appreciated a hot, caffeinated beverage in a long time—maybe ever. She points out the crack in the hardtop over the upper deck. We talk a little about Zona and wonder if the others will have any luck finding her.

Margot says she thinks we're being watched. I know what she means. After scanning the beach, I gaze inland at the dense, dark woods. We listen for sounds, but hear nothing, except the morning birds. Then we discuss the storm. As bad as it had been, it could've been way worse. The boat appears undamaged, so far as we can tell.

It isn't long before the other three rejoin us, saying the walkable part of the beach gives way to steep cliffs. No sign of Zona, though they saw several footprints in the sand nearby.

I pore over my still-damp map of the area. According to where we think we are, there shouldn't be terra firma. It should simply be a wider part of the river. After mentioning this, I drop the bombshell:

"I believe we've washed up on an island."

Eyebrows raise and chins get scratched. Without waiting for further response, I tell the three others how Margot and I had felt like we were being watched.

"More reason to get the engine started, just in case the folks around here aren't too neighborly," says Leon.

The two men head for the boat.

Kali, Margot, and I speculate about what could have happened to Zona.

Kali thinks either she fell off the boat during the worst of the storm, or she leaped overboard. I agree it was probably an accident. While Zona could sure be moody—in fact, she has been the surliest of the crew—I don't think she would have killed herself.

What I want to say, but don't: In Zona's obvious attempts to steal Leon from Kali, it definitely looked like she was going to reap the bounty.

We all knew it. It would've made far more sense for Kali to have been the most distraught, the most—dare I say, suicidal. Do the others suspect Kali of foul play? The thought crosses my mind, but it's unlikely. Nothing about her fit the profile of a killer. Plus, she isn't nearly as physically strong as Zona. Could someone else aboard have done away with her? While we all wanted to strangle her at various times—some of us more than others— we were all too busy trying to keep ourselves alive during the storm.

Leon is especially upset by her disappearance. The rest of us, while shocked, don't feel especially sad. Only yesterday, we discovered Zona had stolen one of Kali's books—an anthology of women poets. Kali found it on Zona's bed and brought it out to shame the accused. Zona had simply shrugged. Four of us had furrowed our brows at her, but Leon had quickly, too quickly, jumped to her defense. "Oh, c'mon you guys! Books around here should be shared, anyway."

I'm about to tell Kali and Margot that I'd just seen someone peering at us from the woods when Kali blurts out how attracted she was to the missing girl. She quickly adds how she also admired Zona for her candor and badass behavior, though Kali was admittedly angry at her for trying to steal her man.

Leon, who is on board, trying to get the engine started, doesn't hear his girlfriend's admission. Had Zona known about Kali's feelings?

Kali then lets us know the last time she and Zona had been alone together was right before we'd seen the topiary animals.

"It was then I'd confided to her about my crush."

"Your crush? On Leon?"

"Cassie, don't be daft! I'm with Leon, so how could I have a crush on him? I mean, I'm attracted to him, for sure. No. I told Zona how I was attracted to her."

"Oh. Okay," I say, looking away.

If Margot is shocked, she hides it well. I know my eyes have nearly doubled in size.

"No, not okay. The woman is gone. It could all be my fault! She seemed pretty weirded out after I told her."

"Kali, I'm sure that's not true!" Margot says, hugging the younger woman.

I try my best to reassure her. "I highly doubt it would've caused her to jump overboard. Remember what we'd just witnessed? First, the singing owl. It went above and beyond ordinary hooting by singing to us. Remember how he'd advised us to turn back? And then we saw our doubles. If Zona hadn't been thrown off one of the outer decks in the storm, the sight of her double could've overwhelmed her. Maybe she couldn't deal with seeing herself in another body. It wasn't easy for any of us, I'm sure."

"Even if that's true, I chose the wrong time to tell her."

"Maybe it was the right time," says Margot.

We then realize Ollie the Owlet disappeared during the storm, too. Margot checks the pocket of her skirt, which she had been spread out to dry on a deck seat, but he isn't there.

After checking each of the cabins and crawlspaces, we realize Ollie is gone. First Zona, and now Ollie. Panic mixes with the sadness of loss.

The two men rejoin us. I suggest a moment of silence for our sweet little mascot and the others readily agree. Tears stream down several faces.

Maybe Zona and Ollie left together, I say. This is met by fresh tears, sniffles, and a few nods.

I feel dazed by Zona's disappearance, but a little less so by Ollie's. The others who slipped away from me: Peter, Giles, and friends who left without letting me know I'd never hear from them again. My mother's body, still alive but her mind gone, and my daughter—her mind very much there, but her physical self in hiding.

The tenuous attenuates.

Is any of this real?

I try to reassure Kalie that no one blames her for Zona's disappearance, when four children emerge from the woods. Fearing they'd vanish if we made a sudden movement, we sit as still as stone sphinxes and barely breathe. They, too, freeze in place, resembling the orphan statues in Doze.

They stand only twenty feet from us. I'm surprised by their bravery. Their tattered and faded clothing suggests they've been here a long time.

Despite their long snarled and straggly hair, their faces are surprisingly clean. Two boys and two girls, roughly aged eleven or twelve.

The girls seem friendlier than the boys, though all smile wanly and warily.

"Welcome to the Island of Lost Children," the taller of the two girls says in a monotone, as if she has rehearsed her opening line a few too many times. Then, sounding more sincere, she adds, "You must've washed ashore from that storm last night. We think it only hit the northern part of the island."

I'm not surprised to learn we are indeed on an island.

The taller girl pushes a smaller girl even closer toward us. The smaller one has something in her hands that is wrapped in large green leaves.

I rise and begin walking over to them.

Instantly, the four leap backwards, and the two smaller kids retreat slowly toward the woods.

Did they think I was going to chase them? Take them hostage?

"I'm sorry! I didn't mean to startle you. My name is Cassie and yes, the storm landed us here last night." I smile more broadly than I usually do, to show we mean them no ill will.

They slow down their retreat. The older girl beckons the others back and they immediately obey. Next, the older girl braces the shoulders of the gift-giving girl and nudges her toward me with the leaf-wrapped object.

"This is for you, Cassie. And the others," says the younger girl, extending her arms.

I thank them profusely, especially the gift-giver, before knowing the contents. The younger girl smiles more widely than before. It turns out to be a wooden music box that plays Barbara Streisand's song "Memories." Three of the music box legs have fallen off, and while the wood is a little scratched, there is a little red velvet lining inside, and the tune, though tinny, is discernible.

After again expressing my gratitude, I invite them to join us around our campfire. Even the boys are now more relaxed, though all the children sit in a huddled fashion. There is something most un-childlike about them. My guess is they're all old souls.

I offer them cookies, as everyone introduces themselves. While they don't appear hungry, their faces light up when I pass out soggy vanilla wafers. They soon confide that they are among twenty children living here. They've lived on the island for almost two years.

I ask my burning question: How did they wind up here?

The oldest boy, Murphy. His shoulder length, red hair, and enormous blue eyes peering keenly from a freckled face, more than hinted his descent from Erik the Red. He paces and occasionally gestures wildly as he narrates the story.

"There used to be twenty-four of us, but four died after we arrived here. We were on a riverboat trip with our parents two summers ago. Originally, there were over thirty kids and fifty adults, plus a captain and staff. Our parents were all members of the same country club. It was a great trip, or at least it was at first. After a few days on the river, our ferry boat missed the proper channel. We saw some pretty strange things on the river banks: a two-headed cow, flying spiders, and even a talking fish! Then, a day or two later, the adults all got sick.

We docked our boat in a place called The Land of Doze. It was there our parents died in their sleep. A few hung on for another couple of days. None of us younger ones came down with anything more than a rash on our stomachs and legs. Some of the kids remained in Doze and the rest of us continued our cruise. I took over the captain's job. Before I knew it, a storm came up and, we got shipwrecked here on this island."

I don't tell him how we are well familiar with Doze or about the orphan ghosts. My crew and I exchange glances. So these are the rest of the orphans who didn't stay in Doze? It doesn't add up. We were told the orphans had been in Doze in the 1990s and it's now 2033. If there are any living orphans, they would be nearly middle-aged by now.

"What happened to the ferry?" I ask.

"It's on the other side of the island," Murphy responds. "Repairs have been made, but it still won't run. It's not like we need it. Lucky for us, we found a ghost town when we were exploring. We discovered several houses, so we didn't need to make our own shelters. There's a grocery store with canned goods and other stuff. Not only do we get fish straight out of the river, but there's a lot of fruit on the island—berries and apple trees. Anyhow, that's the story. There's a little cemetery outside town. Not very many tombstones, so we think the people must have up and left. At first we wondered if they died from the same thing as our parents, but we never came across any dead bodies."

"Why didn't you build a raft to take you to the other side of the river?" asks Vincent. A logical question. I appreciate someone else helping me give the kids the third degree.

"What he means is it's not like crossing an ocean," I add.

"You're kidding, right? Maybe you don't know about the crazy current?"

We shake our heads.

"It's amazing your boat wasn't torn to shreds, and that you landed here at all. We've seen plenty of others try to pull ashore, but few with any success. Sometimes the current even runs backward. Also, we think you adults have pretty much made a mess of things. Us older kids decided for the group. Some of the younger kids cried like babies at first, but it didn't take much convincing."

There is a lot to digest in his baffling tale. I am tempted to ask what year this is, but it isn't the right time. Such an odd turn of events. I've always considered myself to be both adaptable and open-minded. How could anyone prepare themselves for this unexpected place and its young inhabitants? This certainly isn't in the guidebooks, but then little of our journey has been. We've all been looking for a pleasant escape, and while there have been pleasant moments, many of our times have been jarring and nerve-jangling. I now see how isolated I was before the river trip. No longer being part of the workforce. Never seeing my daughter, hearing news of skirmishes in the interiors and borders of states soon to become separate countries and always worrying about the increasingly empty shelves in the grocery stores and not hearing any word from the rest of the world.

For all its difficulties, I much prefer life on the water with the constant change of scenery, not to mention my several companions.

Vincent asks if artwork is disappearing from the island, the way it does in other places.

Perplexed, Murphy and the older girl, Aurora Lee, raise a brow in near unison. She is taller than the other children, reed-thin, with a ghostly pallor. Her blond hair is almost white, and she has large and watery aqua-blue eyes.

Vincent further explains how paintings, poems, and stories have been vanishing, except in certain places like Doze or on riverboats.

"We've drawn a lot of pictures on rainy days here on the island. They're all here as far as we know. I'm the only story writer here, and I think they're all still in my spiral notebook," responds Aurora.

"I make up tons of stories, but have never bothered writing them down. Some I've maybe forgotten," adds Murphy. "Is this the reason I forget them? Is this like the flu, but it attacks your memory?"

"No silly, you're forgetting some of your stories simply because you're stupid and don't know how to put them in writing!" Aurora Lee scolds him. The two continue to bicker playfully. It's obvious they are deeply connected.

I interrupt them to let them know one of my passengers is missing. After describing Zona to them, I ask for their help in our search for her. I'm touched by their concerned expressions. This certainly doesn't seem to be a *Lord of the Flies* outpost. They immediately agree to help fan out along the beach.

Murphy and Aurora Lee confer in private for a few minutes. They are clearly the ones in charge. After returning, Aurora Lee asks if we'd like to see their town. She seems nervous, but is either friendly by nature, or aware of the importance of being friendly.

"If you do want to see it, we'll have to warn the others first," Aurora Lee says in a hushed, furtive tone. "We'll tell them who you are and why you're here. Some of the little ones might panic when they see such tall strangers. Also, five of the little ones are sick. Remember, it's been a year since they've seen adults."

"I thought you said it was two years ago?" I ask. A warm wind rustles furtively through the trees.

"Well, yes, but we did see one adult after that time."

Aurora Lee doesn't elaborate, and I don't want to pry. Something tells me we'll have plenty of time to try to solve the mysteries. I like how protective she is of the younger kids. We agree to go our separate ways for a couple of hours, and promise we won't wander into town unless they escort us.

• • •

Leon doesn't believe Murphy's story about vacationing with their parents, though he believes there is likely a ferry on the other side of the island.

"Did you notice how he couldn't look at any of us while he was talking? He kept shifting about, and I don't know, there was just something disingenuous about his tale."

Leon is probably right. However, Vincent will not let him have an easy win: "Despite your astute observations, why do you always have to be so cynical?"

"Me cynical? Man, I thought that was your department."

There has been little friction between the two men on our journey. With what I know about human nature, this surprises me. Is their good rapport going downhill?

The strange feeling I'd had when we first set foot on the island returns. My anxiety, plus something else, gives me the chills. There is something about the breeze that feels odd. When Leon was talking, his mouth was moving slightly out of sync with his speech. I can tell by their baffled faces that the rest of the crew feel like something is majorly wrong, too. Did they notice this, too? I am afraid to ask.

RIVER VOICES

Margot

Did we know about the Island of Lost Children before arriving here? I thought Cassie had said something about it, but maybe I dreamed it. It looks so familiar. No matter, we're here and the storm is over. I don't think I've ever been as sick as I was during those wretched hours. Dizziness and nausea lasted for hours. Symptoms would subside, but then worsen. Cassie felt as wretched as I did, though she complained more about her stomach than the room spinning. I truly wanted to die. But I didn't, and here we are on this serene and lovely island. It would feel like paradise, were it not for Zona and Ollie having gone missing. No one recalls seeing either of them during the worst of the storm. Could they have disappeared at the same time? I can't shake a feeling something is not quite right about this place, but I feel a sense of belonging, too.

Vincent

Could this be the island paradise of my dreams? Since I was a kid, I've wanted to live on an island. Maybe I've finally escaped the word-plagued world. Maybe now I won't have to look over my shoulder all the time. There's something peculiar about the kids we met; something is off. A shame about what happened to their parents and how the kids became orphans. While they're all scruffy, and some of them stink, they sure don't look underfed. I get the feeling we'll need their permission if we want to stay here. Maybe some of the crew will leave, and that will be okay, better than okay. I wouldn't be surprised if Leon gives a hard time to those of us defecting. I'll feel a little bad bailing on Cassie, but she's a good enough captain to get the boat back to its owner. Margot and I could truly begin our lives together here, and if I'm not mistaken, I think Cassie feels a sense of home here, too, despite its strangeness.

Leon, Kali, and I just returned from a thorough walk along the beach, searching for Zona. No sign of her body. While there's a chance she could turn up, I doubt we'll see her again. Do the others sense my detachment? I'll do my best to hide it, but I can't help but feel relieved. Someday, I'll explain it all to Margot. That is, when the time is right.

Kali

Me and my big mouth! I just blurted out to Cassie and Margot about my attraction to Zona. Why did I? Did telling Zona how I felt, cause her to take her own life? While it's true that the possibility exists that she fell overboard, she was one messed-up girl. The others never realized how crazy she was—even Leon. I hated how the two women looked at me like they felt sorry for me after I told them. I think I've about had it with this group bonding thing. Like the others, I can't help but feel intrigued by the island, but part of me feels like we should leave as soon as possible. I'm looking forward to a tour of the town, and afterward, I hope the others feel like we should return to the river road. There's something not quite right about this place.

Leon

I've got a bad feeling about Zona. I'll have to remind the others about my premonition, not that it'll much matter. If she's gone, she's gone. We had some enjoyable times, many of which I'll always remember. Wish I could talk about her with Vincent. Not that doing so would lessen my sadness. I found my blues harmonica. Think I'll play Sonny Boy Williamson tunes. Maybe "Blue Bird Blues" under the shade tree over there—the one standing aloof from the others. I'll make that song my own. It'll help my anxiety, plus maybe playing it will help rid me of this sense that there is something not right about the island, despite its beauty.

DAY 20

So far, no trace of Zona. The children helped us search until nightfall yesterday. As a reward, the crew and I made an enormous meal and asked them to join us. It surprised me they didn't hesitate for longer than a minute. The fish tacos went over big, though I couldn't eat one. I haven't been able to eat fish since my perception of them changed on this journey. Afterward, we told stories and sang around a crackling bonfire.

A mutual trust is growing, though both groups seem a little leery of the other.

After admitting we felt a little lost, we sang them the theme song from *Gilligan's Island*. The children knew it, too, and sang along. I mentioned to Murphy and two other kids how it's amazing that this 1960s TV show is still popular today in 2033.

"What do you mean 2033?"

"What year do you think it is?" I asked him.

"It's 1993, lady."

"Don't be ridiculous!"

Three of the other children overheard us and laughed amongst themselves over the idea of it being 2033. But then I recalled how they claimed to have lost their parents in Doze. That would have been in 2031. Something's not right unless there were two separate incidents in which a group of children lost their parents. We were only told about the one in Doze, which happened back in the 1990s. This would coincide with what Murphy was saying. Best to play along, so I told him I was joking. Later, I will tell the crew.

Did we enter a time slip when we wound up on this island?

. . .

It's the following day. I have yet to tell the crew about Murphy thinking it's 1993. And is it possible for the river to run backward? Whenever I've looked at it since we got here, the current is flowing steadily downstream.

Four tour guides (the same kids we'd first met) lead the adults through the town. I've been hoping our phones would work here, but they don't. Ever since Zona went missing, I've felt even more anxious about not being able to get a hold of Melanie. What if Murphy is right and we are back in 1993? It would then make sense that we can't get a phone signal. Melanie wouldn't even have been born. Could time, as well as the river, be in reverse? What if what I think is downstream is really upstream?

It's like a Hollywood tour of a western stage-front. I know we haven't gone back further in time—say to 1833—because the storefronts look like movie props. I ask if the town has a name and the kids just laugh. Murphy, wearing a lopsided grin, says they've had several discussions about what to call it, but decided 'Town' is the best they can come up with. Well, Town even has a saloon. A single street runs down its center with stores on both sides. I am surprised to see a few residential side streets. It's much smaller than Doze or some of the other towns we've seen.

I had expected to see more of the remaining children, but there are only a few sitting on wooden chairs outside the general store. Younger than our tour guides, they stare at us with faces much older than their years. One girl smiles and waves, but the others have furrowed brows and arms crossed over their chests. Their clothing is dirty and raggedy. They remind me of the unhappy orphan statues we saw in Doze. I whisper this to the others, and they readily agree.

It is odd to see a town without adults.

Vincent strides over to the girl who'd smiled at us, but she runs into the door-less store. He waits for her to come out, but she doesn't.

Murphy raises his voice and scolds Vincent for approaching her. He paces like he did when we'd first met him. Hadn't Vincent only just told us being too friendly was a bad idea because the children might view it as a trap? He tries to explain how the girl is the spitting image of his daughter, Tara, who had died during the worst of the latest pandemic.

We promise Murphy that from this point on, we won't approach the children unless they come to us first. I'm sure they must feel intimidated by our sizes. While the buildings need fresh paint, it's surprising how intact and clean they appear—at least the facades.

"What pandemic?" Murphy asks after pulling me aside so the others won't hear. I keep my whispered answer brief. He laughs nervously and says he is glad it's 1993 and that it hasn't yet happened. He obviously doesn't believe us and no doubt thinks we're from Mars.

We first tour the general store. While there are a few items on the shelves, Aurora Lee tells us there is a back storeroom that contains a fair amount of food, especially canned goods. A strong odor of rot prevents us from lingering at the shelves. The others notice it, too, though none of us can discover the source. Flies are buzzing in the windows. All the counters are sticky, and the floors are dirty.

Next to the General Store is a women's clothing shop. Aurora Lee admits they had ransacked all the clothes, leaving only a few things on the racks. "The styles were so old-fashioned and ladylike, but we did our best to make use of the material." Emma, second in command to Aurora Lee, is clearly wearing a woman's blouse as a dress. The pink sleeves reach her fingertips, so she keeps rolling them up.

Beyond the clothing store is a dusty-looking hardware store, and a restaurant the children use as a gathering place.

The restaurant, according to Bennett, had been a fun place to go until they had eaten all the food. He is a tall beanpole of a boy, and the cuffs of his faded jeans barely reach his ankles. His sandy-brown bangs curtain his eyes. He strikes me as more upbeat than Murphy.

"And the saloon is a place where the little ones liked to play hide and seek," chimes in Aurora Lee. One moment she looks like an urchin in need of a good scrub, but the next—she is ethereal and otherworldly in her delicate beauty. She further explains how, in their first days on the island, Murphy and she had locked up the booze in a back storage room.

"Good thing we did, or we would've had a bunch of drunken kids stumbling around," she adds.

"Not even Murphy knows where I've hidden the key."

"Do, too!" says Murphy. The two squabble as they lead us to a large house off Main Street, an attractive old Victorian house with a large wraparound porch. Wicker furnishings are shockingly white, as if freshly painted. We are told five kids live there, sleep most of the time: three of them can sit up to eat a little, but the two others are now too weak to feed themselves. The older kids take turns caring for them. They'd all fallen ill within the last couple of weeks. Until then, life had been a little easier.

They turned two downstairs bedrooms into a makeshift hospital ward. The three kids, who aren't terribly ill, are together in one room. It's large, with three beds side by side. There's also an area for play. When we walk in, two of the sicker ones are sitting at a small table coloring. I'd guess them to be about five or six years-old. They glance up briefly at us before resuming their coloring. Another child, a boy of around eight, sits cross-legged on an unmade bed. He shouts at us: "Hey, who are you big people? You need to go and leave us be!"

"They're visitors here, Peter. No law against it," Aurora Lee says, crossing her arms in front of her chest. Peter, the name of my former husband...

"Only other kids can visit. I thought that's what Murphy said."

"No, he didn't," Aurora Lee intervenes. "Say, Pete, where's that plane you made yesterday?"

"Josh smashed it with his stupid old foot."

"I told you I didn't mean it!" Josh yells. He is one of the two kids coloring.

Aurora Lee pulls out a new coloring book from a box in a cupboard. Something tells me the younger ones wouldn't have survived this long without her.

"I'm sorry, Peter, but here's a new one. Looks like you'll be busy again today, too."

As we return to the hall, she explains how they'd come across many untouched toys in cupboards and on closet shelves of the houses in town.

The former inhabitants must have been well off, as evidenced by the nice furnishings. Almost all the furniture is Victorian and plushy, with lots of velvet-covered couches and padded armchairs, grandfather clocks that have stopped ticking, cabinets of glass figurines, fireplaces in most of the rooms, and paintings on the walls. And the people in the paintings are from the Victorian era. I feel their eyes following me.

The drawn shades in the other first-floor bedroom darken the room. Two small children are asleep in single beds with makeshift rails so they wouldn't tumble out. A potent odor, even worse than the rotten food in the general store, hangs heavily in the air.

Aurora Lee puts her index finger over her closed lips. All of us remain near the doorway, except for Margot. She tiptoes right up to the first bed, places her palm on the forehead of one child, and then does the same with the other. Afterward, she stands there staring down at them until Aurora Lee tugs at her sleeve.

Once we are back in the creaky-floored foyer leading out, Margot informs us how the two little ones have high fevers. We debate whether it could be the pandemic. While it doesn't seem likely, whatever it is could be catchy, so we agree to wear masks if we see them again. I feel faint and lean against a hallway wall.

"We've got to do something! How long have they been this sick?" Margot directs her question to Aurora Lee.

"Over a week, I think. Their fevers break, but then they come right back. At first, they were both eating a little, but now we're lucky if we can get them to take a few sips of water."

"Well, they won't last too much longer unless we get them to a proper hospital. Why haven't you taken them off the island? There must be a boat that works!" Margot's stern voice catches everyone's attention.

"You think we haven't tried?" Murphy snaps. "There are two boats here. One is an old motorboat, and the other is the ferry we came here on. Me and a few of the older kids have tried a bunch of times to get their engines going."

"Maybe we can help you," says Vincent, who until now has said little. "That is, if you let us. We could take the sick children to a town on the mainland so they can get proper medical attention. It could save their lives."

"Aurora Lee and I will talk about it and let you know. I think you strangers have seen enough, so you'd better return to your boat. Strangers—especially grownup strangers—aren't welcome to stay here for long. This is our chance to start over. Even if we can't give the sick kids the proper care." Murphy explains with amazing calm, barely raising his voice. His three compatriots nod at what he is saying with arms crossed over their scrawny chests. The stern expressions on their young-old faces tell us they mean business.

"There was one adult who would visit us here. We met him maybe a month after we first got here. Jimmy brought us stuff from the mainland. He also told us about what was going on in the world. Hearing about the fighting on the mainland made us decide to never return. Jimmy was a great guy, and we were even going to invite him to stay with us, even though he looked like our enemies," Murphy adds.

So, Jimmy is the adult the children had known a year ago.

"What happened to him?" I ask.

"We don't know. Some of us would meet him down by the dock, from time to time. He just stopped showing up, so something must have happened to him. Jimmy wouldn't have just abandoned us. We didn't want his spirit to play tricks on us, so we had a goodbye bonfire for him. Now we just want to be left alone." A tear trickles down Murphy's dirty cheek.

I thank them for the tour and the generosity they've shown by allowing us to remain as long as we have. The adults and tour guides look at me like I've slapped them. I truly don't mean to be so abrupt. Aurora Lee nods, sniffles, and holds the door open as we depart.

· · ·

Once back at the boat, my crew has a meltdown over the sick children. I don't. I'm sure they're wondering how I can be so calm. Worried they think me indifferent, or insensitive, I do my best to explain my background, especially from my doula days.

First, there was Anna—a young mother who found out she had terminal cancer during her pregnancy. I'd been a doula for less than a year. I met her when she was seven months along. Anna expected me to opt out after explaining to me the odds were against her living through labor and delivery. The determined intensity of her dark eyes shining out of her pale face told me otherwise. I agreed to help care for her newborn, regardless of whether she would be there. Her husband's sweaty palms and darting eyes told me all I needed to know about his thoughts on the matter.

She lived for two weeks after giving birth to a healthy baby girl. She passed away in my presence with the baby cradled in her arms. Anna had a smile on her lips. When her husband held the baby's face close to her mother's for one last time, the baby's tiny fingers reached out to touch the already cool mouth. My wish was for that baby to take away the sweet memory, but I knew it was doubtful she would.

I lost it. Anna's grieving husband had to console me. I agreed to help him out for an additional couple of weeks. It was such a sad and difficult time.

And then there were the twins. Less than a year following Anna's death, I cared for Connie following the birth of her identical twins, Maxie and Mark. They weighed in at seven pounds and seemed healthy. A week after their births, Mark unexpectedly perished. Maxie, his identical twin, refused her mother's milk and turned her rosebud mouth away from formula. The pediatrician could find nothing wrong with her. I could see in her tiny features, a resolve that she wouldn't remain here without her twin. Her cries became weaker and weaker. Connie was inconsolable. While I did the little I could for them, the situation left me heartbroken. I decided the only way I could continue being a doula was to become more detached. And thus, I became so.

• • •

If we don't leave soon, the islanders could become hostile. Maybe they have weapons. I don't know why this hasn't occurred to me before now. And if they do, they probably know how to use them, and won't hesitate if they felt threatened. Maybe they already have. There could be something more to the story about Jimmy than we've been told.

"Well, crew, I guess it's time we follow that river road again," I say, after explaining my coolness toward the sick kids. We are sitting on the beach to better enjoy the warm afternoon sunshine.

"What? And just leave those sick children? Could you be any more heartless?" Margot scolds me.

"Heartless? Are you that naïve, Margot? You seriously don't think those kids might have a few guns stashed away? I don't think they're bad kids, but I don't believe Murphy's story about Jimmy simply having disappeared was the entire truth. Do you?"

Vincent rushes to her defense. "I don't think Margot is as naïve, as you think, Cassie. She's just got a real soft spot for kids. I do, too. Can I please tell them more of your story, Margot?"

"Before you do," I jump in, putting my hand on her arm, "I've got to tell you guys something Murphy said last night. He claimed it was 1993. Remember how they also claimed to have lost their parents in Doze? It sort of adds up."

No one says anything for a couple of minutes.

"Since he's the group's leader, of course they believe him. How would they know any better? Maybe he got amnesia after losing his parents in Doze. That would explain it, right?" asks Leon, pushing his glasses up to the bridge of his nose. He raises a thick brow.

"What about Aurora Lee? She laughed when she heard me claim it was 2033."

"C'mon on gang, would it really surprise you if we had indeed entered a time slip? At least it's my favorite decade. Margot's, too. We were just kids back in the 90s," says Vincent.

"Let's hope once we're back on the main channel, we'll be back in 2033," I respond. I don't think this is the time to tell them my hunch about the river running backward, even though it could support my view. The information might be too much of a head-scratcher.

"Really, Cassie?" Vincent asks with a smirk. "2033 sure has felt like it's been near the End Times to me. Remember the girl I saw in town? She not only looked like my daughter, Tara, it was like she was Tara. Maybe Tara didn't die, but came here instead."

Faces wince in pain. Had they all been simultaneously tasered? I imprint my hands in the sand, but as soon as I remove them, the fine grains shifts back, leaving no indentation. None at all.

"Maybe time's doing weird things because it's already the End Times and as the saying goes, 'The End is nigh.' But if we've entered a time slip, maybe it'll be postponed for us—unless we find our way back," adds Leon.

It's clear the others find more credibility in Vincent and Leon's viewpoints, but at least they don't gaslight me. I don't argue my point, except to add that it's all more than a little strange. The latter point is something we can all agree on, although it's obvious they—particularly Vincent—don't want to dwell on such a baffling issue. "If you don't mind, Cassie, I was about to tell a story about Margot and her love of children."

Margot makes a face but nods.

The day feels almost summery, so I remove my shoes and bury them in the cold sand while Vincent speaks.

"I've told you how Margot was caring for a lot of kids the day I met her, right? She'd take them to this park every day before escorting them back to a community center. They were all refugees—illegal aliens. When word got out how they were rounding up children who weren't here legally, she immediately set out to find families willing to take them in. It didn't take her long. Most of them were childless couples living in backwoods areas, off the grid. Having to say goodbye to ten kids was one of the hardest things she's ever done. That's why soon after, she became mute. It broke her heart."

"There's a little more to it, my love," says Margot, grinning. Is it my imagination or has the gap between her teeth disappeared? How can that be?

We wait for her to explain, but she jumps to her feet and points down the beach at something in a patch of reeds. Without hesitating, we sprint over there.

The body of a young woman is lying on her stomach. She has very short, dark hair. Zona? It can't be. Her pale arms and legs are without tattoos.

Leon drags the body from the reeds and onto the shore. Vincent helps him roll it over. We all gasp at the bloated, white face of Zona. It's definitely her. Still pretty, despite the disfigurement. But how could the tattoos have simply vanished from her arms?

Leon falls to his knees. Vincent vomits.

Kali, Margot, and I can only stare. It's like we've frozen in place. After what feels like a long time, I leave to scrounge up a tarp from a storage container on the boat.

Both Margot and I are shaking as we dry off Zona's limbs. Afterward, we wrap her body up in a blanket and roll it tightly in the tarp. We then carry it closer to the boat. The odor is so nauseating I hurl my breakfast and part of last night's chow. Margot almost does likewise.

As there are no signs of foul play or self-harm, we surmise it must have been like we originally thought: she'd simply fallen off the boat in the storm. Or she'd jumped, Kali adds. Since Zona wasn't much of a swimmer, this is a definite possibility. Even the best of swimmers would have drowned that night—unless someone had pushed her. But the only one who might have had enough animosity toward her would have been Kali, and she doesn't strike me as being capable of murder.

Kali whispers to me that Zona's tattoos had been vanishing, one at a time. They disappeared several days ago, so her death wasn't the cause. Another mystery.

At first, I feel more shocked than anything else. We can't contact her parents since they are missing, and we don't know names of friends—if she had any. How little of life she'd tasted. I only hope she'd enjoyed some of the journey. How to go forward with the trip with one of my crew now dead? If we are now in the 1990s, at least she hasn't yet been born. If we hadn't discovered her body, I'd prefer to think of her as still being alive in 2033, but there is no way this could be the case.

I return to *Silver Lady* and make my way down the narrow passageway to Zona's cabin. There must be a clue. The poetry book, stolen by Zona and discovered by Kali, appears to be missing again.

Kali joins me. We clean up the messy little room and then bundle up a pair of jeans and a few black T-shirts. Could the book have had anything to do with her death? I write it down as a clue. I feel vaguely guilty about packing up her stuff, as it seems way too soon to be doing so—but I've got to burn up some of my frenzied energy. Kali must feel the same.

Next, I roll up Zona's sleeping bag. A few other books that she never returned are in one of the cabin's corners. We gather them up, along with several bracelets that did not belong to her, and set them on the dining room table.

We reason the bracelets must belong to Margot, as she is the only one who wears them. Zona had adopted an attitude of "mi casa es tu casa." I can't help but laugh because whenever anyone had asked if we'd seen something that had gone missing, Zona had always so innocently shrugged her shoulders.

Vincent and Margot head to town to inform either Murphy or Aurora Lee of the discovery. Since Zona's body had washed ashore with no evidence of foul play, we now have a little reassurance there's no murderer, or murderers, aboard *Silver Lady*.

. . .

We hold a funeral pyre on the beach.

It takes most of the afternoon to collect enough wood and carefully arrange it. Rather, we help the children gather it, since this is their third beach cremation. The first two had been for young children who'd perished shortly after they'd arrived on the island.

After the adults carry Zona's tarp-wrapped body on a makeshift stretcher to the waiting wood, it is the children who situate it on a platform and then set the wood on fire. It takes a long time before all is in order for the burning. The adults are numb, except for Leon, who mostly sits on a beach blanket with another one wrapped around his shoulders. He rocks back and forth. Kali doesn't comfort him, but a couple of us, now and then, rub one of his shoulders.

Before lighting the fire and after explaining how they came up with what has now become a ritual, the older children paint our faces with blue and purple swirls and black teardrops. As they do so, they teach us a couple of their made up songs. Here's one of them:

Body gone, but spirit sings
Let us leap in your joy glow

So glad to know you
And we always will

We gift your body to the flames
Then leap in your joy glow

Goodbye, for now, our friend

We gift your body to the sun
As we leap in your joy glow
So glad to know you
And we always will

So, this is how a new civilization starts up. I can't help but be awestruck. To read about it is one thing, but to experience it is quite another. No one cries, but the somber mood will prove hard to dispel.

Next, they have us form two rows: adults stand in the one closest to the pyre flanked by the many children. Before lighting the fire, those of us who'd known Zona say a few words. We remain standing, but step slightly forward and turn to address the mourners.

I begin:

"I admired Zona's spirit, despite her hostility. She must have been through a lot of crap before we knew her, and that's why she was so defensive. Who wouldn't be? Sometimes she'd turn to me like she wanted to confide, but couldn't quite make herself vulnerable enough to do so."

The children look at me like I'm speaking Greek.

"She could have a wicked sense of humor and she 'got' poetry. I'll give her that," Leon adds. "Plus, she had a raw, savage sexiness to her." The blue and purple teardrops contain real ones that slide down his face, smearing the painted ones.

His unabashed admission earns him a point or two in my estimation. I think his comments go right over the heads of even the older children. Two of the older ones snicker, so maybe I'm wrong.

Kali turns her face away, but does not disagree. She takes a couple of steps forward and adds how it was too bad Zona had never known her parents' fates. She sounds sincere and more empathetic than I would have imagined.

"I wouldn't over-think it," Vincent says with a yawn. He doesn't address us, but stands facing the pyre.

Margot steps forward and turns to face us. "True, but if someone had killed them, poor Zona didn't have any closure." She also says how it's a shame Zona's life was cut short.

Vincent shifts about uncomfortably during the moving ceremony—especially after listening to the children's death songs for a second time. While I've seen him tap his foot before, it's a curious response. It's possible he is bored, uncomfortable, or both. Maybe he is just one of those people who have a hard time facing death.

I am amazed at how quickly Leon collects himself.

Then Aurora Lee stands up. "We didn't know this lady, Zona, but we know this: her spirit's trapped on the island, just like the children we lost. After her body is gone, we'll preserve her ashes with the others by a small waterfall. We'll sing to her and calm her spirit so it doesn't attack us."

Do they truly believe this? It shouldn't surprise me. Maybe this place is called The Island of the Lost Children—not because of the living children, but because of the ones who died. It's another form of homage, another way to keep grouchy ghosts at bay.

Murphy dumps a few containers of charcoal fluid on the large stack of wood. The rest of the children fan the flames. It isn't long before an enormous fire roars.

The children leap and dance around the body as it burns. Once again, they sing the happy death song—for it can hardly be called a dirge. "Body gone...We leap in your joy glow!" This time, it is only the first line that is repeated in a loud monotone as they dance.

Margot plays her flute to the children encircling her. One of the little girls reaches out to touch Margot's braid, but quickly withdraws it, as if she's experienced a shock. I can't identify the haunting yet comforting melody. My guess is she made it up for the occasion.

Next, we stand in a single line in front of the fire, holding hands, and swaying side to side. No more words get spoken, no more music plays, but a strange enchantment remains constant in the air.

DAY 21

Today's been quieter than usual. We practice Qigong on the beach for over an hour since we haven't for so long. I wind up incorporating yoga poses with the fluid motion of Qigong. It's as if I'm choreographing a strange but lovely dance. Even Margot is amazed. We follow it up with a thirty-minute group meditation that lasts longer than the ones we've done on the boat. Everyone agrees they feel better afterward.

I ask Margot about the missing gap between her teeth. She shrugs and says she's never had a gap—I must have been seeing things. I know what I saw, I want to say, but bite my tongue.

Silver Lady will soon head downstream once again. Hopefully, downstream isn't upstream. It's a good thing they repaired her engine and swabbed her decks.

Aurora Lee and Murphy stop by while we are having coffee to tell us we need to leave, and the earlier, the better. Their coldness, especially after the funeral, catches me off guard. We can only nod in response.

I am in for a further shock. Fewer of us will be traveling the River Road together, as Margot and Vincent have decided to go their separate ways. While Margot had made it clear that she wants to help the sick kids, I'm not prepared. It's too soon after Zona's funeral. Tears well in my eyes, but I collect myself, and give them both hugs. I'll miss Margot, though Vincent, not so much, as I truly think he's been looking for wiggle-room to leave, despite his enchantment with the river.

Now, Leon's gone off with Vincent to the other side of the island to work on the ferry. Once it's repaired, Vincent and Margot will take the sicker children to the nearest hospital. They discussed this last night with Murphy and Aurora Lee, who hesitantly agreed. After telling us their plan this morning, I told them we'd be happy to wait for them. I was about to implore them to reconsider, but Vincent raised his hand to stop me from saying anything further. They have decided that if the ferry is in good enough shape, they'll continue on—without us. No doubt the couple of weeks of togetherness have been more than enough for them.

While I'm disappointed, I get it. I really do. They are a new couple, if not exactly a young one. Due to Margot's interest in children—and in getting the island children well, I wouldn't be surprised if she stayed near the hospital until they are healthy. Maybe Margot and Vincent will even remain long enough to find homes for them or adopt one or two themselves.

Something tells me Aurora Lee and Murphy agreed to let the couple take the sick children to the mainland, providing Leon, Kali, and I don't remain on the island in their absence. For a moment, I think of asking for clarification, but it would be pointless.

As captain of *Silver Lady*, I must sign a written agreement stating that we will, under no circumstances, either report the lost children to any authorities or discuss my knowledge of the Island of Lost Children with anyone. There is also a place for Leon and Kali's signatures. Murphy informs us they are preparing a similar document for Margot and Vincent.

I wonder what year it will be at our next stop.

DAY 22

I can still see the island. Leon and Kali have joined me on the upper deck as I drive us down the River Road. No doubt Zona's absence helped them rediscover each other. For the longest time, we wave at Margot and Vincent, and they wave back. For the first time in quite a while, the boat feels spacious.

Someone else waves at us from the edge of the island's point.

"Is that Zona? It must be her, but how can that be possible? She looks as alive as any of us!" Leon shouts with eyes almost popping from his face. He removes his glasses.

All three of us are flabbergasted.

"ZONA!!" I yell, but it is too late. She has already vanished into the woods behind her.

If it was truly her, whose body had we burned? No, this is sheer nonsense. The woman standing there must have been someone else or —

"Remember how we saw our doubles back before we got to the island? Maybe that's who this was." I can't keep the quaver from my voice. They nod in unison, both beyond baffled. Anything's possible when you're on a magical river.

There is a single moment when it feels like a giant wave rocks the boat. I tell them it could mean we've re-entered 2033. Eye-brows raise—but no eyeballs roll.

Before saying our goodbyes to Vincent and Margot, I had suggested we try meeting up with each other in the future. While everyone agreed, they further agreed not to set a date or place. Realidad, if we could ever find it again, might be our best option.

And now that Vincent and Margot are no longer aboard, I can't help but wonder how much further Kali and Leon will travel with me. Maybe believing we had developed a deep bond is wishful thinking on my part, but it's a way to cope with the sadness of the group disbanding. Before now, I hadn't realized my attachment to the entire crew—the sense of community we've shared. Truly empathetic people, like those four, are in short supply in this world.

It's now been a couple of hours since we docked. I go below deck to check out Zona's former cabin. There, on the bed, is the women's poetry anthology. The one Zona stole that had been missing for a second time. I bring it out to the deck and ask if either Kali or Leon knew the missing book had turned up. They both look surprised. Then, I inform them I found it on the bed and mention how her sleeping bag was unzipped and stretched out across the bed frame.

To report their astonishment would be to understate their reaction. They follow me back to Zona's former room to see for themselves.

Kali seems a little too surprised. How little I actually know her!

First, I discover Zona's phone in her backpack. After charging it for a few minutes, we search and find a few of the pics she took before the storm. One of the kookaburra, and another of a few of the sand sculptures in Realidad. A third is of a group of people on a riverbank—the last one's too blurry to make out. Had she taken one of our doubles? All the rest of her photos have disappeared. We eye each other suspiciously.

Then Leon locates Zona's diary beneath the mattress. On the second page, she'd described her fears of being on the boat with her parents' killer. He reads this aloud. Leon's eyes swiftly scan the page and he flips it to the next. Kali snatches it away from him.

She reads aloud.

The next couple of pages describe Zona's views of all of us, including her attraction to Leon; how she thinks Kali's a twat, and that sometimes, I could be a hovering mother whore. She also writes that if she doesn't get off at the next town, she might do something she'll later regret. She doesn't specify what exactly, at least not at this point in her diary.

Large tears form in Kali's eyes, but she quickly wipes them away.

Leon pushes his glasses up and then shifts jerkily back and forth, as if there is sudden turbulence on the boat.

Not the sweetest of girls. Just when I'm feeling happy about Zona's demise, Kali reads further about how she'd planned on contacting Jerry Wilson, the private investigator, because she was worried Vincent, and maybe Margot, knew something about what happened to her parents.

Could one of them have killed Zona because they suspected she knew too much? What had she known?

There are three blank pages followed by a description of the dinner she ate in Doze. Evidently, she'd enjoyed the cuisine.

Leon snatches the diary back and flips ahead a few pages. I can tell by his flustered expression that Zona had also described her time, or times, with Leon.

Then his eyes rest on what he'd been looking for. A look of shock crosses his face as he removes his glasses, rubs his sweaty nose, and scratches his head as he reads:

Waiting for the right moment to gift Vincent to the fish. I don't know how I've let so much time go by living on a boat with someone who knew about what happened to my parents. I'll get it out of him one of these days.

Kali and I agree to do our best to notify Jerry Wilson and let him know what we know. He should probably be informed about her death, at the very least. Now he will have two mysteries to solve—or at least a single complicated one.

"But what do we really know? A few lines from a girl's diary? That's all we have. Zona could have died from foul play—or not. She wasn't the most reliable source. But if Zona was correct, and Vincent and Margot, or Vincent alone, killed her to prevent her from finding out what had happened to her parents, then she hadn't merely slipped during the storm," I pause, before continuing.

"And what did the couple know? Zona had no clear-cut proof unless she could've gotten Vincent to admit it. I doubt he would've murdered her simply because she knew too much. I might not always be the best judge of character, but I can't believe he would do such a thing. While Vincent can be moody, he simply doesn't fit the profile of a killer. It doesn't add up. If Zona had been murdered, someone must have pre-meditated it."

Leon makes a further claim. "And since he confided everything to Margot, she would've known about it. No way can I see her as having been an accomplice to something this horrific! Even though the storm could've been the perfect cover, the very act of throwing Zona's body overboard would've taken some planning."

"You're right, Leon, unless Vincent didn't tell her about it and it had been an act of impulse on his part," says Kali.

Leon pushes his glasses back on his nose and scratches his chin. I nod, but make no comment. I don't bring up the fact that Leon, too, is a suspect. He has a temper and had been having an affair with Zona. They could have had a lover's quarrel and push could have come to shove. But, no, that didn't add up either. He was a good and decent man.

And while Kali has more of a motive for murder than most of us, she'd done nothing that would lead me to believe her capable of carrying it out. She often acts saner than the rest of us. At one time or another, we have all probably wanted to throttle Zona. While we are all capable of murder, the likelihood of us committing it is remote. Maybe I'm wrong.

I suggest returning to the island. After all, we'd all seen Zona, though it could have been her ghost. Nothing will surprise me about this strange universe. Why not find Vincent and Margot and confront them?

Leon thinks it a bad idea. Kali does, too.

At the very least, I respond, we should notify the investigator.

They don't argue about this, but Kali says, "Times are so different now, especially with the civil war breaking out. Something tells me they—the investigators, like law enforcers, have more pressing issues to deal with."

Still, we can't just pretend Zona's death never happened.

Leon, changing course, adds: "Think of the peculiarities and illusions we've seen along the river. From seeing our doubles, the crazy Owl Town, that circus...how can we trust what we see, when maybe life really is just a dream?"

He makes a good point, but there still needs to be some accountability, some bit of logic, or the chaos will overwhelm us. Are the chances for justice to prevail less than before? If I know anything, it's that the universe has its own way of getting even, even if we find it incomprehensible. I hope to have the final say.

"Call it karma, but the creeps and killers aren't getting away with their crimes these days. I could be wrong, but I doubt it."

This is met with eye-rolling and smirks.

We try to settle into our changed circumstances, but it isn't all that easy. The feeling of strength and solidarity of the entire group is gone. Still, the three of us get along okay, so that's something. We agree that Margot and Vincent will be good foster parents. None of us brings up how something is unsettling about Vincent. He's a good guy, but he's been concealing something. What if he knows what happened to Zona's parents, despite his denial? Maybe he was responsible for Zona's death. While I doubt Margot knows the full truth, I wouldn't be surprised if he had clued her in. Did this influence their decision to remain behind? And yet, how caring of them. Best for now if I don't mention my doubts about Vincent.

"With society unraveling by the month, if not day, I doubt Vincent and Margot will have an easy time finding families to take in the children, providing the sick kids pull through. If they can't, I'm sure they won't abandon them," I tell the couple. They readily agree.

We then discuss the island. What are the chances the remaining children will be okay for long? Leon has his doubts, but my hunch is they are better off there than most other places. Kali doesn't have an opinion on the matter, except to say if we had returned to the island, maybe the children wouldn't have been there—they could well have been figments of our imagination.

Leon and I concur that while we've had a few group hallucinations, the Island of the Lost Children isn't one of them. The possible time-slip remains a mystery.

We next talk about the hot and cold spots, along with the near certainty that the further south we go—the greater the risk of the Vanishing to occur with written words. The river water feels a great deal warmer here than it did before the horrific storm. Does this mean that artworks or written work will vanish? Perhaps even my captain's log is in jeopardy of disappearing. I don't have the attachment to it that Leon and Kali have to their poetry. However, I'd sure like to have the log as a souvenir of our times on *Silver Lady*.

The two sit with me on the top deck as I steer us down the mighty river. We are alert once more to the living paintings along the riverbanks. Now that we are further south, and deeper into spring, the vegetation is greener, and the air feels summery. The air is rife with braided smells of rotten eggs one moment, and sweet river grasses, the next. Hopefully, the evenings will continue to cool down nicely. Frogs croak and turtles watch us from shoreline rocks. I cross my fingers that the worst of the spring storms were over.

There are fewer bald eagles, but more blue herons and pelicans. I miss the northern bluffs, but the variety of trees in this region is amazing. Here, the river has widened, making it now impossible to see both sides of the banks clearly.

I tell the couple about my earlier fear that the river would run backward, the way it did during the last storm. When we left the island, I worried we wouldn't continue going down the river and that the *Silver Lady* wouldn't be allowed to return home. They agree that if it was going to be a problem, we would've realized it by now.

We pass many more boats than we did before. I haven't yelled, "Ship, Ahoy!" since the early days of the trip. Boats of all varieties and sizes: houseboats, ferries, motorboats, barges, and kayaks. Sometimes we pass by fishermen. People often wave and are friendlier out here on the water. Maybe they're that way in much of the South, despite the hostile mood in the former states. Again, we see the middle-aged woman and her teenage companion relaxing on a raft. We wave at them, but they only give us quick nods of recognition.

After all that we've seen, this more typical scenery is a welcome relief. But it is after leaving Realidad that I begin to—occasionally—lose my sense of time.

Then, a disembodied voice—Zona's voice—calls out loudly with an eerie clarity:

"You think you've seen this before.

You think you know reactions to all situations –
How it's all going to go down.
Newsflash: you don't!
And it's a long time going home.
A long time clinging to the branch
Above that roaming river road."

Wasn't this what Zona's double shouted at us days ago? Leon and Kali declare it to be the same poetic chant. I've got to keep my eye on the river ahead, but the couple searches the riverside through binoculars.

No, Zona, I don't think I've seen this before. As for feeling like I (or we), have been clinging to a branch above the roaming river road, there is no doubt some truth to that. And yes, I don't know when I'll be home, or if 'home' exists anymore. Maybe we take it with us wherever we go, or maybe it's an illusion, a necessary one at certain times in our lives.

. . .

When I see the speedboat stealthily sneak up to our port-side, cutting its engine, I know we are once again under attack by pirates. Then again, maybe Melanie had gotten in touch with the river rangers and insisted on having them take her deranged mother into custody. Surely, pirates had better things to do.

They make us pull into a boat slip nearby a riverside town. It doesn't help that the guy (one of only two) who climbs aboard looks like a nasty relative of Smokey the Bear.

It turns out they are actual river rangers. They stop us simply to give us the news that the Coast Guard Pirates have been arrested. I let them know they had robbed us several days ago, but we are otherwise okay. Did we file a report afterward? Sheepishly, I admit we hadn't because of circumstances. No point going into it.

Have they heard of the Ladies in Waiting?

"They're the only other pirates we've encountered," I tell Jim, according to his name tag.

At first, he isn't sure, but after describing the tough and nasty-smelling group, he has little doubt. "Oh, you mean the Kayak Pirates. Yeah, we've heard lots of stories about them, but so far have never had the pleasure of meeting them." After taking some notes, he scolds us again for not having reported the incident and not to hesitate if there is a 'next time.'

I feel strangely reassured that the world is still partly working the way it should. Justice is sometimes served.

RIVER VOICES

Leon

Now that the gang's busted up, I feel restless and out of sorts. Things with Kales have gotten better without Zona on board. No sooner had I begun to miss my new friend, Vincent, when I learned he was a murder suspect. If he did indeed take Zona's life, I want nothing to do with him. And while I didn't get to know Margot well, I admired her musical talent, and how caring she was with those sick kids. There's a kind of innocence about her I find charming. If Vincent has a dark side, she'll be the last to know. Even if he does, I think he wanted to help those kids, too. People are complex; we've all got our secrets. Also, the possibility exists that Zona is still alive.

The three of us all saw her on the tip of the island as we floated away. She appeared too solid to have been a fucking ghost. I'll be the first to admit, I'm tired of this dreamland bullshit. If it truly was her, then whose body did we find in the rushes and weeds? As sure as I am of sitting on this boat deck, it was her body, and we must have been staring at her double— or a ghost. The doubles we saw before were real people, so it could be true that we had entered a parallel universe. This would explain hearing Zona's voice calling out to us a second time.

After finding out we were back in 1993 on the Island of Lost Children, what year must our doubles have been in? Since they looked like we do in 2033, it must be the same for them. If our science was more advanced than it is, I'm sure there's an explanation. A parallel universe, though plausible, is hard to get my mind around. Cassie and Kali don't understand why I'm all riled up about it, but the better question is, why aren't they? How can they be so cavalier, so easy-breezy about all we've seen? Maybe they're pondering it, too. Cassie's always writing in her captain's log.

And while I've got scads of poems memorized, I don't like the thought of losing my latest verse in a hot spot. Could it be that artwork and rough drafts of poems and stories are winding up in some other world? Hell of a chance finding them there when I can't even keep my writing organized here. Something tells me it's soon going to be time to find a landlocked place to call home for a while.

DAY 23

Much has happened in the last several hours. Soon after my last log entry, we stopped at a town—the first one we'd seen since the island. I noticed a couple of missed calls from Melanie, but when I tried calling her, her phone would ring a few times, and then go dead. The call didn't go to voicemail or tell me her voicemail was full. Could something have happened to her? Had someone broken into the apartment? I pictured her beautiful but startled eyes when I'd last seen her and how she'd only opened her door far enough to see me standing there. Had someone else barged their way in? Minneapolis wasn't as crime-ridden as some of the other cities, but what if that had changed? Happy path: there was something simply wrong with my connection or her phone. Kali and Leon tested their phones, but had no problem placing calls.

Not only do we need gas and provisions in town, but I'm curious to see if it has a hospital. If it does, I'll bet this will be where Margot and Vincent bring the children. However, it's a town with no name—the second nameless one we've encountered.

As we walk toward downtown, we stop a woman out walking her dog to ask if there is a local hospital. She laughs at us, as if it's somehow funny that we don't know of it. After telling us how to get there, she tells us the town was once called Victory.

All went well until rioting got out of hand about a year ago. Authorities imposed martial law and stripped the town of its name. After a few weeks, the police put a stop to the violence. Those in charge enforced the radical idea of taking away not only the town's name but the names of places and people.

"We've all become unnamed," the woman says, adding flatly how it took some getting used to. She's known as 'the woman with the little white dog.' The townsfolk identify each other by their appearance or occupation.

"No one likes it," the woman continues, "but it became essential to be nameless since we have a few factories in the area where they make munitions, and a few secretive weapons that no one knows much about."

"So, were the name of the town and other names removed because of this, or because of Martial Law?" I am confused.

She doesn't have an answer.

I ask her the year. She assures me it is most definitely 2033, but looks at me like I'm the one who's crazy. Thankfully, this relaxes my breathing.

Next, Kali asks her if the artwork disappeared here, as it has been in other places. I am glad to see Kali has become more assertive. Does it have to do with Zona's absence?

The woman laughs sarcastically, and responds, "Who has time to make art these days?" Her little white dog barks, as if in agreement.

We thank her for the information and move on. While the names of the town stores have all been removed, new ones replaced them: HARDWARE, RESTAURANT, GAS STATION. I've never seen some place so nondescript. Also, the all-white residents make Leon feel uncomfortable with their hostile stares. He is furious. Who can blame him? We decide to fill up the gas tank and leave while we can. No way did we want to remain in Town a second longer than necessary.

"What's happened to our world?" I ask the other two once we are back on the water.

Leon is quick to respond. "I'm not going to sit idly by, Cassie. Float by passively. No way! I've decided I've been river cruising long enough. The next town we stop at, I'm going to say my goodbyes. My anger is a part of my identity; I've realized that now. My poetry can stir even mediocre minds, so I'm going to fight for social justice by giving readings everywhere I possibly can."

He reluctantly allows Kali to get off the boat with him but explains to her the rough time he could well be facing. "You don't know how mean the world can be, Kales."

She declares that she'll follow him anywhere, even if she is still upset about his feelings for the late Zona. "How do I know you won't do it again with someone else?"

He kisses her on the forehead.

"Don't try to pretend like you never had feelings for her," she snaps.

"I never said I didn't, girl. But seriously, you'd be better off with Cassie. I don't trust life on the mainland. At least for now," Leon says, placing his hand on Kali's shoulders.

"But I can't imagine being without you…"

"I want you to think about it. The next river town isn't for another few hours, if I'm reading the map correctly."

While I haven't connected as deeply with Kali as I had Margot, there are moments when I truly think of her like a daughter. I well recall being her age and feeling ambivalent or confused; times when the path before me was so murky, I couldn't see a path at all. My heart goes out to her, and while I'm far from wise, I'm a good listener, and my shoulder is always available to cry on. Kali knows this, but she's always been wild about Leon. It's a shame, but her lack of trust will affect their relationship. At Kali's age, she doesn't understand—*can't* understand—until she goes through it herself.

Almost half of the poems Leon and Kali have written since our journey began have disappeared from their notebooks. It helps, but only a little, that the ones they'd typed on their phones and laptops are still there. Leon says that, curiously, the ones which vanished were the ones he'd memorized. My captain's log remains on the pages, as did some of my on shore journal entries.

Drifting down the river, time stands still, but then speeds up—like it did when the Coast Guard Pirates boarded the *Silver Lady*, though now in a more enjoyable way.

There's no longer an overpowering need to get wherever we're going because, of course, we will. River Lesson: as long as you're moving in a certain direction, you can let go of time.

DAY 25 OR 26

I'm writing on the boat deck at New Leaf's fairly large marina. A splendid sunset is stealing my focus. Soon, it'll be just me and *Silver Lady* in the foreseeable future. It will be just the two of us taking on the world. I'm banking on the fact there will be a future, despite a few major factors: the civil war, a possible resurgence of the plague, the hot spots becoming more plentiful, as well as the likely recurrence of encountering pirates. The Vanishing shows little signs of waning. The Internet is now defunct. No one yet knows why. Cell phones only work for calling and texting—when you can get a cell tower signal. The signal seems fairly strong here.

I finally got a voicemail from Melanie. What a relief! She's doing okay but says the violence is getting worse in all the cities and has now spread to smaller towns. Nightly looting, car bombs, and buildings set on fire are the new norm. People don't walk after dark since nightly curfews are in effect. She begged me to leave the boat anywhere and to just come home!

I try calling her back, but she doesn't answer. I wanted to let her know I'm safer here on the river, but will certainly begin thinking about my return. Much tongue-biting may need to be done to keep myself from telling her about my encounters with pirates.

. . .

Although *Silver Lady*'s still docked in New Leaf, Leon, Kali and I said our goodbyes a short time ago. I'll miss them, but maybe our paths will cross again. They want me to consider moving here, too—that is, if it works out as well for them as they're hoping. Life seems better here than in Doze and even Realidad. It's attractive, boasting three bookstores in one block, trailing petunias from flower pots hung on lampposts. And then there are the poetry nights at the bars. Realidad has a poetry scene, but not as lively a one. Like other places, New Leaf has a problem with artworks vanishing, but not with written works.

Still, it's too far away from home for Melanie to consider moving. There would be little point in trying to convince her. Other parents learn to live far away from their adult children. Why can't I?

Within only a couple of days, Leon and Kali had signed an apartment lease, and they'd also signed up to read poetry at a coffee shop. Leon says he's heard how looting and vandalizing happens way less here than in other places. Could it be because it's overrun with poets and other sorts of writers? Makes me wish I was one, though I question how long New Leaf will be impervious to the violence and craziness occurring elsewhere. No doubt, poets and writers are often better thinkers than the general population, which may make them less prone to violence, though studies have shown that poets, in particular, have more mental health issues. Haven't we always known that artists, of all kinds, are generally more sensitive?

My guess is you must be a poet, author, or visual artist to be granted residency. That would rule me out. But can't anyone just say they're an artist and come up with a portfolio of abstract sketches? And surely, any literate person can feign to be literary just by typing up simplistic poems likening the sun to an orange. I wanted to talk to Leon about this, but never got the chance.

Where to go next? My busy life never allowed me to wax philosophical about life. This journey is forcing me to become more reflective, if not exactly sagacious—at least when I'm not in survival mode. The main reason I wanted to take this trip was because I've always wanted a houseboat vacation. I wanted a break from the city stress. I've always been in service to others, first as a mother, a teacher, and then as a doula. And for at least the past twenty-five days on this ostensible vacation, the best parts have been getting to know my fellow travelers. Sure, there have been the magical bits of scenery along the way—those living paintings, some of which I'll remember, others I'll forget or have already forgotten, but it is those I've met along the way that I will best recall. Sharing moments with them. Therefore, I know that my upcoming solitude will be necessary, but difficult.

It's been strange to practice my Qigong without the others. Still, it feels good to keep up the practice. At least I'm no longer self-conscious about parts of me that are beginning to sag. I no longer worry about being judged, at least not like when I was younger.

If these are the End Times, what will happen to the Island of Lost Children? Will I return to the 1990s when the world ending seemed possible, but improbable? Or will returning be impossible?

Another concern is the hot spots the further south I travel. My entire captain's log could well vanish without a trace. Who doesn't want to record the trip of a lifetime, right?

Once again, I try to contact George Sherman. No answer. According to my calculations, it should only take me a couple of more days. I'm not worried. If it takes longer, I'm sure George won't mind.

· · ·

I'm swabbing the decks with a mop, doing my best to clean and straighten up the interior. As soon as I enter Zona's small cabin, that strange feeling I always get there comes over me. I open the bottom drawer of the small chest next to the bunk. A page from her diary stares up at me. It must have been her last entry. Why hadn't I noticed it before?

Any minute, a storm is coming... V. finally told me more about seeing my parents. His father had hired him to kill them. The day he was supposed to do it, he hid in the backseat of their car, waiting for them to come out of an apartment building. Then he held them at gunpoint and made them drive to a wooded area a few miles from town. His father followed behind in his car...V. marched them into the woods. About a quarter mile down a dirt trail, he told them he wasn't going to kill them, but they needed to run and never look back—to leave town immediately—not let themselves get seen...After they took off, he fired the gun in the air twice. V.'s father, the former mayor, died of a heart attack that same night. V. never saw or heard from my parents again and left town himself right after his father's funeral. So whatever happened to my parents? Knowing V. didn't kill them, but let them go free, gives me new hope.

RIVER VOICES ON SHORE

Leon

Cassie told Kales and me about Zona's last diary entry. It's good to know Vincent didn't kill her parents. The question remains about what happened to her. Guess we'll never know.

I can't believe our good fortune. New Leaf seems like the town of my dreams, but pinch me, hard, because it sure feels like I'm dreaming (though different from the unreality of going down the river). The poetry scene here is hopping, and the population is diverse. And so far, the townsfolk seem well-educated. Since most are writers or artists, this makes sense. It's said that written works aren't vanishing, unlike paintings and people.

Before arriving here, I thought it might be best for Kales to remain with Cassie, but no longer, as she's about as excited by this place as I am. Who knows if we'll make it as a couple, but with any luck, we'll do alright. I feel bad for Cassie. I think she wishes she was more than a dabbler in the arts, but we all make our choices. Plus, she still feels the need to get *Silver Lady* back to its owner, despite not being able to contact him. She's also disoriented about time. If I didn't focus so much on the present and future, I would be, too. She could be in jeopardy of losing her captain's log due to the Vanishing. I hope it's just the river trip, causing Cassie to lose her clarity.

Kali

I told Cassie she should spend her time here writing poetry. I'd be happy to edit her poems. Afterward, we could put together a decent enough chapbook for her to present to New Leaf's Poet Laureate. That's what Leon and I did. Even though it would make her eligible for residency, she feels it would be phony. Apart from a few romantic poems from high school, the only writing she's ever done has been in the captain's log. Visitors can only remain here for a week. Well, I'll miss her and hopefully we'll all meet up in Realidad for a reunion at some point.

I've got to admit, I'm excited to be here. The seventeen days on the river have given me enough fodder for scads of poems! I can't wait to have time to usher them forth, from the very depths of my being.

Weird about that final diary entry Zona wrote. It must have made her feel a little less hostile toward Vincent and feel more hopeful that her parents are still in the world.

DAY 27

My bluebird has returned! Perching on a rail, he proudly displays his beautiful blue feathers and red breast. I ask him if he is the original Blue— my long-lost friend. Given the strange machinations of the universe, it could be him, right? He doesn't answer, of course. Even if he's not the former Blue, he has taken an edge off my loneliness.

I'm half expecting my log to disappear now that I'm back on the water. If it does, I'll be sad about it, but it's a risk worth taking—one I've known about since the beginning of the river journey. It's even riskier now because of the prevalence of the hot spots. While no one doubts the existence of hot and cold spots, or their effects on objects, we don't know what causes them. I must keep this in mind and not freak out.

When passengers were aboard *Silver Lady*, I had little time to write. I had to thieve the moments when I could. Now that I'm alone, it feels like there's all the time in the world, though there isn't. Sometimes lately, a second takes an hour, but when I think an hour's over, it's only been a few minutes. Snippets of conversation and fleeting images of those on board with me keep looping through my head. How nice it was to have company after two years of isolation due to the pandemic! While I've missed Melanie, I'm no longer as pre-occupied; missing her is an occasional deep but dull ache, rather than a burning throb.

There are a couple of truths I need to remind myself of. First, while we all see the same world (in a given world), it breaks up into many smaller ones because of our various perspectives. And second, perspectives change the given world.

A few of us loved the Island of the Lost Children, but a couple of us were creeped out by it. Maybe it wasn't the island itself, but the children who charmed us. Still, Leon, Kali, and I were eager, though apprehensive, to return from the 1990s to the present. Not so Margot and Vincent. Vincent wanted to remain, because he romanticized island life, and also because of his possible crimes. As long as Margot was with Vincent, I don't think it mattered where she lived. Zona would have liked it there, and I think it would have changed her for the better. We were all horrified over her death—except Vincent. He pretended like he was, but he didn't fool anyone.

Zona allowed no one to be more than superficially kind to her, and she certainly didn't allow anyone to care for her. Why not, when we all wanted to know who she was? Maybe she would have changed in time. I felt bad for her about her parents, the missing journalists. And certainly, Vincent felt even worse after abducting them. I'm glad to know she knew some of the truth, if not what ultimately happened to them. I'll never understand why Vincent didn't let her know, long before he did. She was so guarded compared to the rest of us. Maybe that's why. Not that any of us were, or are, open books. At least the rest of us were somewhat vulnerable to each other. Friendships that formed will hopefully last, even if we never take another boat trip together.

So here's my plan: whenever I get to the marina, I'll do my best to find George. If I can't locate him, I'll either leave the boat there and then rent a car for my trip home, or I'll resume life on the river. Eventually, maybe some of us will meet up in Realidad.

I've decided to stay on the main river channels. I doubt I'll see the surreal scenery we saw in the coves or along the banks of the smaller branches. Kind of sad, but those living paintings came at a cost. I often pass other boats, sometimes several at a time. Lots of friendly waves—vestiges of Southern hospitality. This is sure different from the northern part of the river. The water is mucky and I sure hope I don't get stranded in weeds.

An alligator just poked its snout from the water. I don't think he saw me and was about twenty feet away from the boat near the muddy bank. Sure hope I don't see more of either him or his buddies.

I have little appetite. Maybe it's because I don't enjoy eating alone, but most food tastes bland. In the mornings, I wake with a start—returned from visits to faraway worlds. It takes a few minutes to come to my senses. I talk to Blue on and off during the long days; he has proven to be a reliable little buddy. Once I've docked in the late afternoon, I'm careful to sip my wine slowly, or else I'd down it like a shot of hard liquor. After a glass, or two, I think about how maybe the others didn't simply go their own ways, but vanished like the artworks. What if my mind has reconstructed events to make them look like the truth? Maybe it did so to help me deal with their sudden exit from my life—making things more palatable, if not exactly sweet. I've heard of this happening before. And time has been playing tricks on me—or have I been playing tricks on time?

We could have been wrong about the river. It might not be any safer here than the mainland. Not only are books and works of art disappearing, but now people, too. And if I were to return to the island, New Leaf, Doze, or even Realidad, there's the possibility they, too, will be gone. Will I be brave enough to test my theory? Had any of the others realized this, too? But no, it's silly. I must be wrong: Margot and Vincent were definitely going to take the sick children to a hospital; Leon and Kali are enjoying their new lives and have turned over a 'new leaf' in New Leaf. While I've had my flights of fancy in the past, I've never experienced a psychotic break. The latter explanation will be the only plausible one if I'm wrong about the Vanishing.

What I still enjoy (even more on my own) are the deep sleeps I fall into at night from the slow, rocking rhythm of the boat.

DAY 28

It's taken twenty-eight days to reach the Ruby marina. In the contract, George Sherman, specified that *Silver Lady* should be returned in fourteen days, give or take a few days. The last time I had phone contact with him, he'd softened his tone because of the Great Collapse and the Vanishing. He said for me to take my time and the main thing was to return the boat to him in one piece, adding he hoped the crew remained safe. After that conversation, I began breathing a little easier. I still can't get hold of him.

Before reaching Ruby, the river again widens and the scenery on both sides has changed. I pass through several riverbanks clogged with crowded market squares. Vendors are out selling their wares. Several of them bark out the names of goods they provide. I am met with aromas, both pleasant and foul. At first glance, it could be a Turkish bizarre, colorful and exotic. But then I notice overripe fruit and grimy merchandise (from plastic toys and kitchenware to old toasters and drain boards) spilling into the river. The river is being used as a junkyard and as a garbage dump. Homeless people are camping out, not in tents, but in cardboard huts, tilted sideways using plastic garbage bags as rain roofs. I can't stand looking at so much ugliness, but I have little choice.

Some watch me as I motor by, others turn away. One shirtless guy, with a yellow-tanned torso and long mangy beard, runs into the river toward *Silver Lady* shouting, "Hey, you! Get back here, cunt!" I know I am too far away for him to be a threat. Still. The sound of his buddies laughing on shore, and his angry growl resounds in my head for hours. Both *Silver Lady* and I feel offended.

Many of the boat slips are empty. The few boaters here look listless and bored.

Ruby is a medium-sized river town, but most of the storefronts are shuttered. Poor Ruby has no rubies. Did it run out of funds or did it fear street conflicts? As I pace one side of Main Street, and then down the other, I wonder how the Vanishing has affected this sleepy town. Could this be why so many shops are closed? At least, the sunset tonight is spectacular. Maybe they often are since Main Street faces west. Little wonder where Ruby got its name. Still, I have no intentions of staying here for long.

Were the homeless people I saw up-river once residents here? No time to ponder about it, as it feels like someone is following me. Every time I turn around, no one is there. This has happened before in my life, possibly several times, but I can't recall when or where. It's one of the worst feelings ever.

After looking over my shoulder too much, I decide to relax in the outdoor café of Ruby's Bar and Grill. It's one of the few places open. A familiar man is sitting at another table-for-two.

After sipping a second cup of coffee with Frank, I feel like I've known him a long time. When I ask him if he feels the same way, he raises his thick unruly eyebrows and scratches his salt-and-pepper goatee.

"I'm pretty sure I saw you back in the sad little town of Byron."

"Yes, that was me. You were playing some pretty moving music on a saxophone. Sounded a lot like Louis Armstrong."

"We were also both at a restaurant in Realidad and then at a poetry reading."

"Were you following me?" I am amazed at the number of places I've seen him.

"Certainly not, madam!"

"Also, you were spraying the inside pages of a book on the riverside, near an abandoned floating bookstore."

"Sorry, I don't recall seeing you there at all. Just a fancy luxury yacht."

"It's a houseboat. Still...what are the chances? You did say your name was Frank, right? I worked with someone by that name. Were you ever a middle school administrator? Years ago—twenty, to be precise—I taught at one."

"No, I'm a failed novelist and an inventor," he sighs.

"Are you a failed inventor, too?" My eyes widen and then close as fast as a trapdoor.

"There is no such thing."

"Then there's no such thing as a failed novelist, since novelists are simply inventors of stories." Gotcha, Frank!

We chat for a couple of more hours at the café, before strolling through Ruby.

I'm still conscious of time, though my grasp of it has improved. Frank tells me how he'd come up with a spray of natural ingredients to combat the hot spots. It consists mostly of the river water. He claimed his invention—an aerator—will preserve art works, be they paintings or poems. So, that's why he sprayed a book near the book boat!

"What about captains' logs?"

"Those, too," he says.

The finer spray for written work gets especially good results, though he's been having a harder time getting positive results for the more concentrated one for paintings and other forms of artwork. He believes the problem might have to do with the water samples being taken too close to shore. The intimate contact between air and water may work best in the deeper parts of the river. He thinks water from the mid-section of the river will have the accurate amounts of this-and-that, which, when carefully sprayed on artworks, should preserve them for an indeterminate amount of time. Finer details, such as how often works of art should get sprayed, still need to be worked out, just like vaccines for the plague.

Needless to say, I am impressed. I tell him about my captain's log and he agrees to spray the mistiest of his mists on the pages so the ink won't run. He can't get over how I have written it all by hand.

Sensing my interest, Frank tells me what inspired him to come up with his cure for the Vanishing. He'd written a story about a man who met a woman in a sleepy river town when objects and people began to disappear, only to reappear days later. A little like the waning and waxing of the moon or romantic love. After writing his first draft, the story disappeared off the page. The only way he could recreate it was by telling the story to others.

The details he'd written down vanished, but not the impetus for inventing the spray.

I want to ask if I looked like the woman, but don't have the nerve—after all, we've only just met.

I then confide in him about my river journey, doing my best to describe the crew and our days on the river and in the river towns. After mentioning this is the twenty-eighth day, I add how my perception of time has become increasingly out of whack. He asks if I'm sure about this, and I reply it's about the only time-related detail I am actually certain about. I take a deep breath and tell him about the Island of Lost Children. I'm not worried about the document I signed standing up in court.

According to Frank, the children lost a sense of time because of being cut off from the world. Maybe they had fantasies about the 1990s being safer than today's world, he says, adding, "Then again, anything's possible."

Also, my experience with time doesn't surprise him. Boaters have told him about a few surrealistic scenarios occurring on the smaller river channels. They seemed to match Vincent's theory about living paintings.

"I have a feeling about you," he says once we are again sitting down, this time on a park bench at the riverside, near the marina. "Now, I don't know that I'm a man who normally believes in destiny, but I'm certain we are meant to be in each other's lives. I'm as attracted to you as I was to my first love in my teens."

"Yet, it's like we've known each other a long time," I say, not wanting to let him know I'm feeling the same way. I don't feel the same compulsion I usually do to fill up silences with talk for the sake of talking. While I've never been one to monologue or monopolize a conversation, I've always been on the talkative side. That is, until recently.

Frank then tells me he has a few errands to run, but promises to meet me back at the café. At first, I enjoy being alone. Scrolling old messages on my email, I take my time eating a cream cheese and cucumber sandwich. Two children chase an escaped balloon. A dog chases them.

The problem is, he should have been here an hour ago if I'm right about when he said he'd be back.

I'm thinking of asking him to crew with me on *Silver Lady*. He could collect his water samples for the sprays he's inventing, and we could get to know each other better. I still can't get over how much he resembles the man I had a crush on decades ago at the school. What could be delaying him? Could he have disappeared? Maybe time just felt like it had slowed down because I'm intrigued by him.

When I return to the boat, I discover Blue has flown away again. Goodbye, my friend.

DAY 31

Frank and I left Ruby a few days ago and are now venturing further south on the long and twisty river road. Here I thought I'd be traveling on by myself, but it turns out I have company. Maybe I'm being too-trusting by allowing him to ride along with me. Life is all about taking chances, right? It's anyone's guess whether we'll remain together for long.

Before leaving the marina, I tried a few more times to contact George, but he never responded. Had he done so, of course, I would have returned this magnificent vessel, albeit reluctantly. I reached Melanie and we finally had a long chat. The curfew she mentioned has gone into effect. The city, once again, had to shelter in place, thanks to a return of the Strangler Virus, as well as the uptick in car bombs, looting, and burglaries. I did my best to conceal my worry. I knew there was no point in trying to persuade her to leave her apartment. She told me about her latest additions to her miniature Utopian village, including a maypole and festival area just outside the village. I asked if she'd carved inhabitants, but she said she hadn't. I tried to describe my present life on the water and mentioned Frank. She didn't say much, but seemed to understand why I may want to extend my trip a little longer. I promised to be careful out here on the water. She promised she'd stay safe.

Frank and I spend hours wrapped in each other's arms. At least they feel like hours—good hours, but not long ones. Who knows how long our limbs entwine! When we're upright, we're usually holding hands and listening to each other's stories with the full attention paid best by young lovers. Sometimes, he'll take one of my mostly silver braids and softly brush it across his face. Once, he even wrapped them about his shoulders like a scarf. We haven't made love yet, as we're trying to take it slowly. It's been ages for both of us. Despite him being a wonderful storyteller, I still know only a few facts about him. He's from Michigan, played the saxophone in college, and has degrees in history and philosophy. He's never had many friends. Married once, but no children. But this is not who the man *is* any more than I'm no one more than a former teacher, doula, mother of one child, and widow. That our identities are infinitely *more* continues to be a source of delight. I would like to hope so.

Frank painstakingly sprayed the most delicate of his mists on each page of my captain's log. I feel much less worried about losing my "baby" thanks to him.

DAY 33

A recent development: Frank's on his way back to Doze since it seems to be where most people are disappearing from. He told me it wouldn't surprise him if he winds up changing the proportions of river water with other undisclosed ingredients—perfectly natural ones. Maybe people and artwork aren't meant to be permanent; we should let Nature take its course and not intervene. Strange, as I always thought one purpose of art was to outlive humans. Initially, he vehemently disagreed, but after further speculation, I was able to get him to see my point. He invited me to go with him, but I declined, saying that someday we'll meet up again. That we kept seeing each other in places along the river meant something, after all. He agreed.

His leaving is one of the many River Lessons I'm trying to master. I can't count all of them, but I recognize the essential ones:

I thought the river adventure would change my life, and it has, but not in ways I would have expected. During inward moments, I thought my feelings for Peter would come back to me, especially as the river has been conducive to me recalling specific times: the trips we took, falling asleep wrapped in each other's arms after making love, lively conversations in restaurants in early phases of the relationship. Still, I can't recall much of what we talked about, only that overall rush and blush of early passion.

During the years of near-total solitude, I was able to relive much of my past. I became too good at it. The present was only a place in which to view my past and to do my best to see it clearly. I did this a little too often. So this life on the river, with often changing scenery, as well as being around others, has been good for me—just what the doctor would have ordered.

What doesn't disappear, and hopefully won't, are the connections I've made on this river ride. Without them, the shifting scenery would have been only props and backdrops moved on and off the stage. Margot, Vincent, Leon, Kali, and even Zona. These were *my* people for this episode in my life. My dear ones for however briefly.

Silver Lady feels enormous, but I'm not lonely. I talk to her and she listens intently. She senses my moods—my joys and misgivings. Still, I find myself on the lookout for our former mascots: Blue, of course, but Ollie the Owlet, too. No sign of either of them. Maybe the dolphin-fish will return and speak again. Maybe this time I'll be able to figure out what they're saying. Maybe because they're not here, my oneness with *Silver Lady* intensifies. It's like our fates are completely connected.

I don't think I'll ever be able to live on the mainland again. It's too dangerous during these times and I'd rather take my chances drifting from one river town or island to the next.

The river in this part of the South is way more congested than I'd expected. Someday soon, I'll turn *Silver Lady* around and head back. I'm curious about whether the places I've seen will look different as I retrace the route. Right now, I plan to meet up with Frank in Doze, but first I'll stop by New Leaf, then Realidad, and the island—if I can find it. There's the chance they'll be gone, but that's the risk I've taken. Such strange and magical places! Maybe I'll even find new ones.

And it's a long time going home. A long time clinging to that branch above the roaming river.

ABOUT THE AUTHOR

Susan Sage has published three other novels. Her novel *Dancing in the Ring* was a Silver Finalist in the 2023 American Writing Awards, as well as a finalist in the 2024 Global Book awards, and a winner of the Literary Titan Award. For several years, Susan taught English at an adult-alternative high school and was a reading tutor for at-risk students. She is ever proud of her grown daughter and enjoys exploring small towns she's never visited before, star-gazing, bicycling, and wine tastings. Although a Detroit native, she has resided most of her adult life in Flushing, Michigan with her husband and two cats.

DANCING
IN THE RING
SUSAN E. SAGE

NOTE FROM SUSAN E. SAGE

Word-of-mouth is crucial for any author to succeed. If you enjoyed *Silver Lady*, please leave a review online—anywhere you are able. Even if it's just a sentence or two. It would make all the difference and would be very much appreciated.

Thanks!
Susan E. Sage

We hope you enjoyed reading this title from:

www.blackrosewriting.com

Subscribe to our mailing list – *The Rosevine* – and receive **FREE** books, daily
deals, and stay current with news about upcoming
releases and our hottest authors.
Scan the QR code below to sign up.

Already a subscriber? Please accept a sincere thank you for being a fan of
Black Rose Writing authors.

View other Black Rose Writing titles at
www.blackrosewriting.com/books and use promo code
PRINT to receive a **20% discount** when purchasing.